THE OATH

THE OATH

Michael L. Lewis

The Book Guild Ltd

First published in Great Britain in 2019 by
The Book Guild Ltd
9 Priory Business Park
Wistow Road, Kibworth
Leicestershire, LE8 0RX
Freephone: 0800 999 2982
www.bookguild.co.uk
Email: info@bookguild.co.uk
Twitter: @bookguild

This work is entirely fictitious and bears no resemblance to any persons living or dead.

Typeset in AldineBT 401

Printed and bound in Great Britain by CPI Group (UK) Ltd, Croydon, CR0 4YY

ISBN 978 1912575 862

British Library Cataloguing in Publication Data.
A catalogue record for this book is available from the British Library.

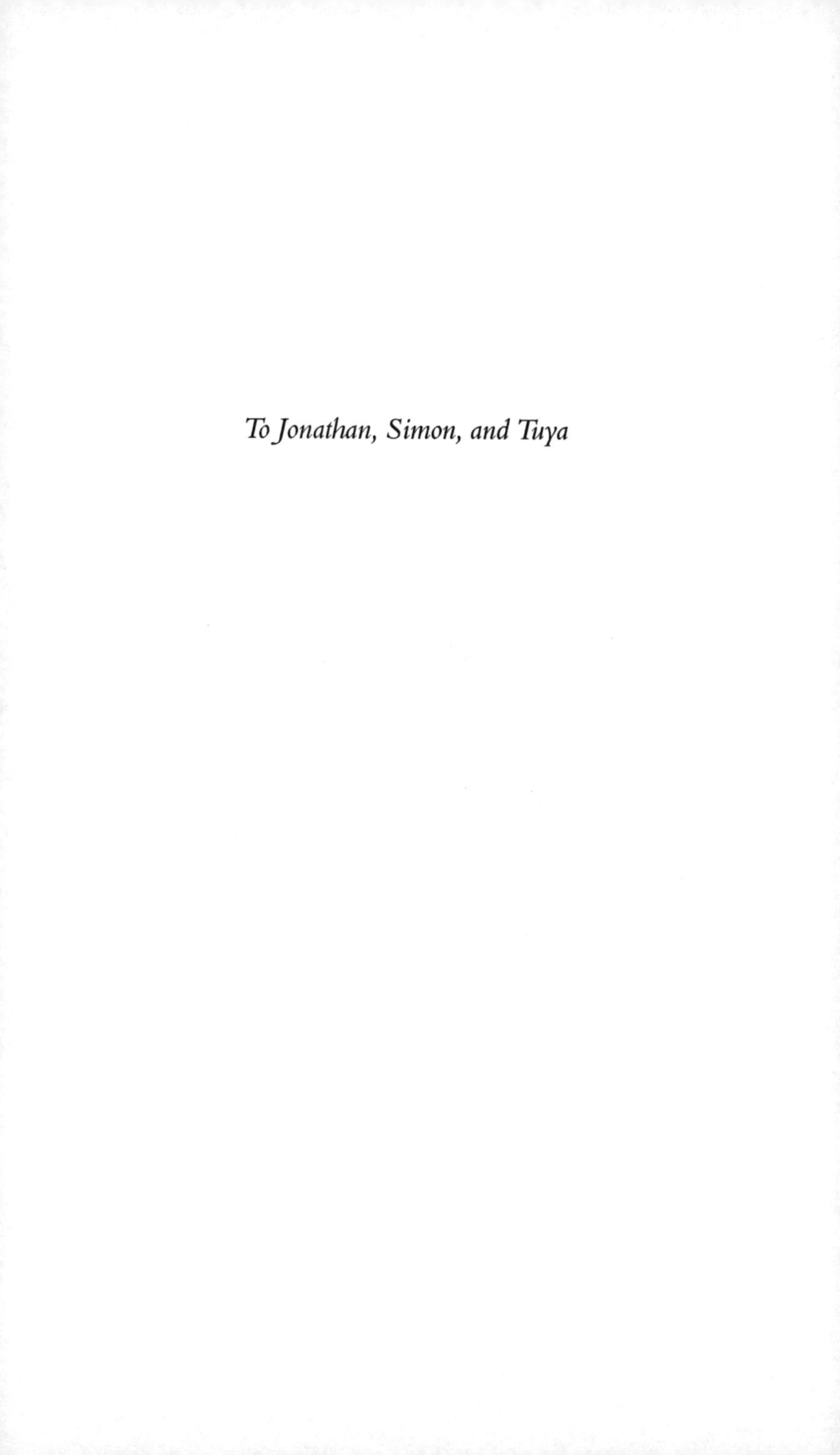

To Jonathan, Simon, and Tuya

This book is for the house
And all I kissed;
But greatly more than those
For children like I was,
If they exist.

– Gavin Maxwell

PROLOGUE

February 1954

The boy's body lay twisted on the stony ground. The observer looked down and was briefly transfixed by the sight of the limp, pixie-faced figure staring up at him with glassy eyes wide open. He recoiled in shock. The boy was clearly dead. *Maybe neck's broken?* he surmised, bending over to close the eyes, then stopped himself. *I mustn't touch the body.*

He surveyed his surroundings to make sure that no witness lurked among the tombstones and placed his palms over his face. *Now they're both dead,* he despaired. As an afterthought, with his gloved hand, he removed a folded slip of paper from his coat pocket and inserted it between the corpse's pallid fingers.

He gazed up at the heaving night sky, shivering with cold. In the moonlight, an occasional snowflake tossed and swirled. Heavenly white flakes would soon blanket the ghastly sight. *I must go now, can't leave footprints in the snow.* Decision made, he turned and walked very fast on the narrow path out of the cemetery grounds in the direction of the House. He never looked back at the bell tower and the fallen boy that lay below.

1

BLACKLEIGH

September 1955

Jonathan Simon reluctantly dragged himself along the corridors of the train until he found an unoccupied compartment. He hoped to sit alone on the long journey to Blackleigh School in Yorkshire. A porter had earlier stowed his heavy trunk and tuckbox in the train's baggage area. Jonathan parked his duffle coat and his carrier bag up on the rack. It contained overnight clothes and personal items, which he liked to keep with him for safety. The thirteen-year-old then leaned out of the open window, hoping for a final glimpse of his mother on the busy platform.

He wished he was still at home, far away from the grunge of the train and the relentless commotion of the station. On the platform clock, he saw the black second-hand count down the last moments before departure.

Jonathan spied his mother making her way towards him through the noisy, bustling crowd; their eyes met. He tried to hide his terror of their inevitable separation and fear of the perilous, unknown world where he was heading.

"I don't want to go," he whispered to her, hoping not to draw attention to himself. "I've never been so far from home. I'll be away from you and my friends. Why send me to this godforsaken place?"

"I've told you, Blackleigh has a fine reputation. You'll get a proper education there," she replied.

"I wish someone could take my place," Jonathan anguished.

"That's enough," his mother said. "You'll like it. Just wait and see!"

"I'll miss you," Jonathan said, blinking back tears.

"I'll miss you too. But I'll send letters," she assured him. "You'll be home before you know it."

"That's if I'm ever home again!" he rued. "Each term lasts three months, and I'll be there for five years except for summer, winter and Easter breaks. That's like forever. Kids tell me the first year is the worst."

A wide shaft of light shone down from an aperture in the station roof. Its rays shimmered down across the platform, tiny specks floating in the pale abyss and fleetingly illuminated the scene. Jonathan saw parents and their sons grouped together. They all looked excited, watery-eyed and tense as they greeted familiar faces, searched for porters, or said their farewells.

Most youths wore beige duffle coats and black scarves with a band of yellow, the school colours. Latecomers hurried along the outside of the train peering into carriage windows, hoping to spy empty seats.

"The other boys look so big," Jonathan shuddered. "I hope no one barges into my carriage… Oh God, I may be the only Jewish boy there. And I'll be teased for my birthmark," he said, reflexively touching his cheek.

"Don't worry," his mother soothed. "No one will bother you. Look, it's almost one o'clock, the train's about to leave. Shall I wait?"

"No. Better go now," he said, biting his lip.

His mother nodded, stood on tiptoe and kissed him perfunctorily on the cheek. "Goodbye darling." She did her best to show her pride in him. "You'll be fine."

Jonathan realised there was no more to say that could alter his fate. "Bye Mum… Write soon," he said with resignation.

"I will."

He noticed a touch of grey in her amber hair that he'd not seen before. It seemed that everything constant was slipping away and beyond his control. He watched her turn to leave and step into the pale ray of light. For him, she had the look of safety and home about her as she slowly walked down the platform until she reached the ticket barrier. There, she turned, waved one last time, lingered and was gone. Jonathan was on his own.

A calm, amplified voice announced that the school train was about to depart. In a final rush of activity, porters hauled sports equipment and other carry-on bags through the last open doors and windows of the train to the awaiting hands of young passengers.

Jonathan firmly closed the door of his compartment, hoping to lock out the world, selected a book from his carrier bag and sat huddled in a corner by the window. He cracked open *Animal Farm* and imagined the book as a shield protecting him from outside distractions, but found it hard to concentrate. His worry about anyone else joining him in the carriage kept reverberating in his mind. *What will I say if someone speaks to me?*

A piercing whistle issued from the far end of the platform, followed by the slamming of doors along the length of the train and jolting him like exploding fireworks. With a lurch, the train started to heave itself imperceptibly forward, slowly picking up speed. Outside, on the platform, an immobilised world of parents, relatives and friends of those leaving glided past the window, rooted like statues where they stood. Jonathan winced at the sound of tramping feet and brash voices in the corridor headed in his direction; the door was flung open.

"Are these seats taken?" a tall pimply faced teen with long oily hair called out to no one in particular.

Jonathan hesitantly replied, "They're free."

"Ace!" the newcomer shouted, turning to others.

Four raucous teens, wearing matching school ties, with yellow stripes on black, barrelled into Jonathan's compartment. They plopped down on the seats and lolled against each other with their bodies, baggage and wild whoops. These second and third year boys could easily tell that the kid in the corner was a new "junior" at the school – a term meant to demean, thus unworthy of their interest.

His heart beating fast, Jonathan pretended to focus on his book, but he couldn't help listening in on their exuberant conversation.

"Wait till I see Jeff," someone croaked in a boisterous voice. "Wonder if he really screwed that girl? If you ask me, his sex life exists only in his thick head."

"Yeah," chortled a tousled redhead with a shower of freckles on his face, "her name's Daisy, at least that's what he told me. Jeff showed me a Polaroid photo."

"What's she like?"

"She's not the prettiest cow in the barn," Red snorted, "but I wouldn't kick her out of bed."

"Hey spastic, I thought you only liked boys," countered an acne-riddled youth; the others sniggered.

Jonathan, uneasy with the turn of conversation, felt himself very much alone. He noticed that it had begun to rain. The speeding train was cutting like a knife through wet ribbons of detached suburban houses, deteriorating streets and buildings, on the outskirts of London. Everything swept by his window: small stations, warehouses, factories, isolated half-lit newsagents, a Westminster Bank, petrol stations, a Boots Chemist, Woolworths, parades of shops, elaborate railway crossings, peeling advertising signs, one for Brylcreem, and now and again a school and an abandoned football field with lonely goalposts and puddles of water on barren grounds.

Steady onward, the train rumbled through an occasional black tunnel, with an eye of light at the far end that grew ever larger until they came out into the open again. Jonathan kept his focus outward, the landscape now endless terraced housing mounted with gleaming wet tiles and chimneys.

Jonathan examined his reflection in the window. He looked like he was dressed for a funeral: short brown hair neatly parted, brown eyes with wire rimmed glasses; and there was that awful reddish birthmark on his cheek that he'd give anything to be gone. Small for his age, the boy staring back at him had an intelligent look and was dressed in his new school uniform, a white shirt and school tie. His black blazer was emblazoned with a large, yellow italic "B" on the pocket, along with traditional grey trousers and black shoes.

Incessant rain splashed against the window. Small spatters fell though the opening at the top, but Jonathan hesitated to close the gap in case others in the carriage objected. His mind wandered. He felt insignificant and helpless as a single drop of rain in the waterlogged scene, where a current of water could carry him away.

His thoughts turned to Elsie and their last conversation in the kitchen when she'd tried to raise his spirits. Forty, short, plump with rosy cheeks and glasses, Elsie came from the historic, northern town of Pontefract. She liked to tell Jonathan that she was especially proud of her birthplace, the original home of Pontefract cakes. Elsie had worked faithfully for his mother in the capacity of cook, nurse and mother's helper from the time he was born.

When he was nine, his father had come back from an early morning run, collapsed in the hallway of their home and died of a heart attack. Energetic and industrious, Sydney Simon worked so hard that Jonathan hardly knew him. He reflected that the shock to his mother was almost too much to bear and Daphne Simon turned to a world within herself. Thankfully, she had the benefit of Sydney's life insurance and she continued to work long hours at the Midland Bank, while Elsie watched over him.

The kitchen, where Elsie made his last lunch, was always filled with the aromas of good things to eat. It was a special place, warm and reassuring, where he loved to sit and chat. He much preferred the kitchen to the more formal dining room.

"C'mon now," Elsie said, "brighten up. Drink your tea. Some boys would call it a privilege to be shipped off to an exclusive boys' boarding school."

"Not me," he replied, his stomach in knots, "I feel terrible. This is an awful year for me and the worst part is to come."

"Now, now. You'll be right as rain," she replied. "You'll make us all proud. Hurry up, your mother will soon be wanting to take you to the station." Elsie came forward and hugged him.

Lost in memories of home, Jonathan fell asleep.

He was jerked back to the present by the voice of the ginger-haired youth, sitting opposite. "You there, in the corner? Tell me your name, boy?"

"A-Are you talking to me?" Jonathan stammered.

"I don't see another fucking *junior* here," he snapped. "What's your name? It's bloody cold, why don't you shut the window?"

"I-I'm Jonathan Simon," he nervously replied, closing the window. "I'm new at Blackleigh."

The red-haired boy scratched his chin, considered this illuminative information and addressed his pimply companion, "Simon says he's new. What about that, Cutler?"

"No shit!" Cutler replied, then quipped, "Do your parents know you're here?"

Jonathan was contemplating how to answer when the blond-haired, blue-eyed oldest member of the group, intervened, "Hey, you guys, lay off." He spoke to Jonathan in a sympathetic voice, "I'm Jack Ridley, in my senior year, but I remember how shitty it felt as a new junior. By the way, at school we refer to each other by our surnames. First names are only for close friends. We're split up into eight separate Houses, where we live and sleep. Which House are you in?"

"Trafalgar… I believe that's mine."

"Right, each House is named after a great victory in English history. We're in Waterloo. As for Trafalgar, Alec Morton is your Housemaster. You must call him 'Sir'. He's in charge, but there are a few despicable seniors in Trafalgar. Watch out especially for Flicker, Sleeth and Tunk. Blackleigh is unlike other schools. Here the five prefects in each House have authority over their domains. Their word is law. Good luck to you."

"He'll need more than luck," the spotty youth chimed in. "Flicker's a power-hungry shit, the other two are about as cold-blooded. They're like viruses, infecting those around them. Flicker has everything going for him, his family has money and connections, he's got good looks, brains and ambition, but he's so damn ruthless. You can never tell what Flicker's thinking. I'll bet he'll end up king of the hill whatever he does. I pity anyone who gets in his way." Then, as an afterthought, "Any of you know how Flicker got that scar on his cheek?"

"I heard it happened at a school fencing match," Cutler offered. "An opponent from another school was beaten by Flicker. He got pissed and lashed out with his foil after Flicker had removed his face mask. The tip of the foil sliced across Flicker's right cheek. What happened next isn't entirely clear, but the next day, Flicker's attacker turned up at the hospital with a broken arm. Even now, when Flicker's angry, his scar seems more prominent, as if it's been seared by a burning poker. There's also that other rumor about him…"

"Yeah, but nothing was proven," the fourth member of the group interrupted. The bespectacled lad talked slowly, with a serious expression. "That Trafalgar junior's death in the old church grounds, last year, was never directly connected to Flicker."

"Not proven doesn't mean he's innocent," Cutler butted in.

"What happened?" Jonathan asked warily.

There was a silence in the compartment; no one wanted to answer.

"Look," Ridley finally spoke up, "just do your best to keep out of the way of those three."

The others in the carriage soon lost interest in him and moved on to a discussion about their classes in the coming term.

Jonathan tried to weigh the impact of their advice. He committed the three names to memory: *Flicker, Sleeth, Tunk*, expecting they'd soon be plotting how to make his life a living hell.

2

IAN GRACEY

Dark figures bustled and shoved one another in the corridor by Jonathan's compartment. Some deferred to others by flattening themselves against doors or windows to allow for those passing through. Juniors instinctively made way for seniors and stood aside while hefty young men scowled with fixed glares and elbowed their way, ploughing on to their destinations. The sounds of cursing, the smell of cigarette smoke and other strange substances hung in the air.

Four doors ahead of where Jonathan sat, two brothers were engaged in conversation. They were the only occupants of their compartment. Harry and Arthur Crown didn't look related. Harry, two years older, was tall with fair curly hair and blue eyes. His rapid speech and hand movements indicated that he could think and act judiciously. He had an engaging laugh, which enjoined others to laugh with him.

Harry was trying to calm his agitated younger brother.

Arthur Crown was short and very overweight. For what he lacked in his elder brother's intelligence, he made up for in his sense of humor. Arthur slumped back in his seat, making no effort to hide that he was sluggish. His body parts didn't seem to quite fit together. Arthur's dark brown wavy hair came to an apex on his wrinkled forehead. His brown eyes and elongated face were bounded by oversized ears. Despite a paucity of handsome attributes, Arthur's mouth occasionally blossomed into a friendly smile. When it emerged, a hangdog grin swept over his features and surprised others. His grin drew them into his confidence and held them with a magnetic quality, as if to say, "I'm about to fuck up… help me!" Occasionally, others did.

"Harry," Arthur said, "if this Flicker character is such big trouble, why then am I, just a first term junior, going to be *his* maid and cleaner out of all the other studies in the House?"

"In the first year, each junior works for two seniors," Harry patiently explained. "Flicker and Croat, like other seniors, share a small room together, where they work and relax. You've been assigned to clean up their place and wash the dirty dishes. They picked you for the job. You don't have a choice."

"But they don't even know me!" Arthur protested. "From what you say, I'm stuck with him! I was only accepted at this school and I'm in Trafalgar House because you're already here. What do I know about washing dishes and mopping floors? Nothing! I ask you, how will this help me later in my life?"

"You'll have to learn like everyone else before you. It's supposed to teach you discipline and humility," Harry said calmly. "The work isn't that hard. Once a week you take up their carpet, hang it outside and beat it to rid it of dust. The rest of your duties are done daily. Dishes and pots and pans go back in the cupboards after you've cleaned them with soap pads. All surfaces get dusted. Rubbish is thrown out in the bins at the back of the House. It's like the way things are done in the army. For God's sake, Arthur, don't make this a problem. And whatever you do, don't get on the wrong side of Flicker, he has an explosive temper."

Arthur looked around in desperation. "Shit, I haven't even started at Blackleigh and I'm someone's slave. It doesn't help that Flicker freaks everyone out. Tell me, exactly, why I've been sent to this prison masquerading as a school?"

"Arthur, you'll have to stop relying on me and start making your own way," Harry said, slightly miffed. "I know you can do it."

Arthur didn't want to be a drag on his brother and resolved that under no circumstances would he go to Harry for support.

Harry couldn't help but smile as he patted his whimsical brother on the back. A cautious knock on the compartment door interrupted them; the door slid open.

"Need you, Harry," pleaded the newcomer in a high-pitched voice, standing in the doorway.

"Hello, Ian," Harry replied smiling. "What's the problem?"

Ian Gracey, who was smaller than Arthur, came into the compartment hauling three cumbersome pieces of hand luggage. His hair was cut in a fringe that complemented his cheerful, angelic expression. His light blue eyes appeared to dance behind his glasses.

"A prefect told me to deliver these bags," Ian said. "The travel labels show they belong to Flicker, Hawk and Bell. Any idea where they're sitting on the train?"

"You're in luck," Harry tossed a thumb over his shoulder. "Hawk and Bell are both in a compartment just along the corridor from ours."

"And Flicker?" Ian queried with a worried expression.

"I saw him earlier at the front of the train with some of his cronies. Try there," Harry replied. "Hey Ian, say hello to my brother Arthur. He's new at the school."

Ian nodded.

"Call me Arthur," the boy replied. "I know the tradition is that they call the elder of two brothers Crown Senior and the younger Crown Junior. Just don't ever call me by that name. It sounds dreadful."

Arthur and Ian exchanged looks and laughed.

"Tell you what," Arthur said, hopping to his feet and relieving Ian of one piece of luggage, "I'll help you deliver these bags you're worried about. It'll give me an idea of what I'm up against at this school. Then, if I don't like what I see, I'll book a return ticket to Manchester."

Ian welcomed the offer. "Thanks, Arthur. I'll take you up on that."

Arthur turned to his brother. "Harry, I'm off with Ian… possibly to meet my doom. If I'm not back by midnight, call Mum and Dad. Better still, from what I heard about Flicker," he indicated the bags, "if I'm away for more than an hour, call the police!"

Ian and Harry laughed uproariously.

Arthur followed Ian down the corridor. They soon found the compartment occupied by Hawk and Bell and delivered their two bags without incident. With Arthur continuing behind him, and already out of breath, Ian turned and headed in the opposite direction, towards the first carriage.

"Now all we need do," Ian whispered to Arthur, "is to find Flicker's compartment, deliver his bag, then leave his imperial presence fast. We don't want trouble, not on the first day of a new term."

They reached the forward cars of the train. Ian noticed some of the light fixtures in the corridors were without bulbs. The two moved on, walking in and out of the draughty darkness. Voices of older boys swirled around them. Sneaky hands tried to grab hold, pinch and obstruct them as they made their way past the compartments.

"We're looking for Flicker," Ian bravely told one hefty boy. "We've got his carry-on."

"You're a butthead, Gracey," the other said gruffly. "Did you steal his bag? Either way, you're fucked."

"Forrester just let us pass," Ian pleaded. He glanced nervously into the next few compartments. In each one, the young men sitting or standing reminded him of wild horses, locked in their stables, frisky and chomping at the bit, as if waiting for a chance to bolt and create havoc outside.

Ian wiped the sweat from his forehead, rested Flicker's bag on the floor and waited for Arthur to catch up. "We've only a couple more places left to check," he assured Arthur, whose face was flushed and sweaty.

The next two compartments were crammed with members of various Houses. The two rested and took another breather.

Ian asked himself, *why am I afraid of Flicker?* He knew the senior was an enigma. Flicker was brainy and funny, but in a sick way. There was something terrifying about how Flicker never forgot even the tiniest slight.

They reached the next compartment. Ian felt goosebumps at the sound of Flicker's distinctive laugh nearby. The window shutters of the carriage were pulled down and he couldn't see in.

"Arthur, this is it, he's in here," Ian whispered. "I'll go in first. You hold onto his bag at the door."

Ian heaved a breath, knocked, slid open the door and entered the compartment. The lights were turned off. In the darkness, Ian could barely make out the faces of the passengers. When his eyes adjusted to the minimal light, he found himself involuntarily shaking with fear. He again cautioned Arthur to stay by the door, then stepped forward in the aisle between the seats.

Ian could see the soft glow of cigarettes on either side, and his nostrils detected the pungent odour of the contraband some were smoking. No one spoke.

Ian inched forward, as if amid a pack of hyenas, alert, waiting to pounce and rip an intruder apart.

Ian recognised Flicker's lanky figure in a far corner. He knew enough to wait until Flicker spoke to him. Through the gloom, he took in the senior's handsome tanned figure, with swept back black hair and rimless glasses, elegantly dressed in a sports coat with an open black shirt. Flicker turned on the reading light over his head, which helped Ian avoid treading on other passengers' feet.

There was an unpleasant smirk on Sleeth's face, a brawny, shaven-head red-faced senior, sitting across from Flicker.

Ian studied Flicker's expression to discern his mood. He took in the scar on his left cheek, tight mouth and piercing, probing, dark brown eyes. Flicker was alert as a wolf, though his gaze at the beer bottle he held in his hand seemed to indicate otherwise.

Ian heard Sleeth say, "Turn off that light, Flicker, it's in my eyes."

Flicker ignored him.

"I said, how about turning off that light," Sleeth raised his voice, "did you not hear me?"

Without looking up, Flicker smashed the bottle against the wall and was instantly standing over Sleeth, swiping the jagged edge of the broken glass in the air, inches from Sleeth's face. Flicker feinted with a vicious jab at Sleeth's throat, who put up his hands to protect himself.

"Never tell me what to do," Flicker seethed.

Croat, Flicker's study mate, jumped up with a look of horror. "Let it go, James, Hugh Sleeth isn't worth it." Croat carefully put his hand on Flicker's left shoulder and applied pressure to the arm that held the weapon.

"I'm sorry, Flicker," Sleeth snivelled.

The apology calmed Flicker as quickly as he'd lost his temper. He pointed at Ian with the broken bottle. "Now, what do *you* want Gracey? Make it quick."

"We, uh, brought your carrier bag. A prefect sent me with it." Ian turned to his companion, still standing in the open doorway.

Arthur wore a stunned, open-mouthed expression; he could hardly believe what he'd just seen.

"Who's that new boy gaping at me by the door?" Flicker asked.

"It's Arth… I mean Crown Junior," Ian corrected himself. "He's helping me."

"I see," Flicker said. "So, he's Crown – the junior?"

Arthur stumbled into the compartment, placed the bag down, and retreated to the door.

The senior's steely gaze fixed on Arthur. "Crown… I assume you're the younger brother of that useless spastic who's already in Trafalgar."

Arthur could only nod.

"Well then," Flicker continued, "I'll contact you soon about your cleaning duties in my study. Now get the hell out of here, both of you."

Ian and Arthur bolted from the seniors' compartment; behind them they heard laughter, led by Sleeth. When

Ian had put enough distance between them and the seniors, he signalled for Arthur to stop.

Ian had nearly reached the same breaking point that he'd experienced years before. Charlie, his younger brother, had died while Ian was with him, alone at home and looking after him. Even though his parents had talked to him about his brother's disease, Ian was unable to understand leukaemia. The adults had explained Charlie's bone marrow deficiency and susceptibility to infection, but Ian always believed that Charlie would get better. He'd been sitting in a chair by his brother's bedside, talking to him.

One moment, Charlie was smiling up at him and the next he was gone. Ian stood in disbelief as he looked down at Charlie, whose eyes were now vacant. He knew that Charlie was dead. With tears streaming down his face, Ian leaned over and kissed his brother goodbye on the cheek.

For nearly a year afterwards, Ian went through each day as if nothing in the world mattered. As time passed, he adjusted to the terrible loss, but felt that he'd never be close to anyone again. He hated everything about Blackleigh, yet he never complained to his parents, who already shouldered the burden of paying the high school fees. Ian didn't want to add to their problems by telling them what happened at school with bullying, drugs, and sex between some boys.

Ian's reflections broke off when he heard the brakes screech and felt the train slow, having finally arrived at their destination. Outside, parked at Enderby's small station, the nearest town to the school, there would be coaches waiting to take them on the short ride to Blackleigh. He stared at Arthur in despair, wondering how the two of them would make it through the term.

3

ARTHUR CROWN

At nine-thirty in the evening, Jonathan arrived at the school in one of the crowded coaches. The first stop was Blackleigh Hall, an imposing main building. Boys living in nearby Houses piled out. Jonathan strained to see some of the adjoining school buildings, but everything was a blur. He waited patiently while the coach made additional stops, letting off more passengers until it finally arrived at Trafalgar House. The driver had said earlier that their luggage, other than their carrier bags, would be delivered in the morning.

In pouring rain, Jonathan, wearing his duffle coat with his hood up, stepped down from the coach amongst a group of housemates. They ran across a sodden forecourt and scrambled through the door of a three-storey brick building where Jonathan found himself in a mad crush of bodies in the entry lobby. They were all trying to force their way to the front of the crowd to look for instructions on the notice board. Jonathan was determined to find his junior dormitory quickly, unpack his carrier bag and go to bed.

Jonathan walked the length of his second-floor dorm until he found his name printed on a 3 x 5 card, taped above an unmade bed. The boy assigned to the adjacent bed was lying on his bare mattress, eyes open, but looking exhausted. Jonathan hoped this was his chance to connect with another junior. He noted that the other twenty-five or so unmade beds in the dorm were rapidly filling up under the direction of two seniors in charge.

"Hello," Jonathan greeted his neighbour tentatively. "Are you new here?"

"I suppose I am," the other replied, "although I've had it with Blackleigh already."

"I know how you feel," Jonathan nodded, becoming more confident, having found someone like-minded. "I'm Simon."

"Simon what?" his neighbor queried.

"*Jonathan* Simon," he corrected himself. "I was told we aren't meant to use first names."

"Well, fuck that rule for a start," the other replied. "I'm Arthur Crown and don't call me Crown Junior. The name's *Arthur*. My older brother Harry is also in Trafalgar, but he's assigned to another dorm for those in their third year."

"Where's your home?" Jonathan asked.

"Manchester, and where do you live?"

"Hendon. It's in north-west London," Jonathan replied.

Arthur took in Jonathan and noticed the reddish birthmark on his cheek. *That*, Arthur thought, *is all I need!* Arthur was self-conscious enough without having to deal with an unsightly blemish on his own face.

Jonathan gestured to the bunks around them. "Why are all the beds unmade?"

"Because we're supposed to handle this ourselves. It's not like home," Arthur said, more to himself, "where the maid makes my bed."

Arthur reluctantly stood up, changed into his pyjamas, gathered his pile of blankets, sheets and pillow case, and made his bed, as did Jonathan. When Arthur had finished his task, the result looked to Jonathan like a careless heap of bedclothes with a pillow plopped on top.

"How many new juniors are there in our House, Arthur?" Jonathan asked, hoping to further connect.

"Only three. You, I and Rayner," Arthur replied. "The other beds are for juniors already in their first year, but two of them are for Diamond, who's a prefect, and Snell, a senior. There's more new boys assigned to each of the other seven Houses. I heard they took in too many boys at Trafalgar last term."

"Our trunks and tuck boxes get delivered tomorrow," Jonathan pointed out, glad to provide some information. He turned to Arthur, whose head stuck out from a heap of blankets, his eyes closed. "Will you be able to sleep tonight in this noisy place?"

Arthur briefly opened his eyes and murmured, "Good to meet you, Jonathan, I hope we'll be friends. I'm lucky – I can fall asleep even in a hurricane."

Jonathan, touched by Arthur's sentiment, was about to reply, when he saw Arthur was already sound asleep.

The windows in the dorm were soon flung open wide by the two seniors; the dormitory lights, hanging bulbs, were turned off, and a prohibition enforced of no talking. But for Jonathan, sleep didn't come easily. He was distracted by snoring, nasal grunts and heavy breathing. He imagined that he was adrift in the English Channel, among the sounds of incessant foghorns from trawlers plugging through rough seas. When he finally fell asleep, it was a fitful one.

★★★

In the morning, Arthur awoke early and looked around. As usual, he had slept well. At the other end of the dorm, he made out the bed where Keith Rayner slept. Arthur recalled that he and Rayner had exchanged a few words before coming up to the dorm. He felt threatened by Rayner's confidence and maturity. The fellow junior was a handsome boy with fair hair and hazel eyes. He told Arthur that he'd already boarded at other schools before coming to Blackleigh. Arthur reflected that unlike Rayner, he'd never been away from home. The idea of his sleeping in a room with twenty-five congealed noses, having to make his own bed, and enduring the chill from wide open windows all appalled him. *What were my parents thinking when they sent me to this hellhole?*

At home, his father, Fred Crown, usually left in the morning, earlier than his mother, and drove his Bentley to their dress factory in Hale. With Harry already at boarding school, he'd gone to a private day school in Manchester. The only other presence at home was Hilda, the German maid. She spoke few words of English and had little to do with him. He tried to avoid her unsmiling face but turned up punctually for meals.

Fred Crown was confident that his elder son, Harry, had a bright future, but often expressed doubts about his younger son to his wife, Fran. "I never know what he's thinking, or what will become of him," Fred often complained. "Arthur's had it too easy. How is he ever going to develop a good work ethic like I did? I came up the hard way."

A week before Arthur left for boarding school, his father had made a concerted effort to change his son's attitude. Fred urged him to spend a day at the dress factory: "Get the feel of the place, son. You'll love it! And you'll get to see how hard work pays off."

"Dad, that's a great idea," he'd replied, grinning with false enthusiasm. "But today's not a good time. There's so much I have to do to get ready for school." Then Arthur asked himself, *Why in bloody hell would I want to spend one of my last days of freedom in a stupid dress factory?* His sole ambition was to be left alone.

Arthur's conclusion, as he lay in bed on his first morning, was that to survive at this new school he'd have to act like a chameleon, invisibly visible, hoping to blend in. Maybe one day, when this was all over, he'd be able to laugh about it. But not now. He decided to make an early start and dress before the seven-thirty wake-up call. Arthur threw back his rug, sheets and blankets, and quietly heaved his portly body out of bed. He shivered until he'd put on his dressing gown and slippers, pausing to look out of the window.

His first view of Blackleigh afforded an idyllic scene. A billowing mist hung over green fields and valleys stretching as far as he could see. In the distance, slightly less than a mile to his right, he saw the remains of an isolated Saxon church and an adjoining high stone bell tower overlooking a graveyard. The church and grounds were bounded by a grim looking barbed wire fence. He'd read in material about the school that the cemetery and tower were all that remained of an ancient village, once located on the site. That whole area was strictly out of bounds for all students.

To his left, a pathway led away from Trafalgar and snaked for some distance to a cluster of buildings around Blackleigh Hall, at one time the manor house on a large estate. The impressive central building was approached by stone steps that led up to the entry doors. Inside, he'd read that there was a large assembly hall, where the faculty and student body gathered, and that was the focal point for school activities. Also, in the main building were the dining rooms, where members of each House sat for meals with their housemates at long tables. Even farther away, he saw the outlines of more modern buildings. Some were classrooms and others looked like more Houses and some faculty residences.

Arthur glanced at Jonathan, still asleep in his bed, and didn't want to wake him. He took out his toothbrush, paste and hand towel from his carrier bag, then tiptoed out of the dorm and headed for the washroom. He knew that his first classes were in the morning, his medical scheduled for the afternoon, and that he and the other new boys would meet with Trafalgar Housemaster, Mr Morton, that evening.

He gingerly opened the swing doors to a large white tiled room with three stained baths and enclosed toilets. Along the far wall were rows of washbasins, mirrors and small lockers, each marked with a boy's name, and placed above the sinks. In the middle of the room was a section for hanging towels, dressing gowns and a place below for shoes. He shivered in the cold.

"I ask you," Arthur said aloud to himself, grimacing in a mirror, "how the hell am I going to live for even a term in this *dump*?"

Arthur had assumed he was alone and was stunned to hear a gravelly voice behind him reply, "So… are you going to survive? The answer: Not a chance! No fucking way, spastic!"

Arthur, in horror, stood still as a tall, muscular senior banged open a toilet stall behind him. The junior didn't want to look directly into the other's face and shifted his gaze downwards at the hostile stranger's bare feet.

The intruder was big and naked, except for his underpants. His shiny head was razor cut. He had a thick veined neck and his broad chest, and sturdy long legs were carpeted in reddish hair. To Arthur, the aggressive creature looked to be over seventeen and was used to having his own way.

His pock-marked, clean-shaven face and almost invisible eyebrows bore down on the new junior with disgust. "Look at me when I'm talking to you!"

With a great effort, Arthur complied.

"Do you have a name, worm?"

His heart pounding wildly, Arthur blinked back tears. "I'm C-Crown, sir."

"Right, Crown. You call me Sleeth, not 'sir'. And know this, I'm your worst nightmare."

Arthur couldn't help himself. It always happened when he became anxious and words failed him. He smiled instead, and when the smile spread over his face it evolved into a hangdog expression, gaping, with his mouth wide open.

"What's so fucking funny?" Sleeth barked, his face growing redder as he spat out the words.

"N-Nothing is funny… I-I'm sorry, M-Mr Sleeth," Arthur stammered. "It's a nervous habit I have. What have I done?"

"I'll tell you. You exist – that's enough for me!"

"Don't I have rights?"

Arthur's towering assailant gritted his yellowish teeth. "You have none. You're not even human. I'll be planning something special for you. Before the term's over, you'll wish you were dead."

"Wh… What did you say?" Arthur gulped, hoping to God that he'd misheard Sleeth's words.

"Beat it arsehole!" Sleeth snapped. The junior was

terrified; he turned to run, but not before Sleeth gave him a swift kick. The piercing sound of the seven-thirty wake-up call sent him hobbling from the washroom and back to his dorm, leaving Sleeth behind, laughing maniacally.

At his bed, Arthur was panting for breath, rubbing his sore butt.

Jonathan sat up and looked at him in astonishment. "What's happened to you, Arthur? You look like you've been dragged by the scruff of your neck through a bed of stinging nettles. Sit down."

Arthur sat beside Jonathan on his bed, still breathing hard. "I just… ran into… a senior in the washroom… I think he's crazy."

"What do you mean?" Jonathan replied, alarmed.

"I tell you, this bully wanted to kill me. I did nothing, but he attacked *me*… said he can do whatever he wants to me. That's not all. Yesterday, I saw another senior, named Flicker, who was ready to slash the same guy's face – the one who just threatened me – with a broken bottle."

Jonathan flinched at mention of the name. "I've heard about Flicker. And there are at least two other seniors I was warned about. It appears we have some real nut-cases in Trafalgar. There's even a rumour that Flicker actually murdered a junior."

"I believe it," Arthur shook his head woefully. "At breakfast, I'll introduce you to Ian Gracey. He was with me on the train when Flicker went ballistic. Ian's somehow managed to survive here for two terms. From what I saw, Flicker's even crazier than the thug who just assaulted me. Can't we report them to someone?"

"Our problem is the code of honour at Blackleigh," Jonathan explained. "Snitching on someone is considered *worse* than the actual offence. And it works both ways: If a junior is caught breaking the rules, the senior won't snitch or report him. Rather, he'll order the junior to report to one of the prefects. They're the ones with absolute power. By this code, the junior must confess his crime to the prefect, who then decides on the punishment."

"Holy crap!" Arthur winced." How long are we considered to be juniors?"

"For the first three terms, I hate to say," Jonathan sighed. "Seniors are in their last three or four terms. Six prefects are selected from among the seniors and one of the prefects is made Head of House. Bottom line, Arthur, there isn't anyone to whom we can report seniors. And even if we could, a prefect is unlikely to punish another senior."

"What the hell do we do? Just sit around and wait to be bullied," countered Arthur, remembering the hairy red antagonist's promise of "something special" for him. To make matters worse, he was selected to clean Flicker's study. "We have to do something. We can't live like this," Arthur insisted with tears in his eyes.

"Yes," Jonathan concurred, "we have to survive like your friend, Ian. We must stick together. We can't let them win."

Jonathan's optimism would carry him through the

next few days. But small decisions, innocently made, on the spur of the moment, would have far-reaching consequences. If he could've glimpsed into the future, then and there, Jonathan would have bolted, bat out of hell, from Blackleigh.

4

HOUSEMASTER

After supper in the main building, the three new juniors in Trafalgar sat in the comfortable surroundings of the Housemaster's office. It was Alec Morton's policy to get to know each new member of his House and arrange for an older boy to show them around in their first few weeks.

The Housemaster, in his early fifties, sat behind his desk, fronted by the juniors in a semicircle, who were balancing cups of tea on their laps. He had a distinguished appearance with light brown receding hair, glasses and a thin moustache. Alec Morton was dressed in his usual black tie, a formal dark grey suit over his white shirt and sweater, plus black shoes. His benign expression hid a genuine determination to help each boy as much as he could. He understood that the maturation of teenage boys was never easy, especially with their rampant hormones.

Alec Morton had been the resident Trafalgar Housemaster for seven years. From experience, he gauged that some newcomers exhibited leadership potential from the start, while others had to undergo a painful rite of passage. To survive at Blackleigh, he knew that each new boy would have to make his own way. It was like a micro journey through life.

He looked around, probing from one junior's face to another. There was an unusually small group this term. He noticed that Arthur Crown smiled nervously in his armchair and avoided eye contact. Unlike his elder brother, Harry, Arthur did not carry himself well. His poor posture and slouching shoulders were a bad sign, as well as his tendency to gape.

"Arthur, when I met your parents," the Housemaster began, "your father told me how he became successful in business. He said that he did not come up on easy street."

"I've heard him tell that story many times, sir." Arthur rolled his eyes.

"Tell me, do you have any hobbies, Arthur?" the Housemaster asked kindly.

"Not really, sir, though I like to follow horse racing. Occasionally, my uncle makes a bet for me," Arthur grinned. Jonathan cringed beside him while Arthur added, "Some bookies take bets for more than just the first three finishes."

"I see," the Housemaster reflected, "horse racing and betting. That's not exactly the kind of hobby I had in mind for you. I was thinking more in line with your playing a musical instrument, being involved in a sport, or perhaps having say, a butterfly, stamp, or rare coin collection." Alec Morton realised, with a sigh, that Crown Junior would prove to be a major challenge. *Will he last? Probably not, but too early to say.*

Morton turned to Jonathan Simon, sizing him up to be immature and alas, self-conscious. "I know this is your first time away from home, Jonathan. How are you coping?"

Jonathan smiled shyly. "Well, the school is going to take some getting used to, but I'll be fine, sir. I already attended my first classes today."

"Good, that's the spirit! And you can always come to me with any academic problems." At Jonathan's impressionable age, the Housemaster mused, he'd face serious pressures in the year ahead. The boy was Jewish with a birthmark on his cheek. Either fact could result in his being bullied. Some of the seniors in the House had become too difficult for even the prefects to control.

There was a knock at the door. "Come in," said the Housemaster, and Ian Gracey entered.

"Ian, grab a chair and sit down," the Housemaster instructed him with a wave of his hand. Ian briefly acknowledged Arthur and sat. "I've asked Ian along because he's in his third term at Trafalgar. Ian knows the ropes and he'll show you three around." Morton liked Ian, who possessed an air of innocence. He knew Ian had yet to make any real friends in the House, but he was coming along at his own pace and presented no problems. The boy, he reflected, would never excel but he was honest and easygoing.

Keith Rayner was the last member of the group. *This one*, Morton thought, *has potential.* "Any problems, Keith?"

"No, sir," Keith said casually. "Things are pretty much what I expected."

"Got the hang of boarding school by now?"

"Yes, sir. You probably know I've been away from home the last five years as my parents live abroad. So I'm used to it."

The Housemaster nodded. Alec viewed Keith Rainer as handsome, polite and self-reliant. Keith, he felt, had a leadership role in his future. He wished that Arthur had some of Keith's self-assurance. *Horse racing indeed!*

Alec Morton glanced at his watch. He was ready to make his traditional speech and pass along the advice he imparted to all juniors. "I want to welcome you to Blackleigh," he began, "and give you a hearty welcome to Trafalgar House. This place may seem strange to you at first, as there's a lot to learn, but the mist will soon clear. Remember to keep up with your homework assignments. A supervised time is allocated for prep every evening in the Houseroom, except on weekends.

"Unlike other schools, here at Blackleigh, the prefects not the faculty, have sole authority to reprimand and punish for any lapses in discipline. I don't expect any of you will encounter such problems. But my office is always open. We, on the faculty, like to think of Blackleigh as one of the great boys' schools in England with a beautiful setting and traditions. I urge you to make good use of your time here.

"The symbol on our school crest is a raven. These birds have abounded in England from early times. They say that if the ravens in the Tower of London ever flew away, the Crown would fall and England with it. You, as newcomers to Blackleigh, are now part of our proud heritage and traditions. I ask you to hold dear the school motto: 'Onward to Glory'. Best of luck to each of you."

That concluded his speech. Morton didn't want to clog up young minds with too much information.

He noticed that Arthur's mind was already wandering off, and the boy had a glazed expression on his face. The Housemaster stood up and shook hands with each junior; then Jonathan, Ian, Arthur and Keith Rayner filed out of his office.

The four of them entered the Houseroom where boys, apart from prefects and study holders, spent most of their free time and did their homework. Each House member had his own locker, where they could store books, personal possessions, and sports equipment.

The lockers comprised small cupboards, with shelves, stacked around the walls on three levels. No wooden door came with a lock, but the compartment doors were kept closed. Inscribed on gold-coloured plates attached to the front of each locker were the names of past Trafalgar House members.

The room boiled with raucous noise and activity. Some were playing snooker on a full-size table, others were talking in groups, reading newspapers or playing ping-pong at one of two long tables, a line of paperback books in the middle placed on edge for a net. Around the walls were black and white photographs of the entire House over the years, with the resident Housemaster, at the time, sitting in the middle of the first row. Twenty or so various sized silver cups, indicative of Trafalgar victories in inter-house sports, were placed along a shelf on one wall of the room.

The three new juniors along with Ian hung together briefly before Keith announced, "I'm heading upstairs to unpack my trunk. Our luggage has finally arrived."

Jonathan had questions for Ian, but he first took Arthur aside. "Say, that went all right with the Housemaster. I had to practically bite my tongue to stop myself from asking about that crazy senior who assaulted you this morning."

"Glad you didn't," Arthur gasped. "We'd be finished here if you'd squealed to a master. Everyone would be out to get us."

"Yes, I know. That's why I kept quiet. Any idea of his name?"

"Sleeth," Arthur spat. "He's a fucking sadist. I'll never forget him… and he won't forget me."

"I've heard that name before," Jonathan reflected. "A senior on the train warned me about Sleeth – and two other seniors here in Trafalgar. You've seen Flicker and Sleeth; Tunk is the other one."

Jonathan and Arthur exchanged looks, sharing a special understanding of what lay ahead. However bad things were for him, Jonathan realised, they were worse for Arthur, who wouldn't fit in at Blackleigh at all.

From where he was standing, Ian heard the two new juniors mention the names of the troublesome seniors. He debated with himself whether he should keep quiet or get involved. Arthur had helped him with the baggage, so Ian felt an obligation.

"Excuse me," Ian said, edging nearer, "I heard you discussing three seniors. Let me tell you what I know." Ian ushered the two over to the trophy shelf. With their backs to the other boys, so no one would suspect they were really talking about the bullies, Ian pretended to tell Jonathan and Arthur about the trophies.

He pointed to a small one. "I don't know Tunk's first name. Keep out of his way. He's always scheming."

Ian indicated a medium-sized trophy. Jonathan and Arthur nodded, feigning interest in who won what. "Then there's Sleeth."

Jonathan said in a low voice, "He's the one who attacked Arthur in the washroom earlier today."

"I'm not surprised," Ian said. "That Nazi bully is always threatening someone. He's like a mean kid who loves to torture small animals."

"Why can't we do something about him?" Arthur asked.

"He's above the law. Sleeth is also influential as head of the Trafalgar Cadet Corps. Everyone joins the cadets at the beginning of their third term, unless for some medical reason you're excluded. Sleeth is a corps fanatic and he can also see cause to reject you. He's often in uniform practising marksmanship at the rifle range. His father is a Major General in the British Army."

"That's all I need to know," Arthur mumbled. "Like father, like arsehole son."

"Then there's Flicker." Ian pointed to the largest trophy. "Arthur, we saw him go nuts on the train with that broken bottle. Last two terms, I worked for Flicker and Croat cleaning their study. Flicker was a taskmaster, complete with white glove inspections. But now, thankfully, I've been reassigned to Diamond and Snell.

Jonathan broke in, "I heard that Flicker had something to do with a junior who died in the old church grounds – is that why they're out of bounds?"

"Now's not the time to talk about that," Ian replied. "But I will say this: Flicker is the most mysterious, and the most dangerous, of anyone at Blackleigh, because he's totally unpredictable."

Jonathan shook his head in disbelief. *This is just a school*, he tried to assure himself, but after listening to Ian, he wondered if he might be in a madhouse.

5

JAMES FLICKER

Sunday, September 1955

A prefect finished reading the Twenty-third Psalm from the pulpit in the chapel. Silence filled the sanctuary. "Let us pray," intoned the chaplain. The Blackleigh congregation knelt on soft pads, provided under each seat. A hush spread over the hundreds assembled and in their black blazers, the crouching flock looked like endless ravens resting on rows of wires.

Minutes later, the shuffling and scraping of shoes echoed off the walls as the congregation rose for the next hymn. An organ swelled through the cavernous chapel and the assembled mass, reading from hymn books and supported by the choir, at the rear, began to sing. As one, the rising surge of voices and the organ fused together.

"Father of all to thee
We breathe unuttered fears,
Deep hidden in our souls
They have no voice but tears."

Somewhere lost in the swell of voices were those of Jonathan, Ian and Arthur. They each hoped that their uplifting words would touch the very fringes of heaven.

Halfway down the chapel, a tall, elegant figure stood by the centre aisle. His white shirt sleeves extended slightly from the ends of his blazer to reveal gold, oval cufflinks. He occasionally sang a few words, but his thoughts were elsewhere. Up closer, one could see a scar slashed across his left cheek. He wore rimless glasses. Occasionally, he'd study those around him. It was difficult to determine his thoughts because James Flicker's face as usual was an expressionless mask.

He had a year remaining at Blackleigh. It was enough time to be made a prefect. If selected as Head of House, he'd jump at the opportunity and stay an extra term. After that he'd go on to university, then work for his uncle's merchant bank in London.

The words of the hymn enraged him, "Father… to thee." He cupped his palm against his cheek. For as long as he could remember, his father, Edward, never cared for him. James constantly lived in the shadow of his elder brother, Nick. His mother, Chloe, meek and fragile, was almost a nonfactor in his life.

★★★

Flicker recalled the last holiday that he'd taken with his family years before. The days were blissful spent hiking and rock climbing with ropes in Somerset. At night, Nick and he slept in twin beds in one hotel room, while their parents had the adjoining suite.

About two in the morning, Flicker awoke to the smell of smoke and found it hard to breathe. A candle he'd lit earlier had fallen onto the carpet and the flames were spreading up from the base of the curtains. Tiny droplets of light, glowing like fireflies, hovered in the air over the blankets. On the ceiling, he saw a jagged crack spreading.

James bounded out of bed and went to his brother. "Wake up, Nick. The room's on fire!"

But Nick was sleeping soundly. He was on medicine for a severe cold, which had knocked him out. James shook his brother but couldn't wake him. Out of his mind with worry, he pounded on the connecting door to his parents' room, but no one answered. James then ran into the outside hallway and knocked on their main door. His father finally opened it.

"Dad, come quick, there's a fire!" James yelled, pointing to the adjoining room.

"What the hell are you talking about, James?" Edward regarded his son sceptically. "It's the middle of the night!"

"A candle fell over… come quick."

James' way to get some of the attention that seemed to always go to Nick was to play practical jokes, and his father didn't believe him. "This isn't funny, James. Go back to bed," Charles exclaimed and slammed the door in James' face.

James repeatedly knocked. When his father opened the door again, James confessed, "I disobeyed your orders and lit the candle for a nightlight. It fell over and now our room is on fire!"

"I thought I told you not to light any candles. Where's Nick?" Edward demanded.

"I'm trying to tell you, Nick's still asleep in our room. I couldn't wake him."

Only now did Edward take him seriously. His father hurried back into his room and James followed. Edward flung open the connecting door. To their horror, Nick's bed now resembled a funeral pyre.

Chloe came up from behind, saw the conflagration and screamed, "Nick! Nick! Nick! Oh, God, No!"

With so much smoke and intense heat coming off the flames they couldn't enter the room. But that didn't stop Chloe from trying, and a wiser Edward had to restrain her.

Fire alarms were going off in the hallway corridor. Men with wheels of rolled up hoses came from nowhere, mounting the stairs. Pyjama-clad guests poured from their rooms.

James Flicker clearly remembered what transpired afterwards. He lived; and Nick died in the fire. From Nick's funeral onward, Edward blamed him and never forgave his surviving son. He didn't speak to James for months.

★★★

Flicker wiped perspiration off his sweating brow. After the guilt his father unfairly put him through, no one would stand in his way again. Flicker clenched his fists. He listened to the last verse of the hymn and tried to suppress his anger.

There was another terrible memory that haunted Flicker. Stephen Rodgers was a new junior assigned to wash and clean for them when he and Croat first moved into their new study over a year ago. Flicker acknowledged that he'd given the sensitive junior a bad time by making excessive demands. The turning point came late one afternoon when Rodgers was cleaning in the room.

Flicker returned early to discover the junior had broken a dish and was trying to hide the shards. The senior snatched his foil off the wall, swiped it in the air in front of Rodger's face and backed him into a corner. "Cross me again," he screamed in rage at the terrified new junior, "and I'll slash your face until you're the ugliest boy alive!" Rodgers curled up in a ball, crying on the floor. Flicker yelled, "Get the hell out of here!"

James had never intended that his threat be taken seriously. He was stunned to learn that the boy had committed suicide that night by jumping off the bell tower in the old cemetery. Rodgers hadn't confided in anyone, and the police reported that they didn't find any note left behind. Of course, Flicker was questioned. Rumours followed that Rodgers had been slowly cracking under pressure at boarding school and the burden of working for both he and Croat was too much for him. There was nothing to directly involve James.

Flicker's uneasy thoughts turned to the more mundane issue of arranging for his study to be cleaned this term. So far, Crown Junior had failed to appear. *Where's that dodo hiding?* The organ surged, and the service ended. He left his seat and joined the crowd heading out of the sanctuary. Flicker pushed his way forward, strode on, reached the main doors and hurried into the night.

★★★

The following afternoon, Arthur returned from lunch to find a typewritten note taped to the door of his Houseroom locker. It was a directive from "JMF" summoning him to his study immediately. Arthur knew who'd sent the note. He imagined Flicker's dark shadow reaching out to grab him by the throat.

With nervous steps, Arthur walked along the corridor, looking for Flicker's study. The first door he passed had only one occupant, David Reece, the Head of House. Arthur hurried past, for fear that Reece might come out and press him into some extra duty. He knew that Flicker's study was located at the far end, and he shared the room with his study mate, Hugh Croat.

Arthur experienced a strange sensation; his legs seemed to resist taking him where he needed to go, feeling like they were about to buckle under him.

Along the way, he heard deep voices and laughter coming from some of the other studies. A few doors were left half-open and Arthur glanced inside. For the most part, the small rooms were in various states of disarray. Some study walls were amateurishly painted, others wallpapered. A typical layout included two desks, each set against an opposite wall, a cupboard, armchairs and curtains. A makeshift cooking area in a corner usually comprised a table, two chairs, a small refrigerator and a meths stove. Above the table was a shelf for prepared snacks. Each study had two bookcases stacked high with books, folders and papers. On many of the walls were taped cut-out magazine pages of tanned, often nude pin-ups, both in and out of bathing suits, with smiling, untroubled faces.

Arthur reached the end of the corridor and shuddered when he saw the door with Flicker and Croat's names. He thought he heard movement from within and softly knocked, once, twice, three times. No response. Arthur turned the door knob slowly and slipped inside.

He was mesmerised by the appearance of the room. One white wall was completely bare except for a mounted fencing foil and a mask. Arthur recoiled at the sight, on the opposite wall, of a framed colored print depicting a woman's face staring blankly back at him. The artist had distorted her features. Her single turquoise eye with long eyelashes was offset to the left of her full red, ruby lips. Arthur wondered why anyone would want to study in a room with such an abhorrent face.

There was also a small black and white signed photograph, in a frame, of the new Prime Minister, Anthony Eden. A "chirp, chirp" startled him. In a corner, a small turquoise feathered bird was swinging on a perch in its cage.

"Wow, it's a bird!" Arthur exclaimed.

"You're observant," an overweight senior, sitting in an armchair, with a blanket over his legs, responded dryly. "It is indeed a bird! Now, what the hell are you doing here?" He had a large face, a receding hairline and thin framed round glasses. He reminded Arthur of a freshly caught fish, with goggle eyes, and an open mouth.

"I-I'm Crown, uh… Junior, and I'm looking for Flicker," Arthur said meekly.

"He'll be back soon. I'm Croat," the senior offered without moving or offering a handshake.

"Maybe I should come back at a more convenient time," Arthur proposed hopefully.

"If you're the bloke who's meant to clean this study, you'd better wait. Flicker's expecting you."

In the silence that followed, Arthur nervously shifted from one foot to the other; but he didn't have to wait long. The door opened briskly and Flicker, wearing a dark blue tracksuit, strode in. Croat nodded in Arthur's direction.

"Ah, Crown Junior," Flicker said. "Where the hell have you been?"

"I didn't know I was supposed to start today," Arthur pleaded.

"What you don't know can get you into big trouble at Blackleigh. I won't tolerate excuses. I should further warn you that when it comes to your cleaning duties, Croat, here, has the highest of standards. Don't disappoint him."

Arthur nodded intensely; Croat looked amused by Flicker's remarks.

"I expect you to be here promptly every morning after breakfast. You'll clean the room and wash our dirty dishes. And make it quick. You'll also have extra work on Thursdays because we entertain guests on Wednesday afternoons. Saturday is white carpet day. Take it up, beat it outside and then vacuum. I'll inspect the room late Saturday." Flicker had gone easy on the new junior so far after what had happened to Rodgers.

"Yes Flicker," Arthur murmured. He didn't dare tell this unpredictable senior that he'd never cleaned or washed dishes before. *Where's the maid, Hilda, when I need her?*

"Another thing," Flicker snapped, "be on the lookout for cockroaches. These incorrigible little bastards scurry across the study looking for food. If you see one, Crown, crush him and remove its remains."

Arthur nodded again but he'd taken in little of what Flicker instructed.

"Any questions?" Flicker shot the junior an icy stare.

"Not really." Arthur shook his head. "When do I start?"

"You've started," Flicker replied.

★★★

Three hours later, Arthur, in a daze, wandered into the Houseroom. He felt his head would burst if he heard any more about carpets and roaches. Jonathan was standing by his locker and Arthur walked over to him.

Jonathan put his hand gently on Arthur's arm. "How did it go with Flicker?"

"He told me what to do." Arthur sighed. "Despite Harry's warning, I think Flicker went easy on me today."

"Watch out, Arthur," Jonathan frowned. "One broken dish or a stain on the white carpet and you'll pay for it. Trust me. Every junior has similar tasks to yours. The only difference is that Flicker is like a keg of dynamite. If something goes wrong, he'll blow his top."

"Jeez, Jonathan," Arthur shuddered, "what am I going to do?"

"Pray for a miracle."

6

KEITH RAYNER

October 1955

An electric buzz sounded ending English Literature, the last class of the day. Keith Rayner noted the assigned chapters of Jane Austen's *Sense and Sensibility* for prep, gathered his books together and strolled back to Trafalgar. Four weeks had passed since the term began and Keith knew his way around the school. It helped that before Blackleigh, he'd lived away from home at private boarding schools where he had to fend for himself.

Keith brushed a hand through his fair hair, sweeping it back and away from his forehead. He recalled his mother telling him that with his good looks, he could win any girl's heart. *But what good is that,* he reflected, *when I'll spend most of the next five years among boys?* Several seniors had already given him admiring glances, but he expected that at an all-boys' school. At his last boarding school, he could have written a scandalous book about what happened in the dorm after dark.

He spent little time with the new juniors, preferring the company of older boys. Keith couldn't tell yet if Simon was up to the challenges of Blackleigh, suspecting he'd likely be teased for being a Jew and having that appalling birthmark on his face. Simon seemed a decent boy but quite immature. And Keith thought it a coincidence that both he and Simon shared the same birthday. As for Crown Junior, Keith had no doubts that he was a hopeless case, and they had nothing in common. The clot foolishly told the Housemaster that his hobby was betting the horses. Keith resolved he'd pass on Crown and try to break the ice with Simon.

He entered the Houseroom, put his books in his locker and went to check out the main notice board in the lobby. A cross-country run was scheduled for that afternoon at two fifteen. He planned to enjoy the run, then do his homework.

Keith was about to leave the House for lunch when he saw Ian and Jonathan approach the notice board.

"That ends my rest I'd intended, this afternoon," he overheard Ian say. "The damn run is compulsory. It's probably five miles. Arthur won't be happy to hear this."

Keith saw the opportunity to make contact and called to Jonathan, "Got a moment, Simon?"

"Yes," Jonathan said, turning around with a look of surprise. "Ian, go on ahead. I'll catch up."

Ian nodded and left out the main door.

Why does Rayner, who barely speaks to me, want to see me now? Jonathan wondered.

"I heard," Keith said when they were standing face-to-face, "that our House initiation takes place soon. All new boys go through this. It's a sick thing the seniors arrange for us to *officially* join the House."

Jonathan was already anxious about the upcoming run, the last thing he needed was more bad news. "Haven't we joined the House already?" he asked, letting out a heavy sigh.

"We have, but the initiation is a school tradition," Keith explained. "Tunk, a senior, arranges it. We don't often see the slimy creep around the Houseroom but when the time comes, he and several other seniors will be waiting for us, without warning, in the washroom. No matter what they do to us, the main thing to remember is not to show fear."

"Let me guess," Jonathan shuddered, "it just eggs them on. Does Crown know about this?"

"No, maybe *you* should tell him."

"I can't tell him about the initiation yet," Jonathan said. "Taking part in the House run will be Arthur's limit for today. What should I know about this *official* ceremony?"

Keith made a sickened face. "To start, Tunk will have us new boys strip naked and get in an ice-cold bathtub. We must hold our breath, dunk our heads, and stay under the water for as long as we can. When we come up for air, we catch hell."

"Catch hell?" Jonathan echoed, involuntarily shivering with fright.

"They put us through sickening torture and don't let up."

"Like what?"

"Like pinch your cheeks, yank your ears, smash your nose. One year, they urinated on a poor kid's head each time he came up for breath."

"How long does it last?"

"For as long as they want. Probably until they get tired, although I hear Tunk never tires of initiations. He gets off on making new juniors suffer."

"My God," Jonathan muttered, "what can we do?"

"Try not to think about it. Worrying won't help," Keith advised. "By the way, there's a cross-country run today. How about we go together?"

Jonathan couldn't figure out why Keith would want to run with him. He replied, "I'm not used to distance running. I'd slow you down."

"Don't worry, I'll match your pace," Keith assured him.

"All right," Jonathan nodded. "I'll see you in the Houseroom after lunch."

Jonathan left Rayner and hurried over to the main building. He needed to find Ian. *The initiation… the House run… why did I agree to run with Rayner?* His stomach was churning. *What will I say to Arthur?*

★★★

After lunch, close to seventy members of the House gathered in the Houseroom for a roll call of their names before the run. There were some for whom attendance was optional. No prefects were present, some seniors, including Flicker, Croat and the illusive Tunk were absent. Members of the cadet corps had an activity elsewhere, and a few fortunate boys obtained medical chits from the House matron, which excused them from the run.

Those waiting were dressed in standard white T-shirts, dark blue shorts, socks and running shoes. The crush of bodies, energy and noise in the Houseroom fused into a steady hum of anticipation.

Jonathan felt tired even though the run had yet to begin. He saw, among the pack, Keith Rayner looking fit and ready to go with his lithe, athletic body. Jonathan signalled to him and Keith nodded back. Jonathan caught sight of Arthur by a window. He was pleading with his brother Harry, who was shaking his head no. Ian Gracey stood alone from the crowd by the Houseroom door.

Ian looked around the crowded room and could sense what others were feeling. He sympathised with those going through their own private pain. Ian knew how it felt; he'd been there himself.

Jonathan stood waiting for the prefect-in-charge to enter the Houseroom. *I shouldn't have agreed to run with anyone, but maybe it'll work out.* He glanced at the House clock on the large mantel. The minute hand had reached the dreaded time of two fifteen.

7

RIFLE RANGE

Charles Hollis strode into the Houseroom accompanied by a mixed chorus of cheers and muffled boos from the assembled runners. Jonathan had been assigned to clean Hollis' study. The prefect was, for the most part, low-key. The House members settled into a respectful silence while Hollis began reading their names in alphabetical order and ticked off those answering from a list on a clipboard he carried.

Jonathan waited nervously; he was interrupted by a touch on his shoulder.

"I'm not a runner," a woeful-looking Arthur whispered, "mind if I go with you? My brother refuses to run with me."

Jonathan wondered how to answer him. At times, Arthur was such a slow walker that he was almost immobile. How could he possibly manage this run? Rayner would go ballistic to learn that Arthur was joining them. Yet Arthur looked so miserable and helpless that Jonathan couldn't refuse him. "Sure, Arthur," he replied. "You can run with Rayner and me."

Arthur sighed with relief and flashed a grateful smile. "Thanks so much. I ask you, Jonathan, how will running help me later in my life?"

"Arthur," Jonathan replied softly, "don't talk during the roll call. Just wait for us outside."

He soon heard his name called. "Simon… Simon are you here?"

"Yes," he replied.

"Then answer the first time," Hollis reprimanded before continuing.

After noting all the names present, the prefect detailed the route of the long, circular run; halfway to Enderby, turning and skirting around the forest, then returning from the reverse direction they took off. The swarm of listeners waited impatiently to be released upon the word "Go."

Jonathan was about to join Rayner, when he was again distracted, this time by Ian Gracey waving. Jonathan realised that Ian too wanted to join him. He was reluctant to hurt Ian's feelings, and having not the slightest idea of how he'd explain to Rayner, Jonathan nodded to Ian and he mouthed, "Outside."

What am I doing? Jonathan wondered. He couldn't keep pace with Rayner, Ian was coming with him, and Arthur couldn't keep up with anyone. Yet Jonathan convinced himself that all would be well and that he'd think of some resolution at the right time. Hollis concluded his speech with ominous words, "I don't want to hear about stragglers. You will all complete the entire run, even if you're not back here by midnight. Now Go!" Hollis sat down at a table.

The mass of bodies headed through the double swing doors of the Houseroom, forced themselves through the lobby and then into the open forecourt in front of the House. Jonathan was pushed on by the surging crowd but managed to grab Arthur's shirt and hold onto Ian's arm. Before he knew it, Keith Rayner was also at his side while other runners flew by, heading north.

"Are you ready, Simon?" Rayner shouted above the noise.

"Gracey and Crown want to come with us. Is that all right with you?" Jonathan yelled back.

Keith looked at Arthur with disdain, then at Ian. "You must be joking," he snapped at Jonathan. "You three won't finish the run even by midnight. I'll see you later… probably much later." He turned and raced ahead to catch up with the others.

"What's his problem?" Arthur frowned. "Aren't we good enough for him?"

"No, if you want to know the truth, we're not," Jonathan replied. "Everyone has left the House. We'll have to think of something fast, otherwise we'll be left completely behind."

Yet, as Jonathan hoped, with Rayner running on ahead, his run with the other two would be easier, and he became optimistic. Jonathan's eyes suddenly lit up and he said with urgency, "Follow me, I've a plan!"

Ian and Arthur obediently fell in behind him, running south, from the back of the House, and hurtled down a grassy hillside.

"Hey Jonathan, where are we going?" Ian called from behind. "We're supposed to be running north. We're heading in the opposite direction from everyone else."

Arthur, also looking bewildered, waited for Jonathan to explain.

"We're doing only half the run. We're starting at the finish line and going halfway around," Jonathan said. "When we reach the rifle range, we'll stop, and hide in the brush. After everyone has run past us, on their way back to the House, we'll join them at the rear. No one will realise that we went the opposite way at the start, then turned around and followed them."

Jonathan had made up his countermeasure as he went along. What a wonderful way, he figured, to resolve how to run with slow-poke Arthur, a frail Ian, and he, himself, who'd never attempted a cross-country run.

"Well," Ian shrugged, "it's too late to catch up with the others. They're long gone, so we might as well take your shortcut."

Jonathan sighed with relief; Ian wasn't going to make a problem. All would be well. Arthur nodded, glad not to have to try miserably to keep pace with the rest of the House.

The three fast-walked in silence. Jonathan experienced a giddy sense of freedom when they reached the bottom of a hill and ran across a meadow. He liked the feeling of cold air against his bare legs and the wind rushing in his face.

Arthur, huffing and heaving, managed as best he could. But he fretted that his legs were going to cramp up any moment. He thought about the rest of the runners going north, sweat-ridden, mud-splattered and practically killing themselves. A smile crossed his face.

They traversed a field of tall grass, slowly jogging on a muddy track that snaked ahead. In the distance, and coming nearer, Jonathan saw the foreboding high brick wall that surrounded the cadets' rifle range. It was a place he knew to avoid.

Arthur fell behind as the other two hurtled down an incline and stopped at a five-foot high wooden gate in the wall surrounding the range. Nearby was a clump of chestnut trees and bushes.

"Jonathan, let's hide behind those trees. We can wait there until the others come by," Ian said. "Your idea's great."

"I can hardly believe this is going to work," Jonathan replied, laughing. "It seems too good to be true."

Muffled voices and repeated bursts of rifle fire issued from inside the enclosure. Jonathan and Ian cautiously peered over the gate. About twenty cadets in denims, leather boots and berets were conducting an exercise. They each carried a rifle and were taking turns shooting at distant targets.

In all the excitement, they forgot about Arthur. Both were reminded of him when they heard him huffing and puffing. He was stumbling down the nearby incline. They tried to signal and warn Arthur, who was now hurtling on like a runaway train, ploughing forward, picking up speed. Arthur finally broke his momentum by crashing into the gate in the wall. He fell on his face on the other side; the impetus of his body having pushed the gate open. Arthur slowly got up, recovered and turned back to Jonathan and Ian with a hangdog grin. "I made it!"

"You scumbags at the gate…" a hostile voice shouted, "Come over here… Move!"

Arthur looked at Jonathan in alarm. "Shit! I know that bloody voice! It's that looney Sleeth! Is he yelling at *us*?"

Before Jonathan could reply, the same loud voice sounded through a megaphone. "I'm talking to you, shitheads. I want you here, on the double."

"Any ideas, Arthur?" Ian furrowed his brow. "We can't run away. They have rifles. They might shoot!"

Arthur shrugged his shoulders. He looked up at the shapeless, white clouds billowing in the sky. "Didn't I say that I wasn't cut out for this school? This looks like the end of the line." With that pronouncement, Arthur grinned broadly and started to laugh. Jonathan and Ian looked at him as if he'd lost his senses.

"What's so funny?" Jonathan shook his head in confusion.

"Nothing really," Arthur managed between guffaws. "Sleeth is nutty as a fruit cake. He thinks he's already a sergeant in the real army and the corps is on a war footing. I knew he'd remember me. Meantime we're fucked, and I can't stop laughing about it."

Tears of laughter flowed down Arthur's cheeks. Then, just as quickly, he became calm. "Let's get this over," he said with finality, "no matter what happens." Then he spun on his heels in the direction of Sleeth.

61

8

HUGH SLEETH

Jonathan and Ian followed Arthur, and the three frightened juniors headed towards Sleeth's ramrod straight figure. They looked like jet-lagged travellers who'd arrived at the wrong destination. Each was sweating, their thighs, calves and running shoes covered in globs of mud. Arthur dreaded to think what Sleeth would do to them, and especially to *him*.

A group of cadets carrying rifles formed a ragged ring around them. Jonathan recognised their faces, being members of Trafalgar. Out of their school clothes and now in military uniform, they looked like stone-faced automatons.

"I'm sorry, this so my fault," Arthur said under his breath.

"No, the shortcut was my idea," whispered Jonathan. "I got us into this."

Ian joined in. "Look, there's nothing we can do.

Whatever happens, don't show these creeps we're afraid." Ian glanced at the other two. Jonathan already showed a tinge of defiance. Arthur's expression was one of sad resignation.

Sleeth's harsh voice broke the chatter. "You three, stop talking. Stand at atten-SHUN!"

Unlike the other cadets in denims, Sleeth's uniform was neatly pressed, his army boots sported a brilliant shine and his gold belt buckle glinted in the afternoon sun. He marched up with two corporals strutting behind him and stopped a few feet from his captives.

"You spastics are trespassing on military property. Have you anything to say in your defence?"

Sleeth's challenge hung in the air like a fizzling track of gunpowder heading towards a pile of explosives.

Jonathan struggled to find the courage to reply. "We weren't trespassing on purpose," he said hesitantly. "We were on a House run and just stopped to rest at the gate. One of us opened it by accident."

The sergeant's scowl fixed on Jonathan. "When you address me in my uniform, boy, call me 'sir'! Now, tell me your name?"

"S-Simon… Simon, sir," he mumbled, feeling miserable.

"What's that red blemish on your cheek?" Sleeth's verbal onslaught made Jonathan feel like crumbling inside.

"I can't hear you. Speak up, berry face," Sleeth commanded.

Jonathan raised his voice, "It's a birthmark, sir."

Sleeth looked down at him and poked Jonathan's chest. "I've seen you before, boy. I never forget an ugly face." Sleeth turned to one of the two corporals behind him who was overweight and wearing glasses. "Corporal Croat, have you ever seen such an ugly mug?"

"No, I haven't, Sergeant," Croat replied with indifference.

Sleeth moved along from Jonathan to Ian. "Ah, Gracey. You of all people should know better than to trespass here. What a joke that a wimpy specimen like you tried to join the corps! I had the pleasure of rejecting you for size." Sleeth drew himself up to his full height and turned away to address the other lanky cadet flanking him.

"Corporal Tunk," Sleeth said, "please step forward and give me your wise counsel. These buggers need a lesson."

Croat stepped back, his opinion and involvement not required.

Tunk had a soft, silky voice and spoke pseudo-politely. "More than glad to assist, Sergeant. Always at your service."

Jonathan knew that Tunk was the person Rayner had warned him about, who took pleasure in the Trafalgar initiations. The ghoulish-looking senior stepped forward, towering over Ian, and placed his palm over his chin in a contemplative pose. Tunk wore a smug look that suggested he enjoyed delicious moments such as this and would take his time.

Jonathan observed that Tunk had dark skull-like

features, and his long face emerged from a thatch of black hair. Most significant, however, was his short tight mouth which, when open, revealed a missing upper middle tooth. For some reason, he'd decided not to have the prominent gap replaced.

Sleeth moved to stand in front of Arthur. "Ah, Crown Junior, my, my, what a disappointment you are! I didn't expect to see you so soon."

Sleeth spent a few silent moments simply glaring at Arthur, then moved on, as if the junior wasn't worth his time. With a swift hand motion, he turned and invited his two corporals to join him and confer. After a minute, a consensus was reached: Sleeth nodded and the corporals stepped away.

"Corporal Tunk will hand down our decision," Sleeth announced.

Tunk stepped forward in the eerie silence. Even the corps members gathered round had grown quiet. "Simon and Crown are new to the school," Tunk said coldly, "unlike Gracey, who is a major disappointment to me, as well as to Sergeant Sleeth. We've decided this is an opportune time for a special House initiation for the three of you." Tunk paused, looking pleased with himself, savouring the moment.

Jonathan tried to stop himself from shaking as Tunk went on, "I'd like you all, if you would, to strip off your sports clothes. I want you boys naked, or as they say, 'in the buff'. Now, if you please… Move!"

Jonathan, in a state of fear and disbelief, exchanged looks with Arthur, who was trembling beside him.

"I've already had my first-term initiation," Ian protested. "None of us deserve this. As Simon told you, we were on a House run, Tunk… I mean, Corporal Tunk, we're innocent, we just stopped to…"

Tunk closed his eyes and shook his head rapidly to indicate he had no patience for Ian's pointless protests.

"My dear Gracey," Tunk said, annoyed, but pretending politeness. He retained his slow, nonchalant speech pattern, "I had hoped to be lenient with you, even though it is dangerous for you to loiter near the range. If you were, as you claim, on a House run, why didn't I see any other runners? May I suggest the simple answer is that there are none? You are a malingerer and your deceitful actions are shameful! You should have thought of the consequences, Gracey, before you decided to throw in with these two arseholes. Apparently, one initiation wasn't enough for you. I hope this time you'll learn some respect."

Arthur was the first to take off his shirt, shorts and underpants. The last to go were his socks and shoes. He stood naked in the chill air with both hands covering his genitals and his white flabby stomach devoid of any definition. Arthur closed his eyes, knees knocking together, and heard the cadets surrounding the three of them hissing and jeering. But Arthur's eyes popped open when Sleeth leaned over and whispered in his ear, "Remember, worm, I said I have something special planned for you?"

Ian, in disbelief at what he'd got himself into, also began removing his clothes. Jonathan undressed, flung his clothes aside, doing his best to ignore the jeers. He noticed Tunk hovering and waiting for Ian to finish undressing. When Ian was naked, Tunk's eyes lingered over Ian's body and genitals. Jonathan wondered why Tunk was staring at him so intently.

Tunk spun and moved near to him. "I see you're circumcised. Are you by any chance a Jew, Simon?"

"Yes," Jonathan admitted, suppressing the anger he felt inside. Despite his lowly junior position in the House, he vowed to never forget this humiliation.

"We have a few of your kind at Blackleigh," Tunk commented. "One's too many, if you ask me."

Sleeth took over. "You three," he commanded, "will run naked to the far end of the range." He pointed to an outhouse. "See that structure? You'll find a foul hole in there. Each of you will dunk your head in the bowl. Then you'll run back here. If anyone's hair is not dripping wet, I'll personally dunk him myself. You'll repeat this exercise three times." Sleeth indicated a scope mounted on the rifle slung over his shoulder. "Crown, I'll be following your every move through the crosshairs. Any slacking or stopping and you'll hear bullets at your heels. Now, move out!"

The cadets booed and laughed at the three naked figures, who nearly tripped over each other when they started to run. Jonathan led the way with Ian right behind and Arthur at the rear.

They hadn't gone far when Arthur complained, "I'm getting an awful cramp. I must stop."

"You can't stop," Ian warned him, "he's covering

you with his rifle. Give Sleeth an excuse and he'll do something crazy."

Jonathan and Ian adjusted their speed so Arthur could keep up. At last the three reached the distant outhouse.

Ian was about to go first into the outhouse, but paused, looking for a possible escape route. *BAM!* came the report of a rifle and a bullet struck the roof of the latrine.

"What are you waiting for? Next time, I'll aim lower," Sleeth yelled.

Ian dashed inside.

When Ian came out with his hair covered in brownish grime, Jonathan shivered with embarrassment for him. He opened the door; the stench in the dark was something he'd never forget; he gagged and had to resist throwing up. He held onto the wall, looking down into a pit filled with the congealed dark sludge of human urine and excrement. Jonathan removed his glasses, took a deep breath and plunged his head down into the murky depths, feeling the wet slime envelop his head. In an instant, he was out again gasping and heading for the open air.

Arthur came out last, bedraggled and almost dropping to the ground. They turned and ran back in the opposite direction. With one foot following another, a frightening emotion rose from the depths of Jonathan's being. It was a fusion of such disgust and hatred directed towards Sleeth and Tunk that he was afraid to discover such an intense part of himself. No matter how long it took, he swore to himself that he'd pay them back, and more.

The juniors reached the grassy area for the third and final time. Like a lifeless doll, Arthur tumbled over and flung himself with his arms outstretched on the ground. There he remained, his hair caked with putrid slime. The two others kneeled on the grass and shook their heads like lowly dogs to remove as much of the filthy sludge as they could. Then, without waiting for further orders, they slowly dressed. They were beyond caring whether Sleeth had any more demeaning punishments for them.

Most of the cadets by now had lost interest and wandered back to the firing line. Arthur turned his head and stared at Sleeth, whose eyes passed over Arthur's exhausted figure with disinterest. Sleeth came over to Jonathan, sitting on the ground and touched the barrel of his rifle alongside Jonathan's blemished cheek. At the touch, Jonathan's neck stiffened, and his body recoiled.

"In less than a year," Sleeth grinned wickedly, "I'll have you in the corps. Then you'll belong to me." He wiped the barrel clean on Jonathan's leg, turned and joined his troops at the firing line.

Tunk approached Sleeth and reminded him, "There's still another new junior, Keith Rayner, due for his House initiation."

"There will be no initiation for him." Sleeth abruptly replied.

"Why not?"

"Because, I said so. Don't question me."

The look of disappointment on Tunk's face was pronounced.

Jonathan and Ian drifted over to Arthur, still heaving with exhaustion.

"Anything I can do, Arthur?" Ian asked sympathetically.

Arthur shook his head. He looked mournful and lost.

Jonathan put a hand on his shoulder. "You did fine. One day, you'll be proud of how you got through this. Now, let's leave this fucking place before they think of something else for us."

9

THE OATH

The crestfallen juniors left the range and slowly climbed a grassy hill on their way back to Trafalgar. By the time they reached the top, they were exhausted. Jonathan slumped down on the grass, and the other two dropped down beside him.

Jonathan found words that echoed what each of them were thinking. "How can we go back to Trafalgar like this? I feel so ashamed."

"What else can we do?" Ian said in frustration. "We can't protest, and we have no rights. If we did complain, we'd be as good as dead. Even our parents won't listen. They're just happy that we're enrolled at a famous school, and they don't want trouble. We have to face this ourselves."

"Sleeth and Tunk treated us worse than animals," Jonathan seethed. "There's no excuse."

"We're nothings at Blackleigh," moaned Arthur.

"Bullies like Flicker, Sleeth and Tunk can do what they want."

"Right Arthur," Ian concurred. "They get some weird kind of a thrill out of making our lives miserable."

"I often wonder about that Trafalgar junior who died a year ago," said Jonathan. "Probably, it was covered up like everything else." His eyes lit up. "You know, in ancient times, people who were wronged would vow to put things right by swearing an oath." The wheels were turning in Jonathan's head. "Why don't we do something like that?"

"It would have to be a blood oath," Ian added. "Knights sealed their oaths with blood."

"I haven't much blood to spare," Arthur winced, "and anyway, we don't have a dagger. Can't we swear a bloodless oath without surgery?"

"But I do have a knife," countered Ian. He produced a Swiss Army knife from his pocket. "I always carry this with me. An oath won't mean anything unless we do it right."

"That'll do fine," said Jonathan.

"What's on your mind?" Arthur asked nervously.

"We can draw blood by jabbing the sharp point of the large blade in each of our thumbs," Jonathan suggested, "then we'll swear an oath to avenge ourselves. Look it's easy…"

Without hesitation, he took Ian's knife, opened the larger of the two blades and struck the point into the fleshy part of his right thumb. He watched as a bright red glob of blood bubbled up on his skin. He passed the knife to Ian, who followed his example. When Arthur's turn came, he closed his eyes and jabbed the blade down hard, missing the tip of his thumb and gashing his palm.

"Aaaah… Get a fucking doctor! There's blood gushing everywhere!" Arthur wailed.

"You're going to live," Ian chuckled, clutching Arthur's bleeding hand. "At least, you've enough blood. Let's bow our heads now, join hands and swear this oath on our lives."

"Isn't that 'on our lives' going a bit too far?" Arthur advanced as they clung together.

"No, it's not. We *are* talking about *our* lives and *our* rights," Ian replied. "Jonathan, this is your idea, say what's on your mind."

Aware of the solemn moment, Jonathan held tight to the other two and looked up at the darkening sky. As one, the three friends raised their bloodied hands to the heavens.

"We three," Jonathan declared, "vow to pay our tormentors back. We must find the strength within ourselves. If anything happens to any one of us, the other two will not rest until the score is evened. Blackleigh has been around for almost a hundred years. There's savage bullying here, which no one dares talk about. This must end. No matter how impossible the task, no matter how powerful the seniors, we swear this solemn oath: To pay them back… and more."

They each concluded by shouting, "I swear!" Jonathan and Ian added the words, "on my life," which Arthur deliberately omitted.

In silence, they gazed down from the top of the hill, where they stood. Serene countryside lay below. Fields of green, some with grazing cows, stretched far into the distance. In the dying afternoon sunlight, the roofs of cottages were flecked with gold. The beauty and tranquility of the afternoon belied the ugliness of their earlier experience.

Upon returning to the House, the three snuck in through the back door. They took showers and went to bed, skipping dinner. Jonathan, overcome with emotion, prayed the Oath would work its magic.

10

FEAR

That night, Arthur, as usual, immediately fell into a deep sleep; but he soon was besieged by a fractured and disturbing dream. While Arthur knew in his mind that he was dreaming, it all felt so real. He found himself wandering among the derelict remains of the cemetery, close to a mile from the House. He was aware that the grounds were off-limits, and to be caught within the fenced boundary would mean a drastic confrontation with the Head of House.

In his dream, Arthur found himself drawn to the base of the bell tower and looking up at the stone surface. The dark opening at the top of the edifice looked so high that Arthur felt giddy. He marvelled that a structure built long ago on this site was still standing, almost immune to the passing of time. Even remains of weathered stone blocks, littered on the ground, retained a noble, enduring grace.

The school was cast in the tradition of the old church with an emphasis on discipline, fair play and honour. But somewhere, in the long link between the past and present, a rupture had occurred, as if the promise of the future had corroded in the present.

Arthur clambered over jagged steps to the left of the open tower entrance. He crossed over a patch of grass and managed to haul himself up onto the top of an awkwardly shaped rock, from where he saw a wire fence with a gate. He jumped down onto the ground and managed to partly force the gate open. Bending down on his knees, he wedged himself through the small gap.

On the other side, Arthur expected to find himself amongst more graves. Instead, he came upon a well-maintained English garden with white blossoming trees. The warm sun at his back, he walked on the soft, green grass to a wooden seat, near the centre of the garden, and sat by a shimmering pool.

Arthur experienced a blissful feeling. Here he could indulge in his wish to be left alone; the terrors of the House stayed beyond the garden walls. Arthur saw himself get up to kneel beside the water and remove his socks and shoes.

He stepped cautiously into the pool, careful not to damage the water lilies, until his feet rested on the shallow, sandy bed at the bottom. The feeling of shivery, cold water on his feet, ankles and legs rippled like chill waves through his body.

Yet among all this perfection in his dream, he grew uneasy. Something was not as it should be. He looked at his reflection in the pool: the mirror on the water surface reflected the sky above. He could feel the wind picking up and saw the cloudless sky transforming into a churning mass of thunderous clouds, streaked with coils of red.

He turned in horror to find the garden in turmoil. Grassy areas were smouldering in heat, the ground was enveloped by smoking, black, bubbling lava, oozing up from the ground in fiery rivulets. Petals fell from roses; tulips and daffodils withered before his eyes. Everywhere he looked, tangled stems were transforming into crawling black and yellow snakes. They wriggled through holes in the fence, dropped down, and slithered in waving motions along the ground. The snakes were coming for him. He raced around, trying to get out, but couldn't find the garden gate. With a swelter of heat, a curtain of flame rose before him and became an impassable wall of fire. Arthur stepped back, and someone grabbed him.

He screamed and woke to find Jonathan leaning over from the adjoining bed, gently shaking him. "Wake up, Arthur! You're having a nightmare!"

Arthur blinked his eyes, felt his heart pumping, and gasped. His cries had woken others in the dorm. Some juniors were throwing objects at him. Two paperbacks caught him on the side of his head and someone threw a hairbrush, which narrowly missed him. A shoe glanced off his arm. Others resorted to verbal insults.

"If you scream again, you spastic, I'll throttle you!" Hawk growled.

"Crown, I'm going to smash your mouth."

The two authorities controlled the outcry. Diamond, who'd just woken, commanded, "Shut up the lot of you. If anyone else makes a sound, including you, Crown Junior, you'll see the Head of House tomorrow."

Silence followed. Most, including Jonathan, went back to sleep. Arthur, too frightened to move, was barely able to breathe. The dorm was quiet again, except for snoring. Arthur tried to stifle the sounds by wrapping his pillow around his head and over his ears. But the ugly nasal snorts kept coming through.

Across the dormitory, he watched two figures climb out of separate beds, leave their partners and tiptoe back to their own beds. He could hear bedsprings creaking in rhythm somewhere nearby.

Arthur thought about his miserable life in the House. He was aware of the tension that seethed below the surface. Changes were taking place all around him. Boys had formed cliques, while others had become full of secrets and hostility. Occasionally, he'd hear fragments of a conversation that stopped when he came too near. They whispered about who had done *it* with whom and who wanted to do *it*. Arthur wasn't clear as to who or what they so intensely discussed, but he had an idea that the subject was sex, about which he knew little.

Yet, Arthur did acknowledge that not everything had turned out for the worst. Ian would sometimes pitch in to help him maintain Flicker's study. Arthur knew he'd be lost without him. One Thursday, Ian was helping him clean up after Flicker and Croat had entertained. The two of them were alone in the study when Arthur found a plateful of smoked salmon slices with an inviting wedge of fresh lemon on the top.

"Do you suppose they'd miss one?" he asked.

"Don't even think about it," Ian cautioned. "You might fool Croat, but Flicker notices everything."

At those times when he tidied up the study alone, Flicker was seldom around. When he did come in, Arthur experienced a chilling sensation even though Flicker, moody and brooding, rarely said anything. He might shoot a stare at an unwashed dish, or an untidy desktop, and Arthur got the message. The study had to look perfect.

On another occasion when Arthur made a rush job of cleaning and washing up, Flicker told him, "If you do that again, what happens next, you'll remember for the rest of your life."

Arthur had no doubt that Flicker would carry out his threat.

School work was another problem. Despite Ian's help, he was always falling behind. They had put him in the lowest class in the school, referred to as "the dustbin," and still Arthur only hung on by a thread. He placed last at the most recent reading-over. Somehow, he'd managed to come twentieth in his class of nineteen.

Arthur was sick and tired of being so hopeless; he began to hatch a plan. It had all started at the impressionable age of five when his older brother, Harry, had scared Arthur practically to death by telling him nightly ghost stories in the bed they shared. Ever since, Arthur believed in goblins and evil spirits. He reasoned that if he could confront his fears and, along with Jonathan and Ian, walk in the forbidden cemetery one night, things might change. The ordeal could possibly help him to grow braver and stronger in his resolve. Right now, he was even afraid to go to the washroom and pee, for fear Sleeth, the red, hairy monster with a shaven head, was lying in wait for him.

11
CEMETERY

On Saturday evening, Trafalgar was all but deserted. Most had gone to the school gymnasium to see *Genevieve*, a popular British comedy film. Jonathan, Arthur and Ian stayed behind to have privacy, and were huddled over a Houseroom work table.

"I was out with my parents this afternoon. We stopped in Enderby," Ian said, "it's a quaint place. While my parents went shopping, I spent an hour in the town library. I checked out old copies of the local newspaper, *The Enderby Times*, looking for any report on that Trafalgar junior who died over a year ago."

Jonathan lit up. "Did you find anything?"

"Only a short article. The report stated that in March 1954, Stephen Rodgers, a student at Blackleigh, died in a tragic accident in the cemetery, near the school. Apparently, he was alone on that night and climbed to the top of the bell tower. Stephen accidentally fell and was killed on impact. There was no inference of foul play. After an enquiry, suicide was not considered a factor and he left no note. His death was described as 'accidental'."

"Did the report mention Flicker?" Jonathan asked, grim faced.

"No, not a word," Ian replied.

To Jonathan's surprise, Arthur spoke up.

"I'm not one for taking risks," he acknowledged. "My brother even says that I'm accident prone. But since we swore our Oath, I've been thinking we should check out the old cemetery some night. I won't make it through this term unless I start to face my fears. Going there will be an exercise in building up my courage."

"We could get ourselves in deep trouble," Ian said, frowning.

"C'mon Ian," Arthur pleaded, "I need to do this. I don't want to be there alone. Even with you two, if I see a ghost I'll shit my pants."

"We wouldn't want that to happen," Jonathan replied, smiling.

"Look Ian," said Arthur, "what do we lose by going there for just an hour? Next Saturday there's another film showing, and before the others return to the House, we could take a quick look around the place and come right back. I've got all the supplies we need. Let me show you."

Arthur went to his locker and returned with a carrier bag. He opened it and placed the contents on their table. "Here are pliers to cut through the barbed wire fence and three torches," he said. "Also, chocolate bars in case we get hungry."

"You mean in case *you* get hungry," Jonathan teased.

"We should wear duffle coats, scarves, running shoes, and gloves," Arthur added.

"I can't believe you've worked this out before you even knew we'd agree to go," said Ian. "You've thought of everything."

Arthur replied. "I hate the idea of it, but I have to do it." He looked at the other two with a pleading expression. "Will you come with me?"

Jonathan and Ian glanced at each other and nodded.

A smile lit up Arthur's face. "I owe you two for this."

"That's what I'm afraid of," Jonathan laughed.

★★★

The following Saturday evening, the three juniors dressed warmly against the cold weather. They left the Houseroom behind the other boys as if they too were going to the film. When no one was paying attention, they veered off in another direction, collected their supply bag, which Arthur had stashed under a bush, and headed to the cemetery.

"God, it's cold. Remind me again why we're doing this?" Ian grumbled. They trudged on, mostly in silence, the wind whipping their faces. The tower, luminous in the moonlight, soared in the night sky and appeared to grow taller as they approached.

Arthur, holding his carrier bag and leading the

way, was soon short of breath and sweating profusely, despite the cold. He clambered on through the tall grass. With his next step, he felt a crusty surface break and putrid brown excrement oozed over his white shoe.

He stopped and turned to Ian, a few paces behind. "Fuck, I've just stepped up to my ankle in cow dung. With this stink, people will know I'm coming from a mile away! Even the ghosts will want to steer clear of me." A grin crossed Arthur's face, "Ian, why do I always end up in the shit?"

"Wow! What a stench!" Ian said, holding his nose. "You don't look for shit, Arthur, but it finds you. Still, I suppose I'd rather be in the shit with you than with anyone else."

"I often wonder why you put up with me?" Arthur said, shrugging his shoulders.

"You make me laugh," Ian replied. "You're out of favour with everyone in the House. But with whom else, other than you and Jonathan, would I agree to go to this godforsaken place?"

The wind was intense and howling when they arrived at the fence barrier, which enclosed the grounds.

The three slumped down, shivering on the grass. Through the fence and beyond uneven mounds of earth, they observed the fallen walls of the chapel, the ghostly tower and the partial remains of stone walls among tall grass and stinging nettles.

"Now what?" Ian exhaled loudly.

Arthur opened his carrier bag, took out the pliers

and clicked them twice. "Now I'll cut a section of the wire and make an opening large enough for us to crawl through."

Jonathan edged away from the foul odour of Arthur's shoe, and watched him grip the pliers around the wire strands. But the wire refused to give. In frustration, Arthur funnelled his hands and tried to cut the same branches of wire from the other side. He gave a sharp yank. The pliers sprang from his hands and fell to the ground, out of reach.

"Sorry, I've fucked up," Arthur sighed. "We'll have to walk around and hope we can find an opening somewhere."

"Maybe this is a sign that we should go back to the House, right now," Ian suggested.

"We can't give up after coming all this way," Jonathan insisted.

At that moment, the three distinctly heard a rustling sound in the weeds nearby.

"What was that?" Ian exclaimed. "Maybe it's a wolf! C'mon, we better keep moving."

They walked on hurriedly, looking as they went for a break in the fencing.

At the far side of the enclosure they were rewarded for their efforts. Jonathan discovered an opening. They shone their torches on a framed wire door that melded into the fence and was partially open. A rusty metal chain, with thick links and a large, rusty bronze lock, lay on the ground nearby.

One after another, the juniors entered the forbidden

cemetery, focusing their beams directly ahead and waving them around in circular motions.

Most of the graves were marked with simple white headstones, and a few of the inscribed slabs lay flat on the ground. The graves were in disrepair. Some had crumbled, decayed by weather and age. Between most of the graves, large dry tufts of weeds grew higher than the headstones. A few sarcophagi, in the shape of coffins, were engraved with inscriptions on the stone lids, and largely covered in moss.

Ian, who had gone on ahead, nearer the tower, beckoned excitedly for Jonathan and Arthur to join him. They caught up with Ian and stood together. At the end of a dilapidated row of graves, was an amateurish, handmade, wooden cross. The three gathered around to read scribbled words written in black marker on the horizontal board: "God bless Stephen Rodgers, 1941-1954."

"One of Stephen's friends must have made it," Jonathan surmised.

Each of them said a silent prayer. Jonathan wondered, *Perhaps Rodgers was another victim of bullying at Trafalgar?*

Ian looked up from the grave to the tower beyond the cemetery. He'd seen the aperture at the top from the House side, but now observed that there also was an opening on the opposite side. He already felt queasy as he was deathly afraid of heights. Anyone standing on the high platform, between the two openings, would have a panoramic view of Blackleigh School, Trafalgar House and the surrounding countryside.

They walked on until Arthur spoke up, "How about we take a short rest? I'm scared half to death."

"All right," Jonathan agreed. He and Ian hopped up on the top of a sarcophagus. Arthur hesitated to join them. "C'mon Arthur." Jonathan patted the spot next to him. "It's this or the ground."

Jonathan offered a hand and helped Arthur up. He turned around and cautiously planted his butt next to Jonathan. "This is crazy," he fretted. "Don't say I didn't warn you if the lid rises up and a corpse yells 'Get off me!'" He settled down, heaved a deep sigh and passed out the chocolate bars.

"How do you feel, Arthur?" Ian asked, "Now that you're facing your demons?"

"Thank God you two are with me. I keep expecting a decomposed hand to shoot up from a grave and pull me down."

Jonathan and Ian chuckled.

"Hey!" Arthur brightened, "I don't know whose coffin we're sitting on, but I can think of a few names I'd like to see inscribed here! How about 'In memory of James Flicker?' or 'Hugo Sleeth?' or 'Tunk' – that gap-toothed slime-bag, whose first name nobody knows."

"Who'd miss them?" Ian scoffed. "I'd go to each of their funerals just to make sure they were really going under!"

"What'll you do if we see a ghost, Arthur?" Jonathan proposed.

"Offer it a Cadbury's chocolate Flake," Arthur mugged. "You two are great to have come with me."

Arthur sat up straight. "Now, I need to do something on my own. Then I'll know for sure I've conquered my fears. I'm going to check out the church. As soon as I'm back, we'll get out of here."

"We'll wait for you," said Jonathan.

The three hopped off the coffin and Jonathan gave Arthur a hearty slap on the back. Jonathan and Ian looked at one another. Both crossed their fingers as Arthur headed off into the dark.

Arthur soon made out that the church was a collapsed ruin. The walls were partially intact, but the front part of the church lacked a roof. Clouds hid the moon and he found it difficult to manoeuvre, even though he had his torch with him. He felt his way ahead, among rocks and overgrown vegetation, and strode on with determination towards the original church entrance, now consisting of an opening with two pillars on either side.

He stood in the doorway at the front end of the church and looked ahead to the far end, where once had been an altar. Beyond, he could see the sturdy outline of the tower.

Arthur edged his way forward and gagged when the strands of a spider's webs pressed against his face. He wiped them away and to his horror, loosened the grip on his torch. It dropped from his hand, rolled away, and the light abruptly went out.

Arthur paused to catch his breath. *What the hell shall I do now?* In the silence, he strained to listen for sounds. He was about to crawl around on the dirty floor to try and retrieve his torch when he thought he heard a noise. *Am I going crazy, or did I hear a door slam?* Arthur didn't want to know the answer.

He spun around in the direction whence he came, tripping over unseen debris as he ran. He recovered, sped on, then jumped over a large rock and ran as fast as he could, huffing and puffing, as if an army of lost souls was hurtling after him. Arthur continued on through tall weeds, passed a familiar tree, and was overjoyed to reach the cemetery.

Without a torch, it was difficult to see any graves in the hazy moonlight. "I'm back!" he cried. "I lost my fucking torch. Where are you two?" He moved cautiously about the cemetery, feeling his way in the pitch dark.

"Jonathan, come on out. Let's go home," Arthur called louder, becoming more anxious. The only sound he heard in response was the rush of wind. He was alone in the ghastly cemetery and didn't know the way out. There was no sign of Jonathan or Ian, and Arthur dropped to the ground in a faint.

12

SECRET CADRE

After Arthur left to explore the church, Ian began timing the minutes until his return. He felt a desperate need to share his unease. "I must tell you," he said to Jonathan, "I didn't want to say anything, but ever since we left the House, I haven't felt well."

"What's wrong?" Jonathan asked.

"That tower gives me the creeps. I can't get the picture out of my head of Rodgers up there, and the fear he must have felt."

"Do you have acrophobia, Ian?" Jonathan asked. He'd sensed this before.

"Yes. I seriously think I'm going to throw up if I stay here any longer."

"Look," Jonathan said, "why don't you go on back to the House? Arthur will understand. Matter of fact, I'll go find him and explain."

Ian let out a sigh of relief. "Maybe, as Arthur would

say, we'll laugh about this later, but not now." With that Ian took off.

Minutes passed; Jonathan waited but still no sign of Arthur. He watched the moon emerge clear and sharp from behind a cloud. Its pale light caught the headstones and stone coffins arrayed in the graveyard. Despite Ian's apprehension, Jonathan began to relax, calmed by the serenity of the scene.

In the moon glow, trees looked like silvery ghosts; unkempt grass rippled like shrouds in the wind, but he was not afraid. Rather, Jonathan sensed a timeless peace around him that fused the past with the present.

He mused that those who'd passed on were no different from those alive, except that they lived and struggled in another time. The challenges they faced were different from those of today, but the goal of making something of value from a short life, that passed so quickly, faced everyone.

Jonathan grew bolder, walking from headstone to headstone, contemplating the faded lives of another era. He shone his beam at an inscription on a granite headstone. The bold, black letters, which made up the epitaph had remained intact: "Will Burton, b:1840 d:1900… My dear husband, loved forever, never forgotten".

How, Jonathan wondered, *can evil prevail in a place where love and memory are one?* He recalled that Rodgers fell from the tower. His death occurred in the cemetery grounds, but otherwise had nothing to do with this place. Whatever caused him to jump, if that's what he did, haunted him before he came to the grounds. Something onerous had occurred that resulted in his losing the ability to cope with life.

Jonathan walked on to try and find Arthur. *I bet he'll be so relieved to see me!* They'd need to leave the cemetery soon in order to be back at Trafalgar before the rest of the House returned from the film.

The way ahead to the church was clear in the moonlight. Jonathan turned off his beam and stepped over heaps of stones. With growing confidence, he hummed to himself, awed to be part of the vast continuum between past and present.

★★★

On the eastern wall of the dilapidated church, a small annex was the only part of the structure still standing, to the right of where the altar used to be. Over the centuries, the room had been adapted to many purposes. In the earliest days of religious fervour, it served as a place for private prayer, and then a study. The room was used and adapted to the needs of the present occupants. Flicker and Croat sat at a table in candlelight.

The rest of the group, four seniors, sat cross-legged in a semicircle, on the stone floor.

Torches were placed at diverse angles, illuminating the cadaverous-looking faces of those present.

Cates, a hefty teen with a pimply face entered the room and said, "I just saw a fucking junior walking through the church, casual as you please, until he dropped his torch. I banged a door and the boy took off, scared shitless.”

“Do you know who he was?” Flicker asked. The senior wore a duffle coat over his white fencing outfit, having come directly to the meeting from his practice.

“I couldn’t say,” Cates shrugged.

“Why didn’t you find out, damn it?” Flicker’s face reddened with anger. He leaned forward and smashed his fist down hard on Cates’ nose. The boy’s head jerked back, his legs buckled leaving him sprawling on the floor.

“Christ, Flicker, why’d you do that?” Cates could feel his nose bleeding. “I think you broke it.”

“Cates, if that’s all it is, consider yourself lucky, you dumb arse.” Flicker immediately regained his composure. “Now, Croat, what’s been arranged?”

“There’s plenty of money in store for all of us. The supplier in Enderby says he can deliver the contraband once a week – but more frequent if there’s the demand. We already have a few reliable senior boys from other Houses to sell it around. All the orders will be placed through them. We won’t be directly…”

Croat’s words trailed off when the group heard a high-pitched voice outside. Croat placed a finger to his lips. All present lapsed into silence.

“Arthur, where are you?” the voice called out.

“Who the fuck is that?” Croat whispered.

Flicker stood as did the group. “I’ll handle this.”

“What are you going to do, James?” Croat asked with alarm.

"It sounds like Simon, that little shit with the birthmark," Flicker growled, "and apparently, Crown Junior is also sneaking around here." Flicker opened the door quietly and was gone.

Jonathan had entered the rear entrance of the church, moments after Arthur made his hasty retreat out the front. Jonathan thought perhaps Arthur had walked into the tower. He crept cautiously into the dark arched entry and found himself in an enclosed area, bounded by four lofty stone walls.

He looked down with disgust; his torch illuminating mounds of dust banking up at the base of the interior walls and a few beetles scurrying across the floor. A rickety wood staircase ran zigzag up to the top of the tower absent a handrail for support. Jonathan coughed after inhaling a cloud of smoky particles and turned his beam upwards. Far above, he could barely make out a platform. Jonathan could hear a rush of wind sweeping down.

"Arthur are you up there?" he called and was startled to hear a rustling sound nearby. *Rats?* Jonathan wondered. He began to climb slowly one step after another.

"For Christ's sake, Arthur, if you're up there, let me know." Six steps up, Jonathan froze. He realised these were the same stairs Rodgers had taken on the fateful night he died; and now Jonathan felt so scared he thought he'd go mad.

A deep voice barked from below, "Hey you! Get the fuck down here!"

Jonathan's heart almost burst with the shock of

seeing a tall figure in a duffle coat at the bottom of the steps. "My God," he gasped.

Flicker made no effort to hide his identity. "Simon," he hissed, "what the hell are you doing here? I don't know why this place attracts juniors, but you dumb fuckers keep coming. We seniors take turns spot checking – and it looks like it paid off."

"I'm searching for a friend," Jonathan said meekly. "We came to explore the cemetery."

"Who?" Flicker demanded.

"Crown Junior."

"Anyone else?"

"No, just Arthur and I," Jonathan lied, relieved that Ian was already heading back to the House.

"What am I going to do with you dumb buggers?" The question was as quixotic as it was unexpected.

Jonathan answered him carefully knowing that one wrong word might trigger Flicker's rage.

"Please Flicker, I swear we'll never come here again. It was an experiment, to try and test Arthur's bravery. Do what you like to me if I break my promise."

"Count on it." An uncomfortable silence followed before Flicker came up with an idea. "If either of you come here again, or if I ever hear of you doing *anything* out of line, it won't be you who pays. I'll take it out on your pal, Crown. The word 'punishment' won't come close to what will happen. The sky will fall on Crown's thick head. From now on, *you* are personally responsible for Crown's well-being. Now get the hell out of here."

Jonathan's heart was pumping wildly. He dashed

back to the cemetery in his manic search for Arthur. His friend had enough to worry about, having already been terrorised by Sleeth. But Flicker's threat, Jonathan knew, was even more dangerous. *Dare I tell Arthur what Flicker said?*

Back in the cemetery, Jonathan waved his torch frantically in every direction, but there was no sign of Arthur. He rounded a sarcophagus and stumbled over a huge lump laying on the ground. He sat up and looked back, flashing his torch.

"Oh, no!" In the beam, he saw Arthur's limp body stretched out.

"Jeez Jonathan, watch where you're going." Arthur slowly rose to a sitting position, rubbing his eyes. "Keep yelling like that and you'll wake the dead."

"Arthur…" Jonathan exhaled his relief, "I thought you were…"

"Hey, I was just talking a little cat-nap," Arthur white-lied, "Where's Ian?"

"Ian wasn't feeling well and took off. Boy, you gave me a shock!"

"Sorry," Arthur replied. "I needed my beauty sleep. Jonathan, thanks for coming with me. I believe I've conquered my fears." Arthur stood up and pounded his chest with his fist. "Sleeth and the rest of those thugs better watch out!"

"I only wish they'd see it your way," Jonathan shrugged his shoulders. "I've had enough of this place. Arthur, promise me you'll never get the harebrained idea to come here again."

Arthur held up his hand, as if swearing, then said, "There's one last thing…"

Jonathan rolled his eyes. "Yes!"

"How am I going to get the cow shit off my shoe?"

Jonathan roared with laughter and gave Arthur a shove in the direction of Trafalgar. He decided not to tell Arthur about Flicker's threat, fearing it'd be too much for his friend to handle.

13

DAVID GOLD

December 1955

The first Saturday in the month was a time of colds, chills, fresh flurries of snow, and the promise of returning home soon for the short Christmas holiday. In the Houseroom, shouts of anger and swearing followed anyone who failed to close the swing doors or open windows and let in freezing air. Boys sat on radiators to keep warm, and nursed chilblains on both their hands and feet.

Jonathan finished his weekend homework and washed up the dirty dishes left for him in Hollis' study. He put on his duffle coat and scarf over layers of clothing and walked to a nearby bus stop, for a ride into Enderby, his first visit there to explore the shops, maybe buy an inexpensive gift or two.

A small green bus pulled up; Jonathan waited as a

few passengers got off. Jonathan paid the driver and found a window seat. He looked out at the school rugby team, known as The Ravens, take the field in their black shirts with yellow collars, black shorts and socks. Cheers erupted from the home supporters crowding along the touchline, scarves waved in the air looked like blackbirds in flight. The opposing team's supporters, mostly wearing red and white scarves, cheered on the opposite side of the field, in anticipation of their team's entrance.

The bus lurched forward and picked up speed. There were only a few other passengers. Jonathan soon found himself being observed by a gaunt figure sitting in a seat on the other side of the aisle. Jonathan, who presumed the stranger was looking at his birthmark, became self-conscious and turned away.

The young man's uniform indicated he was from Blackleigh. He carried a dark blue duffle coat and was immaculately dressed as if he'd been delivered, fully clothed, from a department store. His smallish head with curly brown hair and blue eyes was out of proportion to his tall, gangly, non-athletic body. Grey trousers with razor-sharp creases complemented his shining black shoes.

Jonathan shot a second glance at him; the boy nodded amicably and said, "I suppose you're a first-year here. What's your name?"

"Simon… I'm in Trafalgar."

"Ah… I am David Gold. I have been at Plessey House for almost a year. And your first name?"

"Jonathan."

"I'll bet you're from London – and you're Jewish."

Jonathan's eyebrows went up involuntarily. "How do you know?"

"I can tell these things. I am too, by the way. We live in Finchley. My father is a very well-known accountant with lots of celebrity clients. I was accepted by at least three schools, but decided to come here. What does your father do?"

"My father died a few years ago," Jonathan said quietly.

David remained silent but moved across the aisle and sat next to Jonathan. "I'm sorry about that," he said solemnly. Then turning towards him, David formally shook Jonathan's hand.

Jonathan tried to smile but felt tears coming. To change the subject, he joked, "I see that you weren't selected to play for The Ravens today. Without you, we'll probably lose."

"Interesting you should say that, Jonathan," David replied, missing Jonathan's attempt at humour. "You may know that there are a few players on the school team selected from Plessey House. I'd like to think that those choosing the team will consider my potential next year.

"I presently suffer a medical problem, a tender heel. That's the reason I sadly miss out on many of our House sporting activities, such as runs and physical training sessions, twice a week. Neither Mrs Cardew, our house matron, nor the school doctor know what to do about it. They think I have an unusual form of arthritis."

Jonathan gave him a bemused look as if to say he didn't believe a word of what Gold said. Yet he was intrigued by David's vaulted opinion of himself.

"Since we're both going into Enderby," Jonathan proposed, "how about we have lunch together?"

"Why not?" David gave a hearty thumbs-up.

They walked from the bus stop along Enderby High Street in search of a restaurant. A farmers' market, situated on the street, offered fruit, fresh flowers and farm produce from small stands. David spotted a restaurant across the street just as they were passing a hardware shop.

Jonathan peered into the window. On display were a series of Swiss Army knives, with one like Ian's. The red handled knife with an engrained silver cross, sprouted two silver blades, a corkscrew and a tiny pair of scissors.

"A friend of mine has one of these," Jonathan gestured with enthusiasm. "There's even something to remove a stone from a horse's hoof."

"I don't need mini-scissors and I don't plan to remove stones from a horse's hoof anytime soon," countered David. "I've enough problems with my own foot. You want to buy a pocket knife, be my guest. I'll wait for you in the café."

Jonathan happily purchased the knife with pocket money his mother had set aside for him, that was distributed weekly in the House. He crossed the street and joined David in the small restaurant at a corner table.

Over tea, boiled eggs, toast and a sliced homemade cake, Jonathan asked, "How are things in Plessey?"

"Jonathan, like I said, I don't involve myself in House activities, because of my medical problems," David explained. "That keeps me out of trouble and away from prefects."

"You're lucky. There are sadistic bullies at Trafalgar, we can't avoid. What about drugs? They're all over the place at Trafalgar."

"Jamais dans toute ma vie," David rattled off.

"What's that mean?"

"It's French, for 'never in all my life'," David boasted. "It so happens that I have an innate talent for languages. Anyway, in answer to your question, I've never seen drugs or heard anything about bullying at Plessey."

"David," Jonathan pressed, "are you sure that you don't walk around in a bubble? Life sucks for the juniors in Trafalgar. Seems all we do is wait for the next outrageous bullying incident. Yet, you say that you neither hear nor see anything. What about sex in your House? You must be aware that every night in the dorms…"

"I don't know what you're talking about," David cut him off emphatically. "Are we discussing the same school? At Plessey, people just aren't into that kind of thing. I also get moral support by attending a Jewish service held every Sunday at 11.00 am, same time as the chapel service. A rabbi comes down from London to teach the few of us who attend. Why don't you join us? It might help you."

Jonathan made a hard face. "I'll tell you why I don't come, David. Things are so bad at Trafalgar that I need to pray hard in the chapel just to get through the next week. The chapel is a house of prayer too, after all. Whether I turn up to your service or not, your rabbi from London won't know how to stave-off bullying."

"He never speaks about bullying. I've never heard about such behaviour either," David said incredulously.

"Really?" Jonathan threw up his hands. "For example, a friend of mine was physically assaulted by a senior in the washroom for no reason on his first day here." He paused, thought about the rifle range episode, but changed his mind. "There's so much more I could tell you, but I see you don't believe me, or maybe you don't want to know."

"I'm just surprised," David said, shaking his head in disbelief. "I assure you, there's nothing like that going on at Plessey. Bullying is, of course, unacceptable anywhere."

"Then you must put your head in the ground and block out everything. I hope one day you'll find a way to face reality."

"And until that day comes," David smiled nonchalantly, "I'll drink my third cup of tea and have the last slice of cake, if I may. My father always says, 'Whatever you do, first look after the inner man.'" David reached for the cake and added, "You may be interested to know that my father gets two complimentary tickets to see Arsenal play their home games at Highbury. Of course, the tickets are for the best seats near the directors' box."

"How nice…" Jonathan replied without interest and looked at his wristwatch. "Shit! With all this talking, we've missed the last bus. We'll have to walk back to school."

"But with my foot condition, how will I make it?" David protested.

"Your heel has to hold up. That's reality! Let's pay and get going."

They commenced the long walk back to the school. While heading up the road towards the grounds, Jonathan was surprised that housing developments on the outskirts of Enderby had expanded even to the boundary walls of Blackleigh. Each newly-built brick house was two-storey with a tiled roof and chimney. The houses all looked the same, apart from the front doors, drain pipes and garage doors, painted in different matching colours.

In one small front garden, a heavy woman with grey hair in a bun was trying to soothe a crying toddler, sitting on the grass. The shoeless little girl was wearing a torn, muddy dress, and a baby was bawling in a pram nearby. To Jonathan's surprise, David acknowledged the woman with a friendly wave, calling out, as if he knew her well, "Greetings! How are you doing today?"

The woman, taken aback, reacted with anger, "You bloody idiot, can't you see I'm busy. What the hell do you want?"

They hurried on. David was confused by her hostile reaction. "I was only trying to be friendly, what's her problem?"

"You live in your own world, David. You're so wrapped up in yourself, I don't think you realise why people react to you in the way they do. The woman has her own problems. She sees you all dressed up and going to a fancy school. It looks to her that you haven't a care in the world. No wonder she's angry."

"Is it my fault that I grew up privileged?"

Jonathan could only shake his head at David's naïveté.

They continued walking, for close to an hour, on the steady uphill approach to the school and finally turned into a wide road, a mile and a half from Blackleigh Hall. David continually wheezed and complained about his sore heel.

In the distance, Jonathan made out two Trafalgar figures, athletes on a run. They'd stopped to talk. Jonathan blinked, wondering if his eyes were deceiving him. The two were caressing each other, then they quickly pulled apart and continued running towards them.

Jonathan was embarrassed to recognise the runners. Keith Rayner was in the company of Holt, a House senior. When they ran past, he and Rayner exchanged glances, both giving each other an uncomfortable nod of recognition.

"Weren't those two from your House?" David asked. "How come you didn't introduce me?"

"Yes, they're both in Trafalgar. Maybe I'll make introductions another time."

Half a mile from the school, both Jonathan and David were shivering; the wind had become more intense and the sky darkened.

"We can make it by the six o' clock supper bell if we pick up the pace a little," Jonathan said.

"I need a break," David whimpered.

"Okay, but let's make it quick."

They sat on the grass, with their knees drawn up. Jonathan could see the lights of the school in the distance. Behind him, he was alarmed to hear laughing and swearing coming from the a nearby grove of trees.

They both turned to see two tall figures in duffle coats come out of the undergrowth. They were accompanied by an even taller youth with a shaved head, wearing a T-shirt and corps denim trousers. The three of them jostled each other and then chucked their beer bottles into the undergrowth. They spied Jonathan and David sitting together and headed towards them.

Jonathan recognised Sleeth; the two other seniors were from Plessey House.

"Sit still and maybe they won't bother us," Jonathan whispered to David.

Instead, David Gold struggled to his feet. "I can't just do nothing and wait here."

But before David could take a step, Sleeth called out, "Hey you spastics… want to have a word."

Drub, from Plessey spoke next. "Looks like we found ourselves some Jesus killers. I know you, Gold. Who's your friend with red crap on his face?"

"He's Simon," David replied nervously.

"Well, I certainly know that shithead!" Sleeth laughed at his private joke. "Term after next, I'll have you in the corps, Simon. I'm waiting for you, especially with your interest in the rifle range."

"We're not looking for trouble, Sleeth," Jonathan said evenly.

"I wouldn't call kicking your arse any trouble," Sleeth grinned. He turned to his two companions. "Get 'em!"

The three seniors raced forward with blood curdling yells. Jonathan felt the breath leave his body when Spear, a freckled thug, clamped pincer hands around his throat. Jonathan tried to pull away, but his assailant was bigger and stronger. From the corner of his eye, he saw Drub grab David from behind by the collar, while Sleeth levelled his large fist in the terrified boy's face.

"Please let go," David begged, "I'll give you my wristwatch, it's brand new."

Jonathan finally broke away and yelled, "Don't give Sleeth anything!"

Sleeth calmly looked at Jonathan. "I'll deal with you in a minute." He turned back to David, "Hand over your wallet, wristwatch and any loose shekels."

Sleeth put his fist to David's face again, then cocked it. David rapidly undid his wristwatch and handed it over, followed by his wallet, then the loose change in his pocket.

"Now, let me go, please," David pleaded. "I gave you what you wanted."

"Yeah, you can go," Sleeth said quietly, flashing Drub a brief hand signal.

In the next instant, Drub spun the junior around and released a hammer blow that struck David between the eyes, almost bowling him over. David, bloodied and shaking his head, looked with disbelief at Sleeth then Drub. He began to sob and bolted towards the school. Sleeth and the two seniors laughed uproariously.

While everyone's attention was focused upon David, Jonathan had removed the knife from his pocket, opened the largest blade, and was holding it at the ready behind his back.

Sleeth turned to Jonathan and snapped his fingers, "You know the drill… watch and wallet."

Jonathan's beloved watch had been passed down to him from his father before he died and was something he'd pass to his son. At the thought of having to hand it over to Sleeth he lost control. With a shrill scream, Jonathan slashed the air right and left with his knife. The two Plessey assailants put up their hands and backed away. But even though the blade came within inches of his face, Sleeth remained steadfast and unblinking. "I won't forget this, Simon. You only get one reprieve. Now, get the fuck out of my sight."

Jonathan turned and ran as fast as he could towards the lighted buildings. He couldn't wait to tell Ian and Arthur what happened. While David paid a heavy price for his surrender, Jonathan had faced those he feared and triumphed. The Oath was now a living force within him.

14

ANTHONY SUMMERS

Just before the Christmas holiday, Jonathan was in the main building, looking at the latest bulletins on the school notice boards. No new announcements affected him, so he decided to head over to Trafalgar.

Jonathan came out of the building, in the cold grey afternoon, and stopped in his tracks. David Gold, impeccably dressed, was coming up the wide steps towards him. Jonathan was furious that David had made no effort to find out what'd happened to him after they were attacked, and he didn't feel like talking.

David looked up as they were about to pass each other and said brightly, "Hello, Jonathan. Well… only six days until the holiday." He let out a throaty chuckle that reminded Jonathan of a hen clucking at feeding time.

"The last time I saw you," said Jonathan, "you were crying with your tail between your legs, leaving me behind with those brutes. Two of them were from Plessey and, of course, they knew you. I'm surprised you didn't introduce me."

David blushed but quickly recovered his demeanour. "What an attitude, Jonathan! If I remember rightly, I allowed myself to be hit." David attempted to illustrate his most recent ailment by weakly half turning his head and grimacing in pain. "See, I can only turn so far until my neck tweaks."

"But you didn't try to find out what happened to me!"

"What do you mean?" David replied, puzzled. "I gave up my wallet, cash and my new watch to those racists. After that, I assumed they'd leave *you* alone."

"My God, what a whopping lie!" Jonathan shook his head in bewilderment. "You actually believe you're some kind of a hero. David, are you dreaming? Open your eyes!"

"What about you?" David gestured the length of Jonathan's body. "You obviously survived in one piece… not even a scratch!"

"No thanks to you."

David looked confused. Jonathan realised that he was wasting his breath and said, "Let's forget it."

An uneasy silence passed between them until David broke the impasse. "I want you to know, Jonathan, that I had tickets to Arsenal over the holiday, amongst other valuable items stolen in my wallet. It was the local derby with Chelsea. My father got me those tickets from one of his clients."

Jonathan made no comment. *Why does David need to boast all the time?*

"Well, I'll see you," David said in conclusion. "I've homework to finish for 'Crazy Abbot'. I usually look up the answers to our math prep. They're in a supplement to our assigned textbook that I sent for. I like to know the correct answers to see if I'm right or wrong."

"David, knowing you, I'm sure you're right most of the time."

"Thank you for saying that, Jonathan. As it happens, at maths, I usually am right. Anyway, have a good holiday." David then added wryly, "Don't do anything I wouldn't do."

"Please David, don't say that. It doesn't mean anything." Jonathan didn't know whether to tear his hair out or laugh it off. He grimaced, and then for some unknown reason, he extended his hand, and they both shook. Jonathan went down the steps wondering how many 'Davids' there were in the world; people who lived in a dream world.

David stood at the top of the steps, watching Jonathan walk away. He was relieved that they had sort of made up, even though David knew that the explanation of his actions was lame. He had other things on his mind and could only cope with so much at one time. Reality, he acknowledged, had come to roost; though he couldn't confide that in Jonathan. Sleeth and his thugs couldn't torture him as much as did his present conflict.

He walked through to the assembly and out onto the far side of Blackleigh Hall. To his left, he saw the first fifteen rugby pitch; recognising he'd never play there, now or in the future. Two unoccupied canvas chairs were left at the sideline. He needed to sit, look up at the sky and try to make sense of his last week. David chose one of the chairs, wiped the seat and settled down.

He adjusted his trousers and noticed a visible whitish-yellow stain on the grey front fabric by his zipper. He flushed with embarrassment and cried aloud, "Damn that macaroni I spilt at lunch. Looks like a gob of semen on my fly!" He always made a point to dress with flair. Neatly pressed, clean clothes helped him feel in control of his life. Now he had to return to Plessey and arrange with the matron for his trousers to be cleaned. That busybody matron would ask him about the stain and how it got there. He wished for a magic wand to remove the smudge himself and change his life at the same time.

★★★

David had arrived at Plessey older than other newcomers in his House. He took the common entrance exam later than others of his age. His father was unsure if David was mature enough for life at a boy's boarding school. Since coming to Plessey, he'd tried to fit in; but apart from his brief relationship with Jonathan, he had no friends. He was uncoordinated and found it impossible to keep up with others on runs or involve himself in other sporting activities. House members soon grew tired of his constant complaints about various medical problems that were likely fabricated.

Despite what he'd told Jonathan, as in the other Houses, sex was an intense preoccupation at Plessey. The topic dominated the conversation in their Houseroom and dorms. By his not talking or thinking about it, David hoped that the subject would go away and have no impact upon him.

It hadn't helped when two juniors played strip poker in the dorm, beside his bed, oblivious to everyone else. He was astonished to see them play their game all the way to the naked finish, each handling and arousing the other's penis. Jonathan was right when he warned him that a situation might arise he'd be unable to ignore. It had come in the form of Anthony Summers.

Only a short time ago, his mind was relatively carefree. David missed having friends at Plessey but managed to ignore all talk of bullying, drinking, anti-Semitism, smoking and drugs for almost a year. The ghastly incident, when he and Jonathan were viciously attacked by the demented racists had shocked him to the core; but he still found a way to explain this to himself as an isolated incident. There was, however, no way to dismiss Anthony.

David recalled how he had participated in an abbreviated one-mile run the previous Sunday, and despite persistent pain in his foot, was proud of himself for finishing, albeit last. He entered the Plessey changing room pleased to see no one there.

Being circumcised added to David's sensitivity about showering with the others. He didn't want to be identified as Jewish if he could help it. No point tempting the bullies. When the four showers were full of boys, he'd watch and wait from a distance while each naked wet body left, and newcomers took their places. They too became mingling bodies, amid steam and constant jets of hot water, until they all finally left to dry themselves, leaving the showers free. Only then did David, with his towel close by, take his turn.

This time, he quickly undressed; and passing a mirror on his way to the showers, was dismayed by the straggly appearance of his nakedness. However, once under the water, his mind eased to the soothing feel of gentle pressure on his body. He could finally relax with no one around. He adjusted the hot tap, taking pleasure in the extra surge of water down the front of his body and over his genitals. He closed his eyes.

He snapped them open upon hearing the shower next to his turn on. Through the steam, David cautiously looked across at the intruder and his young, tanned body covered in a watery sheen.

A hand touched his arm, giving him goosebumps.

"Turn down your hot water – it's coming over to my side."

"Right," David replied, fumbling with the tap adjustment.

The modulated voice was provocative. David recognised the newcomer as a first-term junior at Plessey. They'd never talked, but David had noticed him on his infrequent attendance at Plessey physical training classes. Anthony Summers was, David thought, one of those good-looking, blond-haired, blue-eyed boys, who had everything going for him. He was popular, excelled at sports and ran like a gazelle.

David took in Summers' well-defined body and glanced at his penis. Summers was covered in soap suds, sliding down his bare torso. Entranced, but trying to appear casual, David watched the foam glide down Summers' muscular chest, flat stomach, well-proportioned genitals and sculpted thighs until it washed away at his feet. To David, in the shock of discovery, Summers' appearance was neither that of a boy nor a man. His form was masculine but infused with beauty, caught in time, before his face and body changed and he grew to maturity.

"I don't know why we haven't talked much," David ventured. "How do you find school?"

Summers took in David with his piercing blue eyes. "School's good, but I missed two weeks with the flu, so I need to catch up, especially in maths."

"Who's your teacher?

"Mr Guttmann. The man's a bore! He needs a rocket up his arse to make him come alive."

David laughed at the thought of the elderly Guttman, nicknamed 'Slug', with his domed head, propelled through space, smoke fizzling from his rear.

"Slug taught me maths last term. Now I'm in the top group with 'Crazy Abbot'," David bragged.

Anthony pondered this a moment, then replied, "If you're that hot at maths, maybe you'd give me some help?"

"Why not?" David felt himself and his erection soar to heaven.

A split second later, David became embarrassed. He bolted and grabbed his towel on the way to the wooden benches in the changing room. His heart was beating fast and he felt heat pulsing through him. David looked down between his legs; his erection spoke with a timeless language of desire – a mind all its own.

David realised that in his haste, he'd forgotten to turn off his shower. But his priority was to dry off and get dressed before Summers came into the changing room. What a fool he'd been to sound off about his dubious academic ability.

David hastily slipped on his underpants and his eyes became riveted to his groin where a leaning tower of Pisa stretched the fabric to the limit.

He glanced along a bench searching for his grey trousers. They were hanging on a metal hook, where he'd earlier been sitting. He grabbed them and hauled them over his legs just as Summers, naked and dripping wet, strode into the changing room. David watched the lithe and sinewy Summers bend over to dry himself with his towel.

"Gold," Summers chuckled, "you left so fucking fast you forgot to turn off the water. But don't worry, I did it for you."

David, trying to nonchalantly hold his towel in front of his pants, blurted out, "Thanks, I don't know what I was thinking."

Summers continued to dry, placing his bare leg up on the bench next to David, flexing his toes. David hardly knew where to look. He felt like he was drowning in the intensity of the moment. Summers, still naked, turned to face him. "Were you serious about helping me? I have to get ready for our final exam two days before the end of term."

"Sure… Summers, isn't it?" David found the words slipping out, "What about the next few evenings in the Houseroom?"

"Great… and please, call me Anthony."

"Okay… I'm David."

Anthony looked directly at him and grinned.

David sat rooted to the bench while Anthony dressed in a T-shirt, shorts and running shoes. When Anthony was ready, he walked to the door of the changing room and nodded at David. "Tonight then."

David found the spontaneous words leaving his mouth: "Don't do anything I wouldn't do."

"I think there's a lot of things you might actually do, David. We'll see," Summers replied in the tone of a challenge. Before David could answer, Anthony was gone, leaving David alone, listening to the *drip… drip… drip…* of water from one of the showerheads.

★★★

David's mind returned from his reverie. He was back sitting on his chair, overlooking the rugby field. David wondered what was happening to him. His mightily constructed wall of defence was coming apart, brick by brick. He closed his eyes and tried to remain calm.

The first maths lesson with Anthony went well as did the one that followed. But he was nervous in the new junior's presence. Each night he was fighting off dark, erotic fantasies that haunted him when he tried to sleep.

The worst part was that David had no one with whom he could discuss his predicament. He considered reading material from his Sunday religious class, but knew that this remedy, so helpful in the past, would not cure his present ailment. One ray of light kept him sane. For once in his life, he felt totally alive.

15

PREFECTS

January 1956

Over the Christmas and New Year holiday, Jonathan felt dislocated from life at home, unable to shed the protective skin he wore to survive at school. He was out of touch with his old friends from his London day-school, before he went to Blackleigh. No one could relate to his predicament at boarding school.

His mother was preoccupied with work. Elsie tried to understand his frustration but was of little help. Although he was peeved at David Gold, he wanted to rise above it and do the right thing. For someone like David, self-absorbed and naïve about what was going on around him, Blackleigh would be tough going.

When David failed to return his phone call, Jonathan wasn't that surprised. Before he realised it, the few weeks of holiday passed by and he was back at Blackleigh.

★★★

The Headmaster had called a school assembly in the main building. An observer, looking down from the highest point in the auditorium would see the black and white marble squares on the floor, and the great space bustling with vitality.

Through three of the four wide entrances around the circular assembly, hordes of uniformly dressed figures, clad in their black blazers with yellow insignias, swarmed in. The fourth and main entrance was reserved for faculty and prefects. Upon entering, many boys looked around to reconnect with friends. Each of the Houses were designated a specific area where to stand for the twelve o' clock proceedings.

Jonathan could hardly manoeuvre through the melee. The stubborn refusal of others to make way for anyone else was characteristic of those at the school. But without direct supervision by the prefects, the crowd freely released pent-up frustration. All around, tense faces tried to press forward to the open circle in the middle of the assembly where the Headmaster would speak at a podium.

Jonathan made his way through Plessey on his way to the Trafalgar section. He was looking for Ian and especially Arthur, sure that his friend would provide an entertaining commentary on the Headmaster's speech.

He winced with pain following a savage punch to the small of his back. "Owww…" Jonathan lurched forward into the boy ahead of him while trying to regain his balance. A second blow, harder than the first, forced him to stagger to the side. He turned to try and identify his assailant, but the crush on both sides was too tight.

Jonathan saw a small opening in the crowd ahead and squeezed into the gap. He angrily turned, wheezing, and recognised the smirking, acne-blotted face of Sleeth shadowing him.

The senior whispered in his ear. "You fuck, you'll pay for pulling that knife on me."

In the next moment, Jonathan was beyond Sleeth's reach and being swept on further by a shift in the tide of bodies. He saw Sleeth stretch out his arm and point to him menacingly, his face twisted into a creepy smile.

You're crazy. Get some help, Jonathan mouthed back.

He looked at the new watch his mother gave him for Hanukkah; his father's watch was stored at home for safekeeping. Ten minutes remained before the scheduled assembly. All around Jonathan were Plessey faces. On a whim, Jonathan decided to look for David, who wouldn't be hard to find with his tall, lanky figure and receding curly hair.

Jonathan saw him in the front, engaged in a lively conversation with a good-looking boy. The image of *Beauty and the Beast* came to Jonathan's mind.

He disregarded the pain from Sleeth's blows, forced his way to the front, and confronted David. "I called you over Christmas but never heard back."

David was unfazed by Jonathan's unexpected arrival; he smiled with enthusiasm and grasped Jonathan's hand as if greeting a long-lost friend. David looked as immaculate as ever, sporting a new black blazer with the letter 'B' on the pocket, embossed in glinting gold rather than the standard yellow.

He noticed Jonathan staring at the letter. "Don't you think the shiny gold is a nice touch, Jonathan? I've had so many compliments. Gold is my name and gold's my game. Get it? Ha!"

"I called you," Jonathan repeated, ignoring David's bluster.

"And I was going to call you back," David responded, "but there was no time at the end of the holidays. We went to Tuscany and came back the day before school. My father needed a break from his accountancy practice near Piccadilly which is always growing."

Jonathan shook his head in frustration at David's pompous manner. "You should know that I just ran across an old friend of ours… Hugh Sleeth."

David burst into a charade of coughing to cover his embarrassment. He quickly recovered his composure and smiled at his fair-haired friend beside him.

"Sleeth, huh?" he echoed. "Tell me, how's the dear boy? In good health, I expect."

"As well as always. He hasn't forgotten us," Jonathan said to goad David.

"Well, you'll have to say hello to Sleeth for me. Right now, Jonathan, I'm too busy and just not able to make time for him." David waved a dismissive hand. "Anyway, I'd like to introduce you to my new friend, Anthony Summers."

Jonathan turned to Anthony. He'd rarely seen such

penetrating blue eyes. But Anthony's heavenly looks went far beyond his face; he had a charismatic glow about him.

"Anthony's on the Plessey cross-country team," David said proudly.

Anthony nodded modestly. "Good to meet you, Jonathan," he said casually, "David helps me with maths and in return I've promised to help him train."

"Sounds great," Jonathan said, amazed at David's interchangeable personality. "But when it comes to David's running, can you improve on perfection?"

"Probably," said Anthony, laughing.

The Assembly was about to start, and Jonathan had his fill of David.

He turned and headed for Trafalgar.

Jonathan first nodded to Keith Rayner, who smiled back. He noticed Tunk leering darkly in his direction, then he edged over between Ian and Arthur; they smiled and the three patted each other on the back.

The outer doors of the assembly shut with an echoing boom. The hundreds in attendance merged into a solid mass, leaving an open circle in the middle, accessed by an open pathway from the main interior door. The setting, with so many black blazers and yellow striped ties, was like a huge, black and yellow donut, with a hole in the center.

A murmur of expectation arose, followed by a hush. The Headmaster and Assistant Headmaster entered, wearing black gowns, each carrying a mortar board. With them was the present Head of School, Chris Mercer. They were accompanied by a phalanx of prefects, including the three from Trafalgar, who were staying on at the school. Hollis and Diamond were among those who had left, at the end of the previous term, and were going to university.

Ian nudged Jonathan. "Which of the seniors do you put your money on as new prefects? Something tells me we've bad news coming."

"Put it this way," whispered Arthur, "I told Ian to expect worse than bad news, so he won't be disappointed."

Their hurried conversation ended when the Head of School ordered "Silence" in a clear, strong voice.

Mr A. S. Stewart, the Headmaster, tall but stooping, glasses perched over his pointy nose, and a rosy complexion, spoke in his Scottish accent. "I am glad to see so many familiar faces. This term, there are some new lads joining us from abroad. I anticipate they will be shown the same spirit of comradeship and cooperation for which Blackleigh is justly proud."

"Foreign students are the only ones who can pay the exorbitant school fees," Arthur whispered. "Wait till they sample the famous Blackleigh generosity of spirit… they'll flee back to their homeland."

Ian and Jonathan stifled a laugh.

The Headmaster looked down at his notes. "We've adopted a practice at our school that prefects are responsible for all aspects of discipline. Prefects enjoy an especial position of trust in our structure. May I remind you that at Blackleigh there is no room for dishonesty, hazing, or the use of banned substances. Such behaviour is grounds for suspension or expulsion.

"I am pleased to announce the names of our new House prefects. They shall replace those who've left. To the young men who will be with us no more, we thank them for their proud service and wish them well. The selection of these outstanding young men, our new prefects, is made in consultation with their Housemasters."

Mr A. S. Stewart called out the names of fifteen newly appointed prefects for the other Houses. Each time the masses in their part of the assembly made way allowing them to walk to the front. The Head and Assistant Head congratulated each one and shook his hand. The new authorities proudly took their places, forming two lines behind the Head. They and the existing prefects were the new power.

The Head paused. He had come to Trafalgar.

"From Trafalgar House, I am pleased to announce two names. The first new prefect is James Martin Flicker, who is currently attending a school fencing match and returns tomorrow." He paused for the smattering of applause. "And finally, Hugh Bradley Sleeth."

These choices can't possibly be worse, thought Jonathan. He felt a hard shove from behind. Sleeth was already pushing bodies aside, thrusting himself forward. He burst through between Arthur and Ian, his eyes fixed on the Headmaster. Sleeth passed the trembling Arthur and hissed under his breath, "I haven't forgotten you, worm."

Sleeth's staunch form seemed barely able to contain the brute strength and energy from his body. He forged ahead unsmiling, shaved head shining, came to the edge of the circle and advanced towards the Headmaster. Sleeth towered over the Head as they shook hands.

"Congratulations, Hugh. I know I can rely on you."

"You can, sir. I'll do you proud."

Sleeth took his place at the end of the first line of prefects, shoulders square, ramrod straight back, his chest jutting out. He silently vowed to teach those newly under his sway, and especially those for whom he had disdain, a new meaning to the word 'discipline'. Sleeth lordly surveyed the Trafalgar section; he couldn't wait to start cracking the whip.

16

DINNER PLAN

Arthur was drowning in homework. He'd already fallen behind and remained the lowest in his classes for another term. He imagined his plight as though floodwater was steadily rising to his chin and slopping precariously below his mouth. Soon, if he didn't improve on his class performance, the flood of unfinished assignments would engulf him.

The first week of the new term went badly, especially when he failed to finish a chemistry project. On Friday, Mr Pincher, known as The Pinch, a science teacher, returned Arthur's incomplete effort after scribbling a large question mark on the front page.

"What's this rubbish, Crown?" Pincher thrust a finger at the paper he'd just handed back to Arthur. "Your work is unacceptable. Do this project again. Turn your finished paper into my office no later than Wednesday morning."

Arthur also had other assignments outstanding; he shared his plight with Ian and Jonathan in the Houseroom.

"I'm swirling around the drain," moaned Arthur woefully.

"It's not as bad as you think," Jonathan tried to assure him.

"You always come through," Ian added, looking over Arthur's feeble chemistry papers.

"But probably not this time," Arthur replied with resignation, throwing his arms wide in a gesture of defeat. "I have this project to redo, two other assignments waiting, and there's maths, as well. Also, Flicker's study must be cleaned tomorrow. There's a new boy from South Africa, assigned to help me, but I have to train him first. What am I to do?"

Ian and Jonathan briefly conferred.

"How about this," Ian suggested. "Jonathan and I will help you today and at the weekend. If necessary, we'll continue Monday after school until you catch up."

Arthur's expression brightened, his loyal friends had thrown him another lifeline.

They spent Friday afternoon working together; Ian and Jonathan made good progress, and Arthur was overwhelmed.

"I want to show you how grateful I am!" Arthur proclaimed. "I'm going to buy some steaks, and I'll cook them for us in Flicker's study tomorrow evening – he and Croat will be gone. Also, Saturday is a film night.

The rest of the house will be watching *Doctor in the House* while we feast in our House.

"I'll order filet mignon from the school shop early tomorrow. I saw Croat do it once. I can buy frozen vegetables, mashed potato, ice cream and tinned fruit there too. They may have to send out to Enderby for the meat."

"Are you sure Flicker will be away?" Jonathan frowned. "It'll be curtains for us if he or Croat return early."

"Don't worry, they'll be gone. Flicker has a fencing match at Rugby. That's in Warwickshire. And Croat is going to London."

"I don't know… this is risky," Jonathan said tentatively.

"You worry too much, Jonathan," Arthur waved him off, "Flicker made it clear they'd be away. He gave me instructions to feed their bird Sunday morning."

"Alright… if you're so sure," Jonathan acquiesced.

Arthur hurried to his locker, grabbed a pad, and started making out a shopping list.

He was so preoccupied that he failed to notice a hush come over the Houseroom. Arthur looked up and was startled to see Flicker, himself, beckoning directly to him from the entry doors. Flicker turned and left the Houseroom with Arthur meekly following.

In the study, the prefect loomed over him. Flicker wore an impressive new tie, all gold with two diagonal black stripes – a prefect's badge of power. Arthur's planned excuses slipped from his mind. He'd accept total responsibility for any havoc, falling back on Flicker's limited mercy.

"I'm sorry Flicker," he blurted out, "on the last day before the holiday, I was in such a hurry to get home that I forgot to clean your carpet. I'll put this right. If you want, I'll…"

How dumb can this toad be? Flicker thought. *He's pleading leniency for some crime, even before he knows why I want to see him.*

"Shut the fuck up, Crown," Flicker cut him off, "I didn't call you here about my carpet, or to discuss anything from last term."

Arthur sighed with relief, was about to speak, then wisely decided on silence.

"As you know," Flicker continued, "a new boy will be helping you with your cleaning duties this term. Tomorrow is the best day to show Wynn what we expect. Croat is out all day Saturday and you already know that I'll be at an inter-school fencing match. I'm leaving Wynn and the study in your good hands. And don't forget to feed the bird."

"I'll show Wynn the ropes," he assured the prefect.

"Right… Then I can rely on you?"

"Absolutely."

Arthur left the study hardly believing his good fortune. He was relieved to be getting Wynn's help. It would now take only an hour and the rest of Saturday would be clear.

He'd start preparing the meal in the late afternoon. What a dinner it would be thanks to Flicker's meths stove! He'd buy plastic knives, forks and spoons, paper plates, placemats, cups and napkins. There'd be no need to use Flicker's utensils and he'd only have pots and pans to scrub clean. He had it all worked out! *How,* Arthur asked himself, *could anything so well planned possibly* go *wrong?*

PETER WYNN

Saturday morning, Arthur would spend an hour or so training Peter Wynn, a good-natured new junior, who hailed from Johannesburg.

"Hello, howsit?" he greeted Arthur. Peter had a distinctly large head, a good tan and swept back fair hair. He observed in his strong South African accent, "I tell you, someone in this bloody study has a thing for white. Maybe the chappie has a guilty conscience and he wants to white-out everything?"

"How right you are," Arthur chuckled. "The truth is, no one ever knows what's going on in Flicker's head."

They cleaned the carpet together, wiped the dusty surfaces and washed the dirty dishes and cutlery. Wynn neatly folded and draped Croat's blanket over an armchair.

"Hey Arthur, can we listen to music on Flicker's record player while we're working?" Wynn asked, noticing Flicker's neat stack of long playing records, mostly classical. He held up two covers: Bizet's *Carmen* and *Glenn Miller Favourites*.

"Don't even think about it," Arthur cautioned. "You shouldn't even touch the records. But he and Croat don't mind if I listen to their radio. I often catch *Housewives Choice*, if I get here early – and later, around eleven, if I don't have a class, there's *Music While You Work*. Both help the time pass quickly."

Arthur scanned the floor. "Your other job is to be on the lookout for cockroaches."

"Surely you must be joking," Peter scoffed. "If I see any of those ugly buggers, believe me, they'll be pancaked."

"One last thing," Arthur advised, "the prefect has a temper – it comes on like lightning. You can tell when he's mad – the scar on his cheek looks more pronounced.

"As for Croat, his study mate, he hasn't much to say about anything. If Flicker blew in his direction, Croat, who looks like a bloated frog, would topple over. Both in this study and at Trafalgar, Flicker is the power and the glory, forever and ever, A-men."

"I can't believe I've come all this way to clean a carpet and police roaches," Peter said, scratching his chin. "How do I answer my dad when he asks me what I'm learning in England?"

"Get used to it," Arthur retorted. "We also have to clean these cupboards, inside and out."

"Arthur, I need to finish up by twelve," Peter said glancing at his watch. "My aunt and uncle are driving up from Manchester to take me out for lunch. It may only be the end of my first week, but I already need a break!"

"I know what you mean," Arthur nodded. "Go ahead and take off. I've got the rest. There's not much left to do."

"I won't argue," Wynn said with delight. "Thanks for the instruction. I wouldn't have missed it for the world." Wynn waved a hand at Arthur and departed.

★★★

At six o'clock, Arthur sat alone in the serene white study looking ahead to the evening. *This will be some celebration!* He preferred to think about the coming meal as "dinner", a more formal description for what he'd prepare, rather than the word "supper", which described the inferior swill served up in the school dining rooms.

He expected his two honoured guests to join him in an hour. Arthur had already arranged three place settings. His secret ingredient, poured lavishly over the entrée, would come from an expensive bottle of Escoffier steak sauce.

He looked over at the colourful packets of Birds Eye frozen peas and chips, stacked ready for boiling. Three plates with Walls ice cream and tinned cherries were set aside for dessert, each to be consumed with a Dainty – a gourmet, chocolate covered, square marshmallow that he often treated himself to.

His plan had worked like a charm! Arthur gazed

around and saw the bird, pecking at its food tray. He closed his eyes and listened to soft pop music on Radio Luxembourg. *Life,* he thought, *could be worse.*

Arthur noticed that Ian had come to the study that afternoon, while he was out at the shop. His helpful friend had taken out Flicker's black meths stove, and he'd purchased a new bottle of methylated spirits. *Ian's thought of everything!* He'd also put the stove and spirits on Flicker's light blue Formica topped table and set aside the steaks in a bag, a bottle of steak sauce, and a pack of butter.

He briefly imagined Flicker or Croat returning early. After an extended period of torture, death would be welcomed. He banished the thought and made a mental note to be extra careful in removing all evidence and leaving the study spic and span after dinner.

Arthur glanced at the coloured print over Croat's desk. The distorted one-eyed woman appeared to be staring directly at him with a look of disapproval. Arthur took the print off the wall and placed it face down on the floor. *Now she can stare all she wants… at the white carpet.*

He felt something akin to a pride of ownership of the impeccably cleaned study. Of course, he'd make changes when he had a study of his own. For a start, he'd paint the walls in a soft color. He hoped one day to share that study with both Ian and Jonathan.

At six forty-five, the rest of the school was in the gymnasium, watching Dirk Bogarde, the famous British actor, in the role of a medical student. Arthur, not far away, stood in front of Flicker's stove, preparing for his unaccustomed role as a chef.

18

METHS MISHAP

Arthur opened the study window to draw out the expected smoke from the cooking meat. Next, he proceeded to pour methylated spirits into the circular tray at the base of the stove. A few drops of liquid overflowed the rim and dribbled out onto the tabletop. The overflow looked like opaque, miniscule drops of rainwater.

He struck a match to dispose of them, rather than wipe the meth tears away with a dishcloth. Arthur wanted to see the fiery colours fuse and lit the three drops, watching them transformed into teeny flames. The flairs looked almost magical on the table and Arthur marvelled at how beautifully the colours blended. He saw spiralling shades of blue, yellow and orange, coiling around each other. The fiery incandescence, as fragile as life itself, rapidly faded into oblivion.

Arthur was so intrigued that he failed to notice his

lighted match had burnt down to his fingers. "Yow!" he cried out in pain and watched spellbound as the hot match fell into the full meths tray. Arthur abruptly backed away and looked on in horror as the tray burst into flames. Within seconds, a raging conflagration roared up from the table. Red vicious tongues of fire leapt to darken the lower paintwork on the plasterboard wall.

He watched helplessly as the flames spread across the table, reaching ever higher over what swiftly became a black, blistered surface. Croat's bird was going berserk, screeching and fluttering from one side of the cage to the other in her desperation to escape. Arthur quickly opened the cage and guided her out with his finger. The bird flew upwards, releasing a final screeching cry before she flew out the open window. She left behind, in her wake, a turquoise feather drifting down to the floor.

The carrier bag holding the steaks was burning along with the paper place settings. Arthur somehow had the presence of mind to seize the open meths bottle and throw it out of the window. He heard it crash on the forecourt below.

"God help me!" Arthur gasped, "I've set the place on fire… Flicker will kill me!" Smoke was stinging his eyes; between sobs and coughing, Arthur opened the door and yelled for help.

The sound of rushing feet pounded along the corridor and both Jonathan and Ian burst into the room to see fire ablaze on the study wall. Ian looked around and saw Croat's heavy blanket draped over one of the armchairs. He grabbed it, and threw it over the table, smothering the flames that diffused into thick black smoke.

Jonathan tore off his jacket, threw it to the floor and stamped out numerous cinders fallen on the carpet.

Arthur looked on in a catatonic state while his friends double-checked that the last tongues of flame had been extinguished. All three then stood in a daze, spluttering and coughing, as smoke drifted through the open window.

Minutes passed. No one else showed up. The three juniors took in the grim sight. In several places, the white carpet was badly burnt; no amount of cleaning would remedy this. The wall nearest the table was blistered and the stove destroyed.

Arthur turned to his friends with a look of defeat. He closed his eyes, opened them again and uttered the unanswerable question weighing on his mind, "Flicker… what will he do to me? I had to free their bird… look around… it's a disaster!"

"How did this start?" Ian asked calmly.

Through tears and gulps, Arthur explained to Ian and Jonathan what he'd done. "Now I don't know what the hell to do. I need a miracle to wind the clock back before this happened."

"Arthur, I need to think," Ian ran both hands through his hair. "This is all too much for you." He turned to Jonathan and said, "Take Arthur up to the dorm, have him change into his pyjamas. Stay with Arthur. I'll come up when I'm done here. Not a word of this to anyone… promise me!"

Arthur, now a pathetic bawling soul, nodded miserably. "I promise."

"Go with Jonathan. I'll take care of things here."

Jonathan couldn't begin to fathom what Ian had in mind, but he presumed that his older and wiser friend knew what he was doing. He reluctantly led the blubbering Arthur out of the room and closed the door behind him.

Ian stood amid the catastrophe. Arthur would be expelled from Blackleigh, but that would be after Flicker had finished with him. Ian was determined to figure a way out of this terrible mess.

He resolved to clean the place as best he could and to beg Flicker for forgiveness. "Some hope!" he gasped aloud.

Ian's first task was to clear away all evidence of Arthur's planned dinner. He found large rubbish bags in the storage cupboard along with a broom, dustpan and brush. He threw the burnt carrier bag, all the plastic knives forks, spoons and napkins, into one bag. These were followed in another bag with the elements of Arthur's dinner. The main course of steaks and frozen vegetables went first, followed by three plates of ice cream, fruit and Dainties. Then he rummaged in the small fridge for any incriminating items brought that weren't Flicker's, such as the pad of butter, steak sauce and a half-used family brick of ice cream. Ian stored the full bags in the corner of the study for disposal later.

Outside, in the corridor, he heard footsteps approaching and his stomach tightened in fear. With a feeling of impending doom, Ian watched the door handle turn and the door open.

Ian looked down, not daring to see who it was, and heard a startled voice. "Shit, I must be dreaming? What the fuck happened? Arthur and I just cleaned this place today. Where's the bird?"

Ian looked up, relieved to see Peter Wynn and not Flicker or Croat.

"The fire was an accident. My fault. The bird's gone – flew out the window. I don't like to ask you this, Peter, but would you help me clean up?" Ian pleaded.

"Okay," Peter nodded, "as long as if you don't involve me."

"I promise I won't." Ian raised a solemn hand. "But what are you doing here?"

"I saw the light on from outside," Wynn said. "I came to check because no one was supposed to be in the study."

For almost an hour, Ian and Peter did their best to restore some order out of chaos. When they'd done as much as they could, Ian turned to Peter and let slip a smile. "Thanks so much."

Peter bent down and picked up something from off the carpet, "Look a memento," he said, handing a turquoise feather to Ian.

"If only I could fly away myself," Ian mused, putting the feather in his pocket.

Peter scratched his head. "If it's okay with you, I'll

take off now. Sorry to see you like this. It looks bad for you."

After Wynn left, Ian surveyed the study with a sad face. He grabbed the two trash bags and took them all the way over to the rubbish bins beyond the Chapel, where he felt they'd never be discovered. His last gesture was to toss the turquoise feather in with the rubbish and close the lid of the bin.

Ian returned to the House and went upstairs to find Jonathan and Arthur. He wondered how everything had fallen apart so fast. But he couldn't fully blame Arthur. He'd been just as eager to have a celebratory dinner and hadn't tried to dissuade him.

Ian opened the door of the junior dorm. Jonathan was sitting on his bed consoling Arthur; no one had returned from the movie yet.

Jonathan said, "I'll keep watch outside the door and let you know when the others come back."

"I always told you this school wasn't meant for me," Arthur moaned. "I feel horrible. I'll never live this down. I've failed both you and Jonathan. Flicker will come after me. My parents will go crazy when they find out."

Ian sat at the end of Arthur's bed. "Don't worry," he reassured Arthur. "The study looks a little better now. Peter Wynn helped me clean up."

"But you said tell no one," Arthur protested.

"Peter happened to walk in while I was there. I just told him that there'd been a fire. Anyone could see that."

"What are we going to do, Ian?"

Ian had been contemplating this question over the

past hour. "You are going to do nothing. I want you to promise me something... it's a second oath. This time it's an oath of silence."

"I'll swear whatever you want."

"You must let me work out things in my own way. Whatever happens next, never, I repeat, *never* admit to what you did."

"But Ian..."

"Swear!"

"Okay, I swear. But I don't understand."

"Just remember what you've promised me. That's all I ask. Now, close your eyes. Ian put his hand on Arthur's forehead. "Sleep well, my dear friend."

When he was sure that Arthur was fast asleep, he bent down and kissed him on the cheek.

Ian found Jonathan just outside the dorm.

"How is he, Ian?"

"Sleeping, thank God."

"Ian, there's something... I didn't want to worry you about it... but I need to tell you now."

"Go on, what is it?" Ian asked, frowning. "You know you can tell me anything."

Jonathan let out a heavy sigh. "That time at the cemetery, when you weren't feeling well and went back to the House..."

"Yes," Ian prompted, "what happened?"

"I went looking for Arthur, then had the shock of my life... I ran into Flicker at the tower."

"Flicker!" Ian gasped. "Shit! What was he doing there?'

"He told me that prefects take turns checking on

the place. But it's how Flicker threatened me that's important. He heard me calling for Arthur in the church, but I never told him that you also came with us. Flicker said that if Arthur or I ever went there again, or if I caused any future trouble, he'd put Arthur *alone* through absolute hell, *rather than me*, knowing we're such good friends. I suppose this was Flicker's way of having me control Arthur, and to curb me at the same time."

Ian reflected upon Jonathan's revelation. "You were right not to mention that before. Flicker's threat would have driven poor Arthur crazy. But this changes everything. Before I thought you and I could share equal blame for the fire. Now I see that Flicker will take it all out on Arthur anyway."

"What can I do to help you, Ian? Anything!"

"I made Arthur swear an oath of silence that whatever happened, he'd never tell anyone that he caused the fire," Ian explained. "If he breaks his promise, then, and only then, can you admit that you and I were planning to have dinner with Arthur, and that he accidentally started the fire."

"Of course, I'll swear to that, but when Flicker returns, who'll take the blame?"

"I'm thinking," Ian replied softly. "Believe me, Jonathan, the best thing you can do is to play dumb – stay completely out of this. And no matter what happens to me, make sure that Arthur does the same. Please trust me. Your complete silence is the only way we can protect Arthur from Flicker's rage."

"All right, you know I'll keep my word." Jonathan

held up his hand to solidify his pledge. "See you in the morning. Let's talk over everything again, first thing tomorrow."

Ian leaned forward and hugged Jonathan. "I want you to know… you and Arthur are unbelievable friends."

"We're friends forever." Jonathan, feeling overwhelmed, went back into the dorm.

Ian knew what he had to do. He went down to the Houseroom, took a small sheet of paper from his locker and wrote a short sentence in block letters. There were only five words. He folded it in half and put "James Flicker" on the front. Then he returned to the study where the smell still filled the air and placed his note, name up, on the damaged carpet.

At ten forty-five, groups of boys drifted into the junior dorm, still laughing over scenes from the film. No one paid any attention to Arthur or Jonathan, asleep in their beds. Sleeth, the prefect on duty came in, opened the windows and turned off the lights. Silence followed.

Moonlight already cast a spell and with its untarnished glow came the tender release of sleep… for all but Ian.

19

PUNISHMENT

The tall athletic figure strode along the path to Trafalgar, the House ahead shrouded in darkness. Flicker was dressed warmly against the chill night air. He wore a black sweater, scarf and trousers under his navy-blue duffle coat, black gloves and elegant black walking shoes.

While away, Flicker had his hair cut short and dyed it a dull white color that contrasted sharply with his rimless glasses and dark attire. He liked his new regal appearance that set him apart from others. Flicker felt empowered and alert. It was good to be active while the rest of the school slept. The prefect looked the part of a chosen one, ascending in the world.

After the tournament in Warwickshire, he'd met with some fencers from Rugby. He enjoyed having beers and discussing the match with the team from such a famous school, one of the oldest in England. Rugby was the birthplace of rugby football and in his early teens Flicker had read about the school, immortalised in Thomas Hughes' book, *Tom Brown's School Days.*

Flicker socialised that evening, assuming a modest persona. As captain of the Blackleigh fencing team, with many away matches, he had the advantage of excluding himself from the Blackleigh cadet corps. All the better since that was the only activity where Sleeth outranked him. A late-night train back to Enderby suited him better than to return to school Sunday morning; since he was scheduled to read a lesson from the pulpit for the Sunday morning chapel service.

Flicker entered the House and rested his sports bag on the lobby floor. He switched on the lights and looked around. The notice board was free of new announcements. He swung open the double doors of the Houseroom, oblivious to the creak of the hinges. Like a dark spectre, he flitted across the room and stood by a window, bathed in moonlight.

His father was almost speechless when James called to tell him that he'd been appointed a prefect. The man finally offered him advice, the only kind of support Flicker ever expected from him. "They've put you in a position of responsibility, James. Remember, don't court anyone's love or approval, that's a waste of time. The only thing people understand from an authority is fear."

Flicker was only eleven when he first heard that admonition. He was summoned to his father's study after using a curse word in front of his mother. Instead of the whip he'd expected, his father had merely given him a harsh warning, the effect of which was far worse than any beating. "If you use that word again, son, I'll throw you out of my house for good."

"Dad, you're frightening me." James cowered.

"I hope so, James. To succeed in life, fear is an advantage. Stomp on anyone who opposes you. Teach an enemy that they can't mess with you. If you have people's respect for your authority, out of fear, you don't have to worry about turning your back on them."

"Yes Dad, I'll remember."

Flicker moved away from the window and looked around the Houseroom. Everything appeared to be in order. The tables were cleared, newspapers out of sight and the lockers around the walls were firmly closed. Out of the window, to his far right, he saw an expanse of heath, and in the distance, the cemetery, the old church and bell tower. At times, he sensed the abandoned grounds called out to him, as one of the few places where he could plan and find peace of mind.

The fencing tournament, in which six public schools competed had gone well; Blackleigh placed second. With replacements for the weaker members of the squad, the team would be stronger for the next match.

Since becoming a prefect, Flicker had spent less time with the shady elements in the school that he once cultivated. The running of the House with the other four prefects became his priority. He was dissatisfied with the admission of too many foreigners. Blackleigh traditions were being discarded to make the school appear more liberal.

Though tired, rather than go directly to bed, Flicker decided to return his foil and mask to his study. He turned the door handle, entered in the darkness, and was met by an acrid burning smell assaulting his nostrils. *What the hell?* He snapped on the light.

Flicker wondered if he'd stepped into a nightmare. He was reminded of the burning hotel room where his brother died long before. *Has Nick sent me a thunderbolt of fire from his grave?* The walls of his beloved study were smeared black and blistery, and the carpet, from Harrods, burnt in several spots. Along with the destruction, the birdcage was empty, and Croat's Picasso print ruined beyond repair. He surveyed the wreckage and could tell that there had been a forlorn effort made to remedy it.

Flicker slumped into his armchair and tried to control his fury. *Someone will pay dearly!* Croat, who usually calmed him down, would not return until the following evening. He leaned forward, slammed his fist on the floor, and shook the pain from his knuckles.

It was then he saw his name written on a folded piece of paper. Flicker snatched it up from the carpet. He read the words, stuffed the note in his pocket and gathered his thoughts. "What a fucking cretin!"

He lunged out of the armchair and left the study. Moments later, he was climbing the stairs, two at a time, up to Gracey's dorm.

He knew where the junior slept and went directly to Ian's bed wringing his scarf in his hands. Ian soundlessly flailed his arms and legs when Flicker wrapped the scarf tightly around his mouth, silencing him. Then he effortlessly picked Ian up and hauled him over his shoulder.

Flicker glided out of the dorm unseen, carried Ian downstairs, kicked open the Houseroom door and set him on a table. "Don't make a sound until I tell you," Flicker hissed in his face. He undid the scarf and propped up Ian, who stared straight ahead with a look of terror.

"Was anyone else involved in causing the fire?" Flicker spoke in a low measured voice. The prefect's white hair made him look demonic.

"No," Ian rapidly shook his head. "Just me."

"I got your note." Flicker took the slip of paper out of his pocket. "What the hell were you doing in my study?"

"I planned to cook myself a steak while you and Croat were away."

"Are you crazy?"

"It's something I always wanted to do since the first time I saw you doing it. When I heard that you and Croat would be gone for the weekend, I saw this as my opportunity."

"How did the fire start?"

"It was an accident. I dropped a lighted match, it fell into the meths tray. After I got the fire contained, Wynn happened by and I asked him to help me clean up."

"Who else was involved? What about your friends Simon and Crown Junior?"

"No one, I swear." Ian held up his hand. "Wynn pitched in to help me clean up, but he had nothing to do with anything before that. I'm the only one to blame. The whole idea was madness. I don't know what came into my head. I'll make it up to you… I'll do anything you say."

"Damn right you will. Get dressed. I'll see you at the base of the old tower in the cemetery. Thirty minutes from now and not a second later. The gate will be open."

"Why there?" Ian recoiled in fear.

"That's where I want to see you, and that's where you'll be." Flicker turned and left the Houseroom.

Ian had no choice. He snuck back into his dorm, careful not to wake anyone, quickly dressed in warm clothes and put on his duffle coat. *Whatever Flicker's revenge is*, Ian realised, *he wants to do it where there won't be witnesses.*

While cleaning up, he'd found and put Flicker's matchbox in his trouser pocket as a further means to implicate himself. One last thing and he was ready: Ian kissed his Swiss Army knife for good luck, pocketed it and left the House.

★★★

As Ian headed across the fields, he was buffeted by an occasional gust of wind. He had lost Charlie and didn't want to lose Arthur. Flicker could never learn that Arthur caused the fire. Any punishment would be acceptable if he could spare his friend.

When Ian reached the fenced cemetery enclosure, his teeth were chattering with the cold. He hurried on around the barbed wire perimeter until he reached the open gate. Ian compelled himself to walk on between the graves until he came to the small entrance at the foot of the bell tower. Flicker was nowhere in sight.

He felt an impending sense of doom; his fate was in another's hands.

Footsteps, then Flicker materialised out of the darkness. "What happened to the bird?"

Ian was surprised by the question. "I felt I had to let it free – in case the fire got out of hand."

"She won't survive a night outside. I'll give you the same chance as you gave Croat's bird."

"I don't understand."

"Climb the tower steps, until you reach the opening at the top. Then I'll tell you what to do." When Ian didn't make a move, Flicker barked, "Go on, start climbing!"

"But I'm terrified of heights," Ian cried.

"I know," Flicker said. "You don't remember telling me, do you? First day you came to work in our study you tried to make a stupid joke about not wanting to climb a stepladder to clean."

"Please, anything but *that*," Ian pleaded, pointing to the looming tower.

"Get going… NOW!" Flicker bellowed.

Inside the church, next to the tower, Ian's eyes became accustomed to the darkness. He gripped his knife and patted the box of matches, making sure they were in his pocket. *Nothing will happen to me, if I have my lucky knife.* He decided not to light the matches until he was well out of Flicker's reach.

Far above, he could see a wide platform and a shaft of moonlight through the front opening. The rickety wood steps zigzagged from one side to the other all the way up. Ian nervously placed a foot on the first step and then the next. He felt bitterly cold and heard the occasional wail of the wind coming through the opening at the top. With determination to overcome his fear and to save Arthur, Ian climbed step-by-step to the top of the first flight of stairs.

He turned on a small landing, held onto the rail with one hand and mounted the next flight, which faced the opposite wall. Ian lit matches as necessary to see the way ahead. As he moved higher, he warned himself, *Whatever happens hold onto the knife and don't look down.*

With each step, he became more scared the higher he went. At times, it seemed that the staircase was whirling and drifting above and below him.

Ian looked up… only one more flight until he reached the top. Ian's anxiety grew until he was shaking uncontrollably. It became a great effort to put one foot in front of another. Finally, drained and feeling faint, Ian reached the very top step, came out on the wooden platform and flung himself down on the uneven floor, heaving for breath.

While waiting for Ian to appear, Flicker mused that whatever the junior had rashly done, he admired his courage. Maybe the fire in the study was a blessing in disguise. He'd grown tired of Croat's creepy print, which he'd pretended to like. And Croat's bird had become a royal pain with all her chirping. *Had Gracey not turned the bird loose, I'd have probably wrung its neck before much longer.*

Yet, there were still questions in Flicker's mind that cast doubt on Ian's story. Why would Ian, generally reliable and cautious, take the absurd risk of cooking a meal in a prefect's study? And yet, Ian had confessed and endured his punishment.

On the platform above, Ian slowly stood up, petrified by fear. In one hand, he held his knife. In the other, he opened his matchbox to discover only one match left. He lit it and hesitated.

He faced the semicircular opening in the tower wall directly in front, and an aperture matching in size, at his rear. He could see the school in the distance and even the dorm where Arthur would be sleeping.

Flicker saw the brief flare of light at the top of the tower.

"Come on out where I can see you Gracey," Ian heard him yell.

Ian was unable to move and didn't notice the match burn down until it singed his finger. He tried to grab that hand with his other and dropped his knife. It hit the stone floor and skidded a few feet in front of him. Ian slowly shuffled forward feeling with his foot until he found the knife. He tried to slide it back towards him; it fell into a wide crack in the floor.

Now what do I do? he fretted, terror-stricken. Then and there, the epiphany came to him. *I don't need the lucky knife.* He said aloud, "This is for Arthur!" He would make Arthur proud of him. He took two long strides forward until he was standing at the very edge of the precipice.

For the first time in his life, Ian felt truly happy, absolved of all fear. He savoured the wondrous moment.

"You can come down now, Gracey," Flicker shouted, satisfied that Ian had learnt his lesson.

Ian was transfixed. He faintly heard Flicker's voice, but he'd only do what his heart told him from now on. He looked outward to the horizon and surveyed the beauty all around. He smiled to himself and said, "I did it. I'm free."

A couple of snowflakes landed on his cheek and as he looked heavenward with the wonderment of this precious moment, a gust of wind caught him from behind. Ian surrendered to the inevitable completely at peace with himself and the world.

Flicker, the observer, watched the boy plummet as if in slow motion. Ian's slight body floated down. In the form of his falling, Ian appeared to accept his fate. No flailing of arms or legs, no scream, just gentle surrender… then a sickening thud when his body met the stony ground directly in front of Flicker.

The prefect was frozen in disbelief. He half expected Ian to jump up and dust himself off. But Ian made no movement. His face was like an angel's who fell from heaven.

Flicker knew that he didn't dare move the body. There was nothing he could do for Ian. With his gloved hand, Flicker pulled out Ian's note from his coat pocket, and placed it firmly between the boy's curled fingers.

Flicker hoped that Ian would be presumed despondent after torching a prefect's study, and had taken his own life rather than face the consequences. Flicker looked up at the sky. It started to snow. He needed to get going so as not to leave footprints. Flicker walked fast out of the cemetery and over the heath towards the House. He never looked back at the bell tower and the corpse that lay far below, clutching the "suicide note" that read, "I'm so sorry – Ian Gracey".

20

INTERROGATION

Arthur first noticed Ian's absence at breakfast on Sunday morning. He checked with Jonathan, who was clueless as to Ian's whereabouts. Arthur was soon asking so many others that he was making a nuisance of himself. Most showed little concern; a few suggested that Ian might be ill or gone home for family reasons. Such vague answers didn't quell Arthur's frenetic state of mind.

Arthur recalled Ian's insistence that he play dumb and that Ian would fix the situation. The following morning, Flicker said nothing to him about the damaged study, although there was talk in the House that a small fire occurred.

Arthur and Jonathan worked up the courage to investigate Flicker's room. While they stood down the corridor, a couple of handymen were bustling in and out. They came with cans of paint and carried away damaged items, including Croat's print, the Formica table and the carpet. The men then posted a sign on the door in red block letters: "NO ADMITTANCE".

Jonathan proposed a plan. "Let's ask Croat what he knows."

"What if he won't tell us anything?" Arthur said bleakly.

"I think it's worth a try," Jonathan pressed. "It was his study too."

They waylaid Croat in the forecourt of the House, coming back from lunch.

"Can you help us?" Arthur implored. "We can't find our friend, Ian Gracey, and no one seems to know where he is. He'd have told us or left a message if he planned to be away."

"Gracey's in serious trouble," Croat replied. "The little bugger started a fire in our study. Flicker is handling the situation on the q.t. Said he found the place in shambles, after chapel, Sunday morning. Boy-o-boy, I wouldn't want to be in Gracey's shoes."

Arthur challenged weakly, "What makes you think Ian was responsible?"

Croat regarded Arthur as if he were an idiot, "It's no coincidence that Gracey disappeared on the same night as the fire. My money says Gracey couldn't face the consequences and hightailed it out of here. Flicker will get to the bottom of this. After all, it affects the school's reputation. If you hear from your dumb-shit friend, tell him that he'd better give himself up before Flicker finds him."

★★★

On Thursday, Jonathan and Arthur were sitting together at a Houseroom table when Peter Wynn walked in and tapped Arthur on the shoulder. "Arthur, you're wanted in the Housemaster's office. They've asked for me too. Flicker is already there with Mr Morton."

"What's up?" Arthur had a sinking feeling inside.

"I don't know, but it's serious business," Wynn said.

"Give me a moment."

Peter left them and waited for Arthur outside the door.

Arthur straightened his tie and put on his jacket. "I wasn't cut out for this," he said woefully.

"Just remember what we promised Ian. We must trust him. I'll wait for you here," Jonathan said.

Arthur walked with Wynn to the Housemaster's study. Beyond the closed door he heard voices. Peter knocked before entering. Mr Morton was sitting at his desk, facing Flicker and two older men.

Flicker sat on the Housemaster's left, exuding a quiet authority. Mr Morton wore a serious expression, with his hands clasped together. The two men wore dark suits and ties. The taller man, thin, in his mid-forties, had greying hair, neatly parted, blue eyes, a moustache and glasses. The burly younger man looked about thirty, clean-shaven, with swept back black hair; a pen poking out of his jacket breast pocket.

Mr Morton indicated where Arthur and Peter should sit. He then looked directly at Arthur. "It's bad news, I'm afraid. I'm sorry to tell you, Arthur... Ian Gracey is dead. His body was found this morning by one of the gardeners near the foot of the old bell tower in the cemetery. He apparently jumped from the opening at the top."

Arthur held his head in shocked disbelief. He was unable to speak and could only watch the Housemaster's mouth.

"We believe it was suicide. We have, of course, notified his parents, who are devastated." The Housemaster went on, "Ian left a note addressed to James Flicker, saying he was sorry. We think Ian was very distressed after causing a fire in Flicker's study. Arthur, he was your friend. What can you tell us?"

Arthur wanted to vomit, then controlled himself. He felt responsible for what had happened to Ian.

The taller of the two men removed a legal pad from his briefcase. "I take it that you're Fred and Frances Crown's son. I'm Detective Inspector Fox. My colleague is Sergeant Bill Davis. This is a sad business… I'll be getting full statements later, but for now, I'm trying to understand Ian Gracey's state of mind. Have you, yourself, been to these cemetery grounds, where Ian's body was found?"

"Yes," Arthur replied, "Jonathan and I went there once last term." He wanted to protect Ian by not mentioning him. Arthur nervously glanced at the Housemaster, whose expression registered strong disapproval.

"Why did you go? Mr Morton informed us that it's off-limits."

"I wanted to test my bravery. Cemeteries freak me out. It seemed an appropriate place to face my fears."

"Did you see anyone else there at the time?"

"No. Jonathan and I separated while we both looked around. Jonathan would have told me if he'd seen anyone." Arthur's expression was blank. The loss of Ian was a terrible blow. He wondered what he'd do without his best friend. He still had Jonathan, but no one understood him like Ian.

Flicker was pleased that Jonathan had kept quiet about their meeting at the church.

"Arthur, did you go to the film on Saturday night?" Inspector Fox continued.

"No, I had too much homework. Then I went to bed early with a headache." Arthur briefly closed his eyes. This was all becoming too much for him.

Fox turned to Peter Wynn. "I understand that you and Arthur Crown worked together last Saturday morning cleaning the study."

"Yes," Peter nodded nervously. "We cleaned and washed the dishes. Then, as I told Mr Morton this morning…" he looked shamefully at the Housemaster, "I went there again in the evening…"

When the detective became aware that Peter was unable to go on, he prompted, "Why didn't you tell anyone that you came back to the study that night?"

"It's the school code not to snitch on each other."

"What time did you come back?"

"I know for a fact it was nine forty-five," Peter replied, "because my aunt and uncle dropped me off at Trafalgar, so I'd be back with plenty of time before lights out."

"And why did you first check on Mr Flicker's study?" Inspector Fox asked.

"When I got out of the car, I could see through Flicker's window that the light was on, and I knew it shouldn't be. I went to check."

"What did you find?"

"The place was a bloody mess after the fire," Peter said quivering. "Ian Gracey was there alone. He said there'd been an accident and asked me to help him clean up as best we could."

The inspector asked, "How would you describe Ian's state of mind?"

"Depressed… devastated… it was terrible for him."

Arthur couldn't focus on the questions that followed. Inside, he was reeling with indecision. Should he tell them that Ian had insisted upon taking the blame for him? He was jolted back to the present, when he heard his name.

"Arthur, listen to my questions," Inspector Fox pressed. "Did Ian tell you about his plan to cook a meal in the prefect's study?"

Arthur looked around the room. Flicker was staring back at him intently, waiting for his answer. "I never thought…"

The sergeant leaned forward, "What didn't you think?"

"Ian didn't tell me anything."

"You're saying that Ian, your best friend, never told you that he planned to cook in the study?" The inspector looked at him sceptically.

"He didn't."

Fox continued, "Tell me about the last time you saw Ian."

Arthur started to sob, then collected himself. "Saturday night in the dorm. I was asleep. He came and woke me."

"Did he say anything unusual?"

"No, he acted normally." Arthur wiped away his tears. "We talked about some homework he was going to help me with in the morning." For the first time, Arthur looked directly at the detective. "I don't believe Ian would take his own life."

"We found Ian's suicide note with the body."

Arthur scrambled for the right words. The best he could do was, "This would not be anything like the Ian I knew."

"We deal with facts, not opinions," the inspector said. He turned to Flicker. "When did you discover there'd been a fire in your study?"

"Sunday at noon, after I returned from chapel," Flicker said with his prepared alibi. "I went to my study to relax. I was stunned when I saw the devastation. I immediately reported the matter to Mr Morton, as well as to David Reece, our Head of House."

"Why do you suspect Gracey?"

Flicker held up his forefinger. "One... he used to clean our study." He held up another, "Two... his disappearance. Both add up."

"How would you describe your relationship with Ian Gracey?"

"I had very little contact with Ian this term," Flicker replied.

Alec Morton interrupted, addressing the detectives. "As I see it, rumours impact the reputation of a school. We already had an unfortunate situation with another junior, under quite similar circumstances. For public consumption, if you approve, I'd like to report that the troubled junior was depressed after causing a fire in a prefect's study and took his own life."

Flicker raised a hand to catch the Headmaster's attention.

"Yes James, what's your thought?"

"Those in the House already know about the fire and Gracey's absence. Since the junior's mental state at the time is a factor, perhaps we could hold a House meeting to quash any rumours and incorporate a short remembrance service to bring some closure."

"Yes," the Housemaster concurred. "James, perhaps you'd select an appropriate psalm and read it at the meeting. You know the kind of thing… Psalm 23: 'Yea though I walk through the valley of the shadow of death, I will fear no evil.'"

The two police officers exchanged looks.

"This has the appearance of a suicide – but we need to complete our investigation," Inspector Fox concluded. "We thank you for your assistance. There will likely be more follow-up questions and we'll be in touch." They each stood and shook hands with Alec Morton; nodded to the boys. The Housemaster was relieved the meeting was over.

Arthur headed for the dorm, mentally drained and wanting to be left alone. No sooner had he reached the door when Flicker appeared right behind him. Arthur's guilt and confusion expressed themselves in the deep flush that came over his face.

"Crown, I want to see you in my study. Now. Follow me."

Without a word, Arthur trailed after Flicker.

Arthur entered Flicker's study and was awe-struck. The formerly all-white walls were now beige, and void of any decorations save Flicker's mask and foil. A light blue carpet graced the floor and the cheap rectangular table, had been replaced with an attractive mahogany one.

Arthur's mouth dropped at the extent of the changes. In a matter of days, the old study had been erased as if it never existed.

Flicker effused warmth. "Crown, before this tragedy, you worked with Peter Wynn here on that morning."

Arthur nodded. He worried that Flicker might start asking difficult questions to trip him up.

"Did Gracey say anything to you about the fire when he saw you in the dorm Saturday evening? I know you told the police that he didn't, but in difficult times like this, things slip a person's mind." Flicker smiled invitingly as if to assure Arthur that he could freely confide in him.

"No Flicker, I swear Ian never said anything about the fire." Arthur started sobbing.

A long contemplative silence followed. Flicker realised that in Arthur's sorry state there was little point in pursuing the matter. It would have to wait. "We'll talk about this later, Crown," he said. "You're free to go."

Arthur, more than relieved, hurried from the study.

Flicker instinctively distrusted Arthur's version of what happened that awful night. *Something isn't right.*

21

MEMORIAL

Jonathan paced up and down in the forecourt in front of the House. On the chill Friday evening, he was dressed in the suit he wore on Sundays, with a sweater, school tie and formal shoes. In a quarter of an hour, the memorial gathering for Ian would commence. Jonathan felt sad and demoralised. He missed Ian terribly – more than he could find words to say; and he failed to understand the callous reaction by most to the tragedy.

He felt isolated; the other boys moved on as if nothing had happened. Jonathan, by comparison, went through his days in a fugue. It was less than a week since Ian's passing and those in Trafalgar hardly mentioned his name; like Ian was never among them as a vital and cheerful presence, with a promising future. *Don't they feel anything?*

Jonathan imagined himself rapping repeatedly on the glass windows of the ground floor studies. He wanted to make everyone understand and acknowledge that a valuable member of the House was inexplicably gone. But no one cared to listen or discuss what happened. Jonathan, however, would never forget the loss of his true friend, like a part of him was gone forever.

He knew Ian would never take his own life. Nor would Ian, with his acrophobia, of his own free will, have climbed the tower. Ian was full of life, with a determination to prevail. Their Oath was a vow to rely on each other, and to never give up on their struggle.

Jonathan had promised Ian, on the night of his mysterious death, that he wouldn't say anything to anyone about Arthur causing the fire – it was their final promise to each other, and Jonathan felt solemnly bound to keep it.

"Simon, I want to talk to you. NOW!" an abrasive, rasping voice addressed him in the semi-darkness. Jonathan was taken aback at the sight of Sleeth, glistening bullet-shaved head, and large pumped-up body attired in a suit and prefect's tie.

Sleeth was the last person Jonathan wanted to see. "I can't talk now," Jonathan curtly replied, backing away. "I'm going to Gracey's memorial service."

"So am I, you little bugger. But first, follow me. This won't take long."

"Where to?"

"The senior changing room. Move."

Jonathan, without further protest, followed Sleeth into the ground floor changing room, which was larger and darker than the upstairs washroom for juniors. His heart was beating fast.

Two second year boys were talking by the sinks when Sleeth entered.

"You two," Sleeth snapped, "get the fuck out of here, now."

The youths looked startled, glanced with disdain at Jonathan and scurried from the room.

When he was sure they were alone, Sleeth stared down at Jonathan. "I want you to listen carefully. In my new position of trust as a prefect, I take my responsibilities seriously. Foremost among them is to clean up the House and remove troublemakers."

The prefect continued with Jonathan's full attention. "Neither Ian Gracey, Arthur Crown nor yourself fit in with our traditions at Blackleigh…"

"Do I have to listen to this now, Sleeth?" Jonathan broke in.

"I'm sure you know more than you've said about this Gracey situation," Sleeth continued, "even though I've no proof yet."

Jonathan remained silent, raging inside.

"So, as I see it," Sleeth continued, "your unacceptable behaviour makes you a liability." Sleeth pointed a finger directly at Jonathan. "You'd better give thought over the holiday to finding another school – one better suited to a spastic like you."

"Do you have anything else to say, Sleeth?"

"If you stay at Blackleigh next term, as a member of the corps, you will be held to exacting standards and I'll make sure…"

"Sleeth, I won't give in to a sadistic bully like you,"

Jonathan cut him off again, surprising himself with his courage. "I won't even fall into the trap of snitching on you to Mr Morton, or any of the other prefects, because I know the consequences. Sick types like you are a disgrace to this school, but not if I can help it. I'm not going anywhere. Now, you'll have to excuse me. I have a memorial service to attend."

Sleeth drew himself to his full height. "Either leave Blackleigh, or I'll make your life so fucking miserable, you'll wish you had. Don't say I didn't warn you."

Jonathan called back from the door, "Sleeth, take a running jump! Stuff you and your threats… I'll take the risk!"

Sleeth, astonished by Jonathan's bravado, was left dumbstruck.

Jonathan took a chair in the Houseroom next to Arthur and Harry. He acknowledged them with a sad smile. The room was half full. Alec Morton and the Assistant Housemaster, P. G. Ring, were present as were David Reece, the Head of House, and all the prefects.

The memorial service was a private House matter. No one outside Trafalgar attended. Mr Morton started with a short introduction and handed over the proceedings to three prefects, who read poetry and psalms. Flicker was attired in a black suit and tie for the occasion. When his turn came, and Flicker started to speak of Ian's death, he held those in attendance under the spell of his commanding presence.

"Friends, we are gathered here to mourn the sad

passing of one of our number, Ian Gracey. Ian, a junior in his third term at Blackleigh, was fourteen years old this January. This tragedy is made even more profound in that Ian never confided in anyone instead of resorting to such extreme and final measures. Had he sought professional help…" Flicker surveyed the room, "or come to any of us prefects for advice, we wouldn't be mourning him today. I know that I speak for others as well as myself when I say that each one would have stood by him in his hour of need.

"The care of those less fortunate and of those facing difficult situations are traditions at Blackleigh. Ian Gracey will be sorely missed by his many friends here. May he rest in peace."

Flicker lowered his head and sat down next to the Housemaster. Alec Morton thanked the prefect for his heartfelt words.

P. G. Ring remained motionless, and apart from an occasional squint, his palms rested on his lap in silent contemplation. David Reece glumly shook Flicker's hand. The other prefects, including Sleeth, who'd nodded their heads up and down while Flicker spoke, were now respectfully silent.

Mr Morton suggested that all present should take a few moments for a silent prayer.

Jonathan looked at Arthur. Grief overwhelmed his friend as he valiantly tried to hold back tears.

The ceremony felt unreal to Jonathan. Ian was dead, and people were going through the motions of mourning in some bizarre charade. It sickened him.

David Rayner, looking around, caught Jonathan's eye and shrugged his shoulders in sympathy.

Tunk's response to the speech was hard to read. He frequently looked at Sleeth, as if watching and waiting to see his reaction.

Sleeth, among the prefects, sat upright during the moment for prayer, a puzzled expression on his spotty, reddish complexion. *What the fuck*, he mused, *is all this time-wasting crap? Gracey's death doesn't change anything other than that one inadequate specimen can be forgotten.* He admitted to himself that it gave him pleasure to contemplate similar fates for Crown and especially Simon. *All in good time.*

Sleeth glanced over at the Greek god-like Keith Rayner, whose athletic toned body he often imagined running naked with him around the rifle range. Sleeth longed for next term when Rayner would be required to join the cadets. Rayner's death, Sleeth reflected, would be a real tragedy. Ian Gracey's death was little more than an accounting adjustment in the school bursar's office.

Sleeth regarded Flicker's tiresome tribute to Gracey as loathsome grandstanding by a potential rival for *his* future position as Head of House. Though he'd never let on, Sleeth longed to stomp on Flicker's odious, scarred face.

The following day, Ian's bed, blankets, sheets and rug were removed from his dorm. His Houseroom locker was cleared, and his clothes and few possessions sent home. The school avoided any public scrutiny. A newcomer to the House wouldn't know that Ian ever existed.

22

TUNK

A few weeks later, after lunch, Jonathan came into the Houseroom laden with school books, planning to catch up with homework. Ian had been such a part of his daily life that Jonathan still had the expectation that he'd see Ian in the Houseroom and that his passing was some figment of a dreadful nightmare.

Jonathan sat at a table and tried to organise his thoughts. With raucous noise and shouting all around him, he found it impossible to concentrate. Transistor radios blasted endless pop music from competing stations. A foursome, holding cues and playing snooker, moved around the table. Jonathan waited expectantly for the clacking sounds of a white ball hitting red and coloured balls, and bouncing back off the cushioned rims of the green felt table surface. Ping-pong players on the adjoining table added to the distracting sounds, as they smashed their tiny white ball from one side of the table to the other over a net of books.

He glanced in frustration at the headlines of both *The Daily Express* and *The Daily Mirror*, and still unable to focus, his thoughts kept returning to Ian. Finally, he resolved to find a more secluded place.

Outside, he saw Arthur sitting mournfully on the grass by himself.

Since Ian's death, despite numerous attempts, Jonathan found it difficult to speak to Arthur about Ian.

Jonathan would often see Arthur wandering aimlessly around the House, lost in thought. Not even a flash of his old smile illuminated his face. This time, Jonathan was determined to break the ice and hoped the right words would come to him.

"Hello Arthur." Jonathan put his books down on the grass and sat down beside him. Both were temporarily silent; soon, they found themselves looking sympathetically at one another.

"Arthur, I know there's little I can say. Neither of us will ever forget Ian, or the Oath we swore. Ian would want us to carry on."

"He was a wonderful friend," Arthur replied, tears slipping down his cheeks. "From the first day we met, when he came into my train compartment, he was always there for me." Arthur gagged between sobs. "He made me feel alive. Now I'm completely lost." Arthur paused and tried to control himself. "You know what's evil about this place? It's the way people have forgotten Ian. The seniors don't give a crap about him.

He was always with us, but for them, he's barely a memory."

"I know," Jonathan concurred. "Except that Flicker did pay him a tribute at the memorial service. That was something."

"Tribute?" Arthur scoffed. "I wouldn't give you half-a-crown – no pun intended – for that sham performance. Flicker made out that Ian was depressed. Are we supposed to believe the crap that Ian should have gone to Flicker for help after causing the fire? If he had, Flicker would've killed him. And why did Ian go back to the cemetery? Nothing makes sense. Trouble is, I gave my word to Ian not to say anything."

"Ian's death taught me something," Jonathan said with a pained expression. "When I think that Ian lost his life, my problems seem small."

"What problems are you talking about?" Arthur strained to understand.

"I've always been self-conscious about this birthmark on my cheek. But what's that compared to what happened to Ian?"

"It's odd you say that," Arthur said. "When I look at you, I don't even see a birthmark. I just take in all of you, inside and out. But with Flicker, Sleeth and Tunk, I notice how they look because they're evil inside as well as on the outside. Flicker's scar looks enormous to me, and so does the gap in Tunk's teeth. With Sleeth, I just see that domed, shiny, bald head and I cringe inside."

"Really? I'm glad you told me." Jonathan produced a grateful smile.

"I'll send you my bill," Arthur replied. "Better still, can you give me a hand with my maths homework?"

"Sure, show it to me. Now you're sounding like the old Arthur."

★★★

On the same afternoon, two figures in uniform, newly appointed sergeants in the corps, walked over to the parade ground, on the south side of Blackleigh Hall. One was tall and thin, looking like a fusion of bamboo sticks pivoting and swivelling on hinges. No one would comment to his face that he needed to fill the gaping hole in the centre of his mouth, or that he had the look of a praying mantis.

Few knew Tunk well, and those who thought they did would agree that he possessed a strange and enigmatic personality. He had no close friends and was only referred to by his surname. It was difficult to make out what percolated in his mind.

Tunk shared a study with an unusual individual, Nigel Snell, who had a pale cadaverous appearance, kept his own company and said little. He could be seen from April to September wearing a floppy white hat while zealously hunting down butterflies. This he accomplished with the aid of a large butterfly net, a killing jar, smelling of ethyl acetate, to asphyxiate victims, and a selection of slides in boxes with glass lids in which he placed insect pins to permanently mount his unfortunate, beautiful specimens.

Members of the House tended to avoid Tunk and Snell's study, which suited both antisocial occupants.

Although Tunk's presence did not generate immediate fear among the juniors, they regarded him with caution. This was evident whenever Tunk entered the Houseroom. The juniors drifted away from the space he occupied. Tunk was aware of their reaction and took pains to cultivate it. He saw it as an aspect of his subtle influence and growing power in the House.

Returning to Trafalgar from the rifle range, Tunk's corpulent companion, out of shape and gasping for air, hurried to keep up with Tunk's deliberately long strides. Croat frequently removed his corps beret and mopped the sweat pouring from his brow with the back of his arm.

"Sleeth knows that next term the corps will get some problem recruits from the House. I'm thinking of Simon and Crown," Croat observed. "I hope those two won't let us down in the House corps competitions."

"With Sleeth's promotion to prefect and as the highest-ranking officer in the corps," Tunk mused, "he's now a major force in the school. I know his aversion to stragglers and weak physical specimens. I expect he'll come down on them like a ton of bricks. I'd like to see that."

"Tunk, there's something I've observed…" Croat reached out to touch Tunk's arm, but Tunk was moving ahead too fast.

"Yes?" Tunk responded with caution, thinking this could be important. He slowed his gait.

"Well, it's about Sleeth," Croat said when he finally caught up.

"Go on."

"I've noticed that he's always checking out Rayner. I also see Sleeth hanging about Rayner in the junior dorm when they're all undressed for bed. Rayner has quite a physique, and I think Sleeth gets off seeing him naked."

Tunk relished this exquisite turn in the conversation. Neither he nor Croat trusted each other but they still maintained a civil relationship. Both were ambitious and liked to ferret out gossip that could be used for any future advantage. Tunk, a skilled scandalmonger, had already noticed Sleeth's fixation on Rayner. The military-minded prefect couldn't keep his eyes off him.

"You could be right, Croat," Tunk affably replied. "Sleeth certainly has a crush on Rayner. Even so, I can't imagine Sleeth doing anything stupid – too much to lose. He has a shot at being the next Head at Trafalgar when Reece leaves."

Tunk noticed how Croat winced at his last projection. Now he simply had to wait for his response and stir the pot.

"I don't see it that way." Croat flapped his hands. "My study mate, James Flicker, deserves that honour. Of course, I favour James as Head, because how else will *I* be made a prefect?"

"And what an outstanding choice that would be," Tunk said, a wisp of a smile crossing his face. This was the part Tunk liked best – scheming. The idea of a nincompoop like Croat becoming a prefect was farcical. Especially since Tunk was already conspiring to become a prefect himself under Sleeth's leadership.

Tunk promptly changed the subject. "It's odd that between those two spastics, Crown and Gracey, Crown, the weaker of the two still survives. Pity Gracey and Crown didn't both jump from the tower together with Simon bringing up the rear."

"Maybe they're all doomed?" Croat proclaimed.

23

DISCIPLINE

Flicker poured himself a tankard glass of dark beer, the head to the rim, and poured another glass for Croat. They chinked glasses in their redecorated study, toasted the future, then swigged down long draughts.

The prefect looked intently at Croat, relaxing in his armchair, nursing the half-empty glass in his lap. It was late and past the time they usually went up to supervise lights-out in the separate dorms.

Flicker sensed that Croat was withholding knowledge and from experience knew he had to coax it out.

"So, Bill," Flicker prompted, "Tunk, that SOB, sees Sleeth as the future Head of House and himself as a prefect. That toothless wonder must be crazy. Is Tunk losing his mind?"

Croat took the bait. "No, he's dead serious. He's also suspicious about Gracey setting the fire in our study – says he didn't have the nerve. The slimy creature is always digging for shit. I'd like to knock out another of Tunk's teeth."

Flicker showed no reaction. He removed his glasses and cleaned the lenses with a tissue. "Let's not over worry. Tunk is ambitious. The difference between you and me, Bill, is that I won't settle for just one of his teeth. What's he up to?"

"Not sure, but Tunk said he expects his friend Sleeth to become Head of House. I did agree with him that Sleeth is moving up in influence."

"You know I want the Head position for myself," Flicker said. "I was going to leave at the end of this school year. If I have a chance to become Head, I'll stay on another term. It'd look great on my resume and my father might even be impressed. Of course, you too would benefit. Tell me Bill, how did you answer Tunk?"

"I said that there's no way Sleeth would be appointed over you," Croat asserted. "And I threw in that Sleeth has a crush on Keith Rayner. Tunk agreed with me."

"Tell me more."

"Sleeth goes easy on Rayner in the House and in the corps. Tunk and I are both aware of this. When Rayner's around, Sleeth gets a bleary-eyed look. Tunk has a sixth sense for this kind of thing. Scandal is Tunk's hobby."

"How does Rayner take to Sleeth's interest?"

"Hates him for bullying in general. He'd do anything to get even."

"Did that tool Tunk say anything else?"

"Yeah, he doubts Sleeth would ever move on Rayner. Too much at stake."

Flicker grabbed another beer, smiling at Croat. He had the spark of an ingenious plan, but the time wasn't yet ripe, and he calmed his excitement. "Bill, this situation has real potential. I know that Rayner takes up with one boy after another… seems to regard sex as a game… thinks with his looks that he's irresistible. The irony is Rayner also has strong qualities that make for a future leader in the House. Has Rayner any close friends?"

"Don't know. He hangs out mostly with a few seniors, but plays the field, like you said. Among the juniors he shows little interest. But I've seen him chatting with Simon on occasion."

"I'm getting an idea, Bill, it's coming together fast, but I'm not there yet. When I'm ready we'll talk further." Flicker let slip a sly smile.

Their late-night discussion was followed by a dull thud, like a bedside table turned over on the floor above them. Flicker replaced his glasses. A tense look flashed across his face. "That came from the first-year dorm. Snell's in charge, but tonight he's not back until late, after his squash match. I'm going up. If you hear rumbling, it means heads are rolling."

Jonathan was anxious about the uproar in the dorm. Absent anyone in charge, Snell, a senior had not yet come to bed, and the prohibition against talking after lights-out was ignored. Whispering in the dorm had begun with a window of unsupervised freedom and soon escalated with the participants abandoning caution. Several boys had left their beds after others beseeched them to join them in theirs. Keith Rayner ran past Jonathan's bed vaulted over a reclining body and slipped into another bed. In the doing, he'd knocked over a bedside table. Jonathan watched in awe as the debauchery continued.

"How are you doing?" someone asked.

"I've run dry," came the answer.

No one paid any attention when two minutes later the door opened and closed. But Jonathan saw a tall, imposing figure standing at the threshold. Others soon sensed the anonymous presence and the room became quiet and tense.

With a swift motion, a hand turned on the lights. Jonathan shielded his eyes until accustomed to the blaze of bare light bulbs. The shadowy figure materialised into the blazing form of Flicker, a mean scowl on his face.

Everyone in the dorm froze – all heads turned in Flicker's direction. A mad dash in the dorm followed to restore order. Jonathan heard a cacophony of sound, with scuffling, groans and harried figures jumping back into their own beds – getting under the covers – some pulling covers over their heads. Then silence.

Arthur had somehow managed to remain asleep, turned away from the door. He abruptly woke, rubbed his eyes, and couldn't understand why the place was lit up.

"Turn off the goddam lights!" he shouted, sitting up. "You'll have bloody Flicker up here before you know it… Oh bugger!" His words tailed off when he saw him in the flesh.

The prefect inhaled deeply and barked, "Silence! You shitheads need a lesson in discipline. Three of you will be an example to the rest. Tomorrow at three in the afternoon sharp I want to see the following arseholes in the junior changing room: Bhasin, Crown Junior and Rayner."

Jonathan felt for Arthur and a wave of nausea passed over him.

James Bhasin, an Indian boy, with a ready smile and a mop of jet black hair, sat up in bed and protested that he hadn't said a word. By then Flicker had already left. The panic-stricken young man shook his head at the injustice.

Arthur closed his eyes tightly dreading tomorrow.

Keith Rayner showed no reaction. At previous boarding schools, he'd endured much worse.

★★★

The following afternoon, Arthur stood waiting with Keith outside the changing room. James Bhasin was already receiving his punishment. Arthur put his ear to the door to pick up the sound. He repeatedly heard a cane swishing through the air followed by yelps of pain.

At last, one of the double doors opened and Jim Bhasin hobbled out. His dark complexion had taken on the colour of a bruised tomato. Tears streamed down his face. Jim saw Crown and Rayner waiting their turn and bit his tongue to stop himself from crying. He tenderly placed his hands over his ass to relieve the hurt.

"Was it that bad?" Arthur winced.

"Don't ask." Jim moved on, step by painful step. "The pain was terrific."

"You mean terrible," Arthur corrected him.

Arthur, next in line, was shaking when he entered the changing room.

Flicker stood in the corner, shirtsleeves rolled up, a long bamboo cane in his hand. "Crown take a spot along the bench. Remove anything from your trouser pockets."

At first, Arthur thought Flicker was showing him special consideration. Then he realised that nothing in his pockets should lessen the impact of the beating.

Arthur looked along the bench gazing at the line of hooks on the wall. His eyes fastened on one unused hook. "Gracey" was the name on the label above, yet to be removed. He stood near to it and felt connected to his departed friend. Arthur saw Ian's reassuring face in his mind's eye. Whatever happened, he'd not show fear.

He removed his wallet from one back pocket and a handkerchief from the other. He tossed both on the bench in front of him.

Flicker quietly asked, "Do you know why you're here?"

"No, I was asleep before the lights came on."

"Bend over, Crown. Put your hands on the bench."

Arthur obeyed, waiting for the swish of the cane and the pain to follow.

"Before I punish you, answer me one question. If I like what you say, you'll walk out of here now. If I don't…" Flicker smacked the cane against his palm.

Arthur rose apprehensively and turned to face Flicker.

"Gracey and you were close," said Flicker. "What else can you tell me about the fire in my study?"

Arthur carefully weighed his answer, then said, "I can't tell you anything. But I'll say this: I never saw Ian depressed. Maybe the reason he's dead is because there's evil around here."

The response caught Flicker unprepared, but he remained unruffled. "What do you mean by 'evil'?"

"I mean the kind of evil where they try to have us believe someone like Ian would commit suicide. Ian jumping from the tower makes no sense. Why would Ian even go there? He was deathly afraid of heights." Arthur said in a firm voice, "Whether you cane me or not, that's the truth."

Silence prevailed in the room until Flicker said, "Collect your things. You can go."

"I can go?" Arthur echoed with disbelief.

"Yes, Crown. Scram."

Arthur glanced briefly at Ian's name, then bounded out of the changing room. By some miracle, Ian was there for him.

Keith Rayner was surprised to see Arthur so soon. "How was it?"

"Nothing I couldn't handle," replied Arthur enigmatically.

Flicker was now looking forward to seeing Rayner, who he'd not selected as arbitrarily as it seemed. He'd say nothing about Arthur, but he'd make sure Sleeth heard about Rayner being caned.

★★★

That night in the dorm, Arthur confided in Jonathan. "Maybe I was lucky, thanks to Ian." Arthur added cryptically, "But if you want to know the truth, I can't take this place anymore."

"What do you mean?" Jonathan asked, disturbed by Arthur's tone of voice.

"You'll see. You know the song everyone's singing, *whatever will be will be, Que Sera Sera…*" Arthur was interrupted by Snell, who turned out the light, and the junior crawled into bed. But Arthur had no intention of sleeping. He had a busy night ahead of him.

24

THEFT

Arthur struggled to stay awake, but dropped into sleep scant minutes after his head rested on the pillow. When he awoke with a start, it was still dark. Arthur groped for his wristwatch, at the ready on his bedside table. "Shit!" he blurted, seeing the time from the illuminated dials. It was three o'clock in the morning. From the sounds of snoring, he was the only person awake.

All that mattered to Arthur in the last few weeks was to get through each day. He'd always been bad at homework. His relationships with others in the House, except for his brother Harry, Jonathan and maybe Peter Wynn, had petered into insignificance. The turmoil inside him devolved into one question: *Shall I confess?*

Arthur knew that Ian's death was somehow tied to the oath of silence between them. Ridden with guilt, and unable to speak of his crime, he felt the need to punish himself. He couldn't take the pressure anymore and saw only one way out of his agonising dilemma.

Arthur sat up and reached for his dressing gown. He got out of bed, cautiously made his way to the door, quietly opened it and walked along the corridor to the end.

His heart was beating fast. In the changing room, he dressed in sports clothes, grabbed someone's sweater and put it on. He carried his duffle coat and gloves.

What he planned to do wouldn't take long. Arthur reached the stairs and like a blind man felt his way down in the darkness, one step at a time. At the bottom, he reached the double doors of the Houseroom and opened them. The sound of squeaking hinges made him cringe as the door swung back behind him.

He opened his locker and took out a torch. Arthur then sat at one of the tables, trembling and breathing hard, until he could ready himself.

He walked by the lockers near his own. Thanks to the school's honour code, none of them bore locks. One after another he opened each door and shone his torch over the contents. *That transistor radio will do fine – as will the Parker 51 pen,* he mused, removing and placing them on a nearby table. He then returned to the next locker and chose another object to add to his collection.

Within minutes, Arthur had a heap of spoils that included three cheap wristwatches, ordinary pens, a transistor radio, pairs of sunglasses, and an assortment of stainless steel cufflinks and tie clasps. He also removed a pound note from a wallet. He closed each locker door, filled up his own locker with the booty, and finally closed his locker, all but a crack, leaving the corner of the pound note peeking out.

For the second half of his plan, he donned his duffle coat and gloves, then exited the side door of the House into the moonlit night. The air was cold, and he shivered while heading across the fields to his destination.

He'd taken this same route with Ian and Jonathan in his earlier determination to face his fears in the cemetery. How they'd all laughed together when he stepped in cow dung! He no longer had a place in his heart for laughter.

Arthur trudged on, breathing hard, but was determined as if some mysterious force drew him to the bell tower. He reached the enclosure and walked around to the far side and the place where he knew an opening led into the cemetery.

The door was shut, and paddle locked but the hinges were so corroded that after putting a shoulder to it he was able to force it open. Arthur walked through the cemetery without regard for the headstones. He wasn't afraid. Arthur continued through the tall weeds and past the walls of the derelict church, until he came to the looming tower.

He looked up to the opening at the top and recoiled with the thought of Ian plummeting to his death. Why and even how Ian had climbed up all the steps in the tower was beyond Arthur's understanding.

The wind whipped through Arthur's hair and he felt a rush of harsh cold against his face. In the night sky the moon was wrapped in clouds. Arthur knelt at the foot of the tower. He covered his face with his hands and felt tears streaming down his cheeks. He cried out from the depths of his being, "Ian, I must confess. The secret's killing me. I need to get the truth out, but I must have your permission first. Please help me, Ian."

Arthur pointed his torch at the tower entry, casting an eerie light on the lowest rungs of the steps.

Arthur hoped with all his being that Ian's spirit would hear him and give him a sign. "Ian," he called out, "can you hear me?"

A minute passed by; then a voice came to him. Arthur knew that he might be imagining it, but Ian's words were as clear in his head as if he was standing right beside him: *Arthur, my dear friend, what is it?*

"Let me tell them the truth about the fire, Ian."

If you must… but not now… you'll know when to confess.

"Will you stay with me, Ian?"

I'll be with you forever. Then eerie silence.

A snowy owl swept out of the opening, swooped and glided in the direction of Trafalgar. Arthur interpreted the owl to be Ian's way of saying: *Don't get yourself expelled.* With no time to lose, he determined to hurry back to the House and return the stolen items.

★★★

Dawn had broken when Arthur reached the House and entered the Houseroom. He was exhausted, barely able to stand. The others had already returned from breakfast.

Peter Wynn shot a startled look at Arthur. "It's not like you to go for an early morning run. What's got into you?"

Arthur was too nervous to reply. He glanced at the lockers thinking that maybe, if no one else came in, he'd have time to return all the items… *If I can only remember what goes where?*

The double doors opened, and a group of juniors noisily entered. One went over to his locker, only two away from Arthur's and rummaged around inside looking for something. Arthur recalled that he'd taken a watch from that locker. It was ugly with a cartoon face that he wouldn't be caught dead wearing. But even if he'd taken the best watch in the world, he wouldn't have wanted it for himself.

Arthur couldn't bear to look up as others drifted into the Houseroom. He raced out, mounted the stairs to his dorm, hoping to find Jonathan to help him fix what he'd done before it was too late.

To Arthur's relief, he found Jonathan at the top of the stairs. Arthur grabbed him with both hands, gulping for air, "Have to talk… matter of… life and death."

Jonathan took one look at Arthur's anguished expression and knew this was a real crisis. "Come into the dorm, no one's there."

Arthur heaved himself down on a bed by the wall. Jonathan sat across from him on the next bed. Arthur grasped his head and cried, "I'm dead! Finished at Blackleigh!"

"Please calm down," Jonathan said. "We swore an Oath to help each other, and I'm here for you."

Arthur's words tumbled out fast. "Since Ian's death, no one seems to care what happened and I've been so depressed. Then I was stressed about the caning, and more so when Flicker didn't punish me. I want out of this place so bad… last night I deliberately took stuff from boys' lockers."

"But why?" Jonathan said with alarm.

"I was hoping to be expelled. I wanted to stand up for Ian, but I didn't know how. I feel completely useless."

Jonathan felt a sinking feeling in the pit of his stomach. He hopped to his feet. "Arthur, we've no time to lose. We've got to put everything back. C'mon, let's go downstairs."

The door flew open and Jim Bhasin burst in. "Thank God I found you two," he said, wide-eyed. "Holy shit's hit the fan. Arthur, they found a lot of missing things, all in your locker. Maybe someone put them there to frame you? It looks bad… Flicker's on the way…"

They heard heavy footsteps on the stairs. The door opened, and Flicker stood at the threshold, expressionless. "Crown, follow me to my study, right now."

"Can I come with him?" Jonathan pleaded.

"Not unless you want the same punishment."

Flicker beckoned Arthur. "Stay close to me. There are some angry boys down there."

They could hear the cries of the mob from below. "We want Crown!" Without hesitation, Arthur scurried after him.

★★★

Flicker guided Arthur to Croat's armchair. The prefect sighed. The witless junior he'd wanted answers from about the fire was likely to be expelled for stealing trivial items from people's lockers. Flicker was amazed that Crown hadn't shown enough sense to hide the petty crap. The boy might just as well have put the items on display so everyone could see what he'd done. For a brief moment, Flicker felt compassion for Crown. He drummed his fingers.

"The Housemaster will see you shortly. Mr Morton will make the final decision about your future based on my recommendation. Why did you steal those worthless articles?"

"I was trying to get myself kicked out of the school," Arthur said meekly.

"Why?"

Arthur briefly held his palms over his eyes. "I've been under so much pressure, and so sad over what happened to Ian. No one seems to care."

Flicker considered the situation. As prefect, his proposal carried the most weight. He had to decide on Crown's fate. He had two choices. The first was to expel him at the end of the term, just over a week away. Or second, to impose a severe judgement on him, which would include caning, removal of all privileges next term and a public apology before all members of the House. Flicker was leaning towards the second choice but decided to question Crown further.

"Is there anything more that you'd like to say?"

"I can't get over that the police closed the case on

Ian's death, ruling it a suicide," Arthur said, his head bowed.

"Why's that?"

"Like I said before, Ian was so scared of heights there's no way he would have climbed the tower…" Arthur swallowed hard before continuing, "… unless he was coerced." Arthur looked up at Flicker. "What if Ian wasn't alone?"

"But Gracey left a suicide note," Flicker said evenly.

"It still doesn't add up." Arthur shook his head.

"Did Ian Gracey start the fire?" Flicker gambled. "Tell me the truth."

Arthur remembered Ian's admonition: *You'll know when.*

Arthur looked at Flicker with his best poker face. "Ian caused the fire."

Flicker gazed long and hard at Arthur, trying to read him, then gave up. "I'm going to write a note. Take it to the Housemaster."

Flicker quickly typed, sealed the note in an envelope and handed it to Arthur.

"Thank you, Flicker." Arthur felt relieved that perhaps there was still a chance he might be pardoned.

★★★

The Housemaster looked at Arthur, who was still holding out hope. "You know the rules Arthur – I highly value a prefect's recommendation." Alec Morton opened and read aloud Flicker's note: "Sir, Crown has admitted to stealing the items in question. I cannot find any good reason for him to stay at Blackleigh. I believe it will be detrimental to all concerned for him to remain another week and leave with the others for the Easter holiday. His parents need to be informed. Crown should pack his bags and depart by train immediately."

Arthur was crushed, he thought for sure Flicker understood it was a mistake and he was truly sorry. He wondered what could have turned the tide against him so abruptly.

"Arthur, I'm sorry. I'll call your parents to explain the situation. I hope you'll find a way to turn your life around. Go and pack your bags." The Housemaster refrained from shaking Arthur's hand and indicated the exit. He told Arthur, now in a state of shock, "Close the door behind you."

Jonathan was waiting in the foyer between the Housemaster's office and the Houseroom.

"How did it go?" Jonathan asked, fearing the worst.

"The only thing going is *me*." Arthur sighed, "Maybe it's for the best."

"I'm so sorry about everything," Jonathan said, putting a comforting hand on Arthur's shoulder. "But you've one last hurdle. We must walk through the Houseroom. Some bastards heard that you were with the Housemaster and came to gloat. No prefects are around. I think they've deliberately stayed out of the way."

"What shall I do?" Arthur threw up his hands.

"Don't show fear. I'll walk with you."

Jonathan opened the door to the Houseroom. They were surprised to see so many members of the House shuffling about, anxiously.

"One of the boys must've put his ear to Mr Morton's door," Arthur suggested, "then ran to tell the others."

The crowd waiting for them lapsed into a tense silence as Jonathan and Arthur came forward. The mob looked like a pack of hunting dogs, ready to attack. They massed together forming a phalanx across the room.

In the front row, a smirking Tunk, along with his study mate, Nigel Snell, was relishing Arthur's plight. "Greetings arsehole, we're here to see you off," Tunk snarled, flashing his eerie smile.

"See what I meant about another hurdle," Jonathan whispered.

"This is no hurdle – it's a wall," Arthur blenched. "I'm going to shit in my pants."

Jonathan stepped forward hoping to affect a retreat from those in front. No one moved or showed any inclination of making a passageway for them. A hissing swelled in the Houseroom.

"Don't move yet, Arthur," Jonathan cautioned, "one mistake and this could turn ugly."

Someone pushed through to the front unexpectedly. Jim Bhasin broke free of the mass and walked the short distance to where Jonathan and Arthur stood.

"You're taking a big risk," Jonathan advised him. "Are you sure you…"

"I may not be sure what I'm doing", Jim cut him off, "but I do know which side I'm on."

Harry Crown drifted to his brother's side. Peter Wynn joined them.

Keith Rayner was the next to stand with the small group. He nodded at Jonathan. "Let's end this now."

Without saying a word, Keith marched forward leading Jim, Harry, then Jonathan, Arthur and Peter at the rear. Upon reaching the wall of rigid bodies, Keith said in a gruff voice, "Make way."

Tunk barked, "Everyone hold your position," and nobody moved.

Keith balled up his fists and repeated, "I said, make way."

Everyone knew that Keith had got into many fights at the boarding schools he'd attended, and rumour was that he always came out the victor. No one had the guts to challenge him. Even Tunk was wary of what the result might be.

The bodies massed before them slowly parted, allowing the group to proceed to the doors at the far end of the room. Arthur held his head high and looked directly ahead.

Tunk, seething with anger, tried to rally the mob, "Don't let them go. Stand firm!"

But Tunk's plea was ignored and the small group left the Houseroom untouched. Arthur climbed the stairs to begin packing.

Jim fell behind the others and lingered in the House lobby. Before he realised, Tunk darted out and pushed him up against the notice board. He viciously clamped a hand around Jim's neck, and yelled into his face, "Get the hell back to India, you little darky. We don't want your kind around here."

"I was born in England and I've lived in Guildford all my life," Jim managed to protest.

Tunk raised a fist and hissed, "Screw you!"

At that moment, Sleeth was returning from the rifle range. He saw Tunk about to hit Jim and shot him a look that said, *Not here.*

Tunk dropped his hands. "All right, we're not finished, you and me, dear boy. Now, get out of my sight."

Jim didn't wait to argue. He raced outside through the House door, slamming it behind him.

★★★

The next morning, Jonathan stood with Arthur and Harry on the platform at Enderby station. In a few minutes, Arthur's train would depart.

"Jonathan, give me a few moments with Arthur," Harry said.

Jonathan nodded and stepped away.

"What have I done now?" Arthur asked, fearing the worst.

"You've done nothing," Harry replied. "In fact, I feel terrible about what's happened. Jonathan spoke to me yesterday while you were packing. He told me how Sleeth had it in for you from your first day here. Why you didn't tell me?"

"You said I needed to make a go of it on my own."

"I'll never forget how brave you've been," Harry said, placing a hand on Arthur's shoulder. "How can I make it up to you?"

"I don't want to go to another boarding school. A day school would be fine. Can you speak to Mum and Dad?"

"I promise we'll find you one in Manchester."

"That's a relief," Arthur grinned. They hugged each other.

"I'll write soon," Arthur said, then walked over to Jonathan. "There's something I want to ask you."

"What is it, Arthur?"

"What do you think Ian would say about the way I walked straight through that mob in the Houseroom?"

"I know exactly what he'd say, 'Arthur, I'm so damn proud of you.'"

The awkward hangdog grin that Jonathan knew from the old Arthur blossomed over his face.

Jonathan held back tears in front of Harry as he watched his friend's train gather momentum out of Enderby Station and disappear round a bend in the track. He'd be on his own next term, the last of the three friends who swore their Oath.

25

JIM BHASIN

Jonathan's Easter holiday passed swiftly. The day before his return to school, the phone rang. Elsie answered and told him, "You've a call from Jim… I couldn't get his last name."

Jonathan came downstairs to take the phone. "Hello?"

"Simon, it's James… Jim… Jim Bhasin," the caller said hesitantly, "from Trafalgar. I looked up your number in the Blackleigh school registry. Is this a good time to talk?"

"Oh, Jim," Jonathan greeted him warmly. "Yes, it's good to hear from you. We're back to school tomorrow. How do you feel about that?"

"Don't' remind me." Jim let out a deep sigh. "Have you spoken to Arthur Crown?"

"Yes. He went away for a few weeks with his family," Jonathan replied. "Jim, I must say, you were brave to walk with us through the Houseroom."

"I felt sorry for him," Jim said, "but maybe Crown leaving is best for him. What a mob! They wanted to beat him when he was already down. That's not justice, it's plain cruelty. Then again, it's Blackleigh.

"I called you because I'm with my parents," Jim went on. "We're in London overnight. They're going to drop me off at Paddington tomorrow while they attend a business meeting. I wondered if you're free for lunch? I've a lot on my mind about school. I'd like to see you. In fact, you're the only person I feel I can talk to about this."

"Sure," Jonathan replied, pleased to discuss the goings on at Blackleigh school with another junior. "Where are you?"

"In the West End, but I can get a bus or the Tube."

"Great. I'm in Hendon. I'll take the 113 bus. Let's meet on Oxford Street, outside the main entrance to Selfridges?"

"Yes. At what time?"

Jonathan looked at his watch. "How about twelve o' clock?"

"I'll see you there."

★★★

They met promptly and took a red two-decker. From upstairs on the bus, they looked at the historic sites passing by. The bus trundled through heavy, noisy traffic along the large, glitzy shops and department stores of Regent Street and ploughed on to the neon-screaming façades of Piccadilly Circus, with the lone winged statue of Eros in the centre. In heavy traffic, they passed the Trocadero restaurant and the London Pavilion cinema on the way to Leicester Square.

Jonathan and Jim got off at their stop and walked to the nearby Quality Inn, which featured good lunches at a reasonable price. They found a quiet table and agreed on splitting the cost of a mushroom omelette, a side of baked beans, buttered toast and a pot of tea. Their lunch was served with two plates.

"It's my second term at Blackleigh," Jim began. "I can't sleep at night worrying what's going to happen next."

"You're not the only one," Jonathan concurred.

"I've seen how you stood by Ian Gracey and Arthur Crown. I'm sure you have your own problems…" Jim hesitated, fearing he might be saying too much, then forged on, "but I was threatened and almost strangled by a senior, who's now out to get me. I'm utterly scared."

"Who are you talking about?" Jonathan pressed.

"Tunk. Excuse me for saying, but I don't like his face."

"You don't like his face?" Jonathan laughed. "Neither do I, but that's only for starters."

"It's just my way of saying I hate him," Jim explained. "He's a racist and he wants me gone. There's no one to report him to and besides it's curtains if you squeal on a senior."

"Believe me," Jonathan nodded agreement, "I understand how you feel. You're smart to take Tunk seriously.

"The bullying and the cover-up goes on," Jonathan went on. "They claim that Ian committed suicide. But Arthur and I know better. There was another junior, Stephen Rodgers, a year earlier, they also say killed himself. Again, the reason why is vague at best. Arthur, Ian, and Stephen all worked for Flicker at different times cleaning his study. But no one is piecing that *coincidence* together. And if I were to point this out my troubles would only get worse."

"What are you saying?" Jim let loose a shiver.

"Sleeth is out to get me. He and Tunk already put me through a degrading initiation at the firing range. And now I'm due to join the corps this coming term where Sleeth is the Officer Cadet in charge."

"Don't we have rights?" Jim asked, appalled.

"There's only one: that's to leave the school and go somewhere else. The prefects, not the faculty, have the power to discipline, and they're duty bound to believe any senior over a junior."

"So, what can we do?"

"I don't see how this can end without a dreadful confrontation." Jonathan frowned. "We juniors just have to stick together. We're fighting a hundred years of ugly tradition at Blackleigh, but sooner or later one of the bullies will make a mistake or go too far. Only then can we stand up for what's right… or pay them back – and more."

26

CHEATING

April 1956

Blackleigh School traditionally opened their grounds to the public on the first Saturday of the Summer term. On the designated visitor's day, families from Enderby and the adjoining residential community streamed into Blackleigh through the main gates of the prestigious school that was otherwise inaccessible to them.

The annual event, which included a fair, benefited a local charity with half the proceeds going to a disadvantaged Enderby school. But the unstated goal was to improve the hostile relationship between the expensive school and its neighbours, most of whom regarded the Blackleigh boys as overprivileged snobs.

Three years earlier, the festival was suspended after a melee broke out. *The Enderby Times* reported that a gang of Enderby youths had used the occasion to make their mark by drawing graffiti on a school building. Four bloodied gang members were arrested and taken into custody.

Two Blackleigh seniors, who denied being in possession of blackjacks, had minor injuries. Parents were notified, and charges pressed against the gang members responsible.

After recent negotiations between Blackleigh authorities and the Enderby Chamber of Commerce, the gesture of opening the school was revived.

The highlight of the event was a farmers' market on the main rugby field near Blackleigh Hall. Enderby farmers displayed their produce together with fruit, cut flowers and potted plants in assorted containers. On sale were home-baked goods with crusty filled delicacies and other gooey edibles. The fair consisted of rides, food stands, a roundabout and coconut shies. There was also an area allocated to booths offering various games of skill, with a high degree of difficulty, to win prizes.

Jonathan and Jim Bhasin mixed in with the crowd after lunch. They enjoyed the festive atmosphere, enhanced by a speaker system with fairground music swirling above the heads of visitors. Lilting sounds of *The Carousel Waltz* and others, fused with children running excitedly from one booth to another, some licking ice cream cones and others, whirls of pink candy floss.

Among the fair attractions were flying swings of canoes with four seats, one in front of the other. Jonathan and Jim heard shouts of joy as the gold-painted chariots descended and swung upwards again.

"Do they have anything like this in Calcutta?" Jonathan asked.

"I've only been there once, but I remember that the fairs and markets were much bigger."

Jonathan turned his head. "I just saw Flicker at the hamburger stand."

"I'll miss out on a burger for now." Jim flinched at the thought of the name. "I still feel the pain from that caning he gave me."

"It wasn't fair that he chose you or Arthur," Jonathan said.

"No kidding. That was bullshit. Flicker chose me because of my dark skin. Like so many people rooted in the past, he sees me as an intruder. But my parents came to England long ago and made a success of their new life. My father employs many British people."

"What does he do?"

"He owns a shoe factory in Luton. But here's the problem. Dad's had to give up many of his Indian values. For breakfast, with his English customers, he must order toast with marmalade and soft-boiled eggs. These days he acts more English than Indian. If he or I tried to maintain our Indian culture, we'd never be accepted. But Flicker and Tunk won't accept me anyway under any conditions. That's why I was picked-out for punishment."

Jonathan shook his head. "It's sad that Blackleigh resists change. They see the world neatly divided between 'us' and 'them'. They only want to hold on to the old ways and old values."

The two passed a series of crowded booths requiring skill to win a prize. The proprietors of these booths were known for being less lenient in rewarding anyone from Blackleigh. The outsiders were not about to give those with a Blackleigh education any more advantage than they already possessed.

Jonathan and Jim stopped at one unpainted booth, decorated with St George's flags, and attracting a good crowd. It offered a game of luck with virtually no skill involved. Players stood around a large circular table, each holding a grooved wooden slide, and placed half-crowns on it. Once a player released a coin, it rolled onto a table covered with small squares with a number, two through ten, inside each square. If a coin chanced to land plumb in the middle of a square, without touching any of the black boundary lines, the player won back their half-crown, multiplied by the number in the square.

Two Enderby brothers ran the booth, both standing in a circular space cut out at the centre of the table. Dirk Williams, the older of the two, at twenty-one, was stocky, with a close-shaven head. He'd been an amateur boxer, and once had his picture in *The Enderby Times* after he was caught poaching game on Blackleigh grounds. His nineteen-year-old brother, Bruce, wore glasses and had a scruffy beard. As the game progressed, they'd move around the inner circle to award winners. More often, their cupped hands scooped up and pocketed the silver coins of losers that settled on the boundary lines of squares.

Jonathan was intrigued by the game and studied those playing. He tensed upon recognising four of them: Tunk, with Croat watching him play; and from Plessey House, Jason, a swarthy senior and Drub, with his muscular build and ferret-like face, was one of the three who'd attacked him and David Gold.

Jason pumped a fist and exclaimed, "No shit, Tunk, you've won again!" He called to the brothers running the booth, "Hey Chief, there's another winner here."

Tunk pocketed a handful of coins from the younger brother.

As the game continued, Drub kept both brothers preoccupied on the far side of the table, pestering them with questions and demands for small change. Meanwhile, Tunk made no effort to roll a coin down his slide. Instead, he placed a half-crown by hand on a high-numbered square.

Jason repeated the cry, "Another winner! Pay up, Chief."

"Can you believe this?" Jim whispered to Jonathan, "talk about injustice… and at a charity event. Doesn't that toothless wonder have a conscience?"

"Doesn't surprise me," Jonathan replied. "Tunk is always up to no good."

The older brother half turned to watch Tunk out of the corner of his eye, just in time to see him centre another coin on the highest numbered square.

Dirk Williams spun around and accosted Tunk,

"I know what you're doin', ya fuckin' bastard. You're cheatin'."

"You didn't see anything. If you don't like the way I play, I'll go elsewhere," Tunk answered pompously. "Now, pay up, or I'll report you to the authorities." Tunk stood defiantly, jingling the coins in his pocket, clearly enjoying the stand-off.

"You can keep what you already stole," Dirk said, "but you're not gettin' nothin' more."

Tunk cleared his throat and spat a wad of phlegm onto the table. That did it. The Williams brothers climbed out of their booth.

"Stuck-up, prick," shouted Dirk, launching a trained fist into Tunk's face.

Tunk staggered backwards, dazed by the blow, knees buckling, trying to stay on his feet.

A crowd immediately circled the fighters. Jason tried to kick Dirk in the groin, but Williams easily blocked his foot and popped his nose with a left jab, dropping him to the ground. Croat promptly stepped back and disappeared among the crowd of onlookers, out of harm's way.

Dirk turned to Drub, who had a chokehold on the younger Williams brother and was hitting him in the face. Dirk smashed Drub with a body blow to the kidney and he doubled up in pain, letting Bruce go. Tunk, seeing Dirk advancing on him, held up his hands in surrender.

Three policemen descended on the scene and separated the fighters.

"You came just in time, officers," Tunk said, holding a hand to his right eye, already swelling. "These two thugs run a sham operation. They should be locked up."

The officer in charge turned to Dirk, whose face was unscathed but the blood on his hands clearly belonged to Blackleigh. "What's this all about, then?"

"The creeps from the fancy school are a bunch-a cheaters," Dirk snarled.

"See," Tunk waved a finger at the brothers, "the troublemakers are already telling lies. I want to press charges."

The officers sized up the scene. Jason sat on the ground with blood pouring from his nose. Drub, unable to stand up straight, held a hand over his lower back. Bruce had been able to deflect most of Drub's punches, thus avoiding cuts or bruises. Blackleigh was clearly on the losing end of the scuffle.

We're taking you two down to the station," the officer concluded, and handcuffs were placed on the Williams brothers. Despite their protests the two were hauled away.

Tunk straightened his tie. "That's what happens when you let in outsiders. They're as bad as fucking immigrants and refugees…" His words trailed off when he noticed Jonathan and Jim staring at him. "What are you two spastics looking at?"

He turned to Croat who'd just reappeared. "Hugh, those jerks running the booth are lucky the police turned up before I kicked their arses."

Croat badly wanted to call Tunk on his bullshit but Flicker had instructed him to stay on Tunk's good side.

Jonathan and Jim turned and left.

"I can't believe this," Jonathan said with disgust. "Tunk walks away and those he cheated get arrested."

"What did you expect?" Jim threw up his hands.

"Jim," Jonathan grabbed his friend's arm, "we can't allow this. You and I saw what really happened."

"But there's nothing we can do," Jim protested. "You know the school code. We squeal to the Housemaster or Head of House, and we're finished. They wouldn't believe us anyway."

"I'm not thinking of the school." An idea was forming in Jonathan's head.

"Huh?"

"We'll tell the police," Jonathan said, his decision made.

"You can't be serious?" Jim pulled his arm away and looked at Jonathan as if he'd lost his mind.

"What about what's right and just?" Jonathan pressed.

"I'm thinking of our survival," Jim countered. "I'm all for justice, England and 'God Save the Queen', but they're not the main considerations here. Why put our butts on the line for two complete strangers?"

"Unless we take a stand for the truth," Jonathan threw out his hands, "we're no better than Tunk or Drub."

Jim stared at Jonathan wide-eyed, then saw that he had a point. "All right," he agreed, albeit reluctantly.

★★★

Alec Morton looked at the two boys in his office with growing concern. He'd listened to their story with a worried expression on his face and kept his palms pressed tightly together. "I understand that you told your version to the police. Just so you know, all charges are dropped, and the two brothers were released. They are grateful to you. Fortunately, no charges were brought against Tunk and his companions. However, the Headmaster gave Tunk a stern warning. But word of what you two did will get around the school."

"Innocent people were arrested," Jonathan protested.

Alec Morton let out a deep sigh. "It's hard enough being juniors. You know that we have an unwritten code of conduct here. I'm sorry to have to tell you both that you've made it much worse on yourselves."

Jim remained silent. Jonathan knew that they'd done right by the two brothers and he'd leave the room with dignity.

The following day, Jonathan found a note in his locker. "See me, JMF." He walked down the study corridor and saw Flicker's open door at the end. Jonathan coughed to announce his presence.

The prefect stood by the window and Croat was reclining in his armchair. Flicker was conflicted about the incident but felt it his duty to maintain the Blackleigh code of conduct. He turned to Jonathan, then addressed Croat, "Please excuse us."

Croat left without a word and closed the door behind him.

Flicker sighed. "I hear you went to the police and

made serious allegations against two members of this House and two members of Plessey. You and Bhasin are headed for serious trouble. You'll soon be joining the corps, Simon. Who knows how many seniors will have it in for you?"

"We told the truth," Jonathan insisted. "But it seems that no one here is interested in that. Yesterday, Mr Morton brought up our unwritten code, but Blackleigh also has a written code standing for truth, honesty and justice. Would *you* allow those two to remain in prison if you absolutely knew they were innocent?"

Flicker paused to reflect, then said with finality, "That possibility would never arise. You ask me what I'd do. My allegiance is to Blackleigh, its reputation and traditions above all else. That's my truth. You'll have to make up your mind where you stand."

"That's easy," Jonathan let slip a smile. "I go to an insider's school but I'm more comfortable being on the outside, especially when right is on their side."

"Ah," Flicker replied, "then we have a serious problem."

27

CORPS

The warnings from the Housemaster and Flicker were manifested when all of the Trafalgar seniors, and most juniors, no longer acknowledged either Jonathan or Jim's existence. Tunk said nothing but looked at them both with unconcealed hatred, as if waiting for an opportunity to do them grievous harm. For the most part, members of other Houses seemed disinterested in Jonathan and Jim. But both boys were well aware that at Trafalgar they'd have to remain constantly on guard.

A separate notice on the House lobby activity board brought Jonathan's attention to more immediate problems. He'd already collected his corps uniform from the armoury. The notice that applied to all members of the school's combined cadet corps, stated that there was a uniform inspection scheduled for two o'clock on the following Monday afternoon: "Assemble on the parade ground at the rear of Blackleigh Hall. No absences tolerated. – Hugh Sleeth, Officer Cadet."

Jonathan vowed to spend the weekend ironing his uniform, polishing his boots and shining belt buckles. The necessity of putting in so much time on these tasks exasperated him. But he was informed that Sleeth's disapproval with any aspect of his turnout would result in a punishment at a time and place of Sleeth's choosing. The thought of having to face Sleeth one-on-one in an isolated setting was something he didn't want to contemplate.

Saturday, after breakfast, Jonathan came into the Houseroom carrying a large cardboard box holding his corps equipment. He dropped it down on a table and looked out of a window. Keith Rayner sat on the rear House steps. Beside him, Keith's army uniform, shirt, tie, belt, buckles, gaiters, denims, boots and his army beret were piled in a heap.

"Hello," Jonathan greeted Keith, uncertain how to begin. "So… uh… how about we work on our corps turnout together?"

"Sure," Keith replied, as if more important things were on his mind, "but I'm due to go for a run in less than an hour. Let's start with the boots."

Jonathan was grateful for whatever time Keith would allot. "I've got a tin of Kiwi brown polish," he said. "How do we begin?"

"It's called spit and polish," Keith said, glad to be of help. "First, you spit on one part of your boot. Then use a duster with a dab of polish to mix in with your spit, then breathe on the surface. You do the polishing with little round circles and plenty of huffing, working on each part of your boot separately. When you finish, you know you're done if you can see your face reflected in the leather."

"I don't want to see my face," Jonathan said wryly.

"Yes, you do. Come on. After the boots are finished, you 'blanco' your belt and gaiters, then shine your belt buckles with 'duraglit', known locally as 'durashit'." He held up a tin.

They worked on their boots for a half-hour until Holt, a senior who often ran with Keith, came down the steps. Holt ignored Jonathan altogether and addressed Keith, "Ready to run? Or are you going to spend all day on your boots?"

Jonathan realised that Keith, unlike him, did not plan to devote much of his weekend to the demands of the Blackleigh corps.

"I'll keep working on my boots," Jonathan told Keith. "Sleeth's out to get me. I don't want to fail Monday's inspection."

"Sleeth's out for me too, but not in the way you think," Keith grinned.

"I've no doubt, I won't fail his inspection."

Keith nodded to Holt, who smiled back. Holt helped Keith collect his equipment and they left together.

A day later, with further help from Arthur's brother, Harry, one of the few who still talked to him, Jonathan completed his turnout.

"Do you think my boots are shiny enough for Sleeth?" Jonathan asked proudly.

"What *shine* are you talking about?" Harry joked.

"C'mon Harry, I can almost see my reflection in the toe caps."

"Jonathan, you've a great imagination."

★★★

Silence prevailed on the parade ground. The area was filled with over three hundred khaki-clad cadets from the school, wearing matching black berets. Standing at attention, eyes front, the uniformed body was still. Each cadet waited to be inspected by their respective House officers.

Jonathan was second from the end of the third line in the Trafalgar section. On his left, and on the outside, was Keith Rayner. From the corner of his eye, Jonathan saw Sleeth, followed by his two sergeants, Tunk and Croat, start their inspection along the lines of cadets.

Sleeth was impeccably dressed, with his boots reflecting like mirrors. He carried a baton under his arm and briefly stopped in front of each cadet. His two sergeants, like subservient courtiers, waited a step behind for instructions. With hawk-like intensity, Sleeth gazed into each cadet's eyes, then looked down at his turnout. Sleeth addressed one after another, made his decision and barked "Pass" or "Fail". His decision was promptly noted on a clipboard by Tunk.

As they neared, Jonathan heard the declaration, "Fail!" followed by Sleeth's scathing criticisms. With a flourish, the officer pulled out a cadet's crumpled shirt from his belt. "I wouldn't use this rag to wipe dogshit off the bottom of my shoe. You are a fucking disgrace… Fail."

Tunk, with apparent glee, wrote an "F" beside the boy's name on his list. Croat stood by, out of sorts, with no particular duty to perform.

Jonathan glanced at Keith Rayner, standing beside him. Keith stood rigidly at attention, shoulders pressed back, handsome in his uniform. But the creases in his trousers looked uneven and his boots were dull, lacking the extra shine Jonathan worked so long to achieve.

And then, Sleeth was standing directly in front of Jonathan locking eyes on him. Tunk immediately wrote down "Fail", jumping the gun before he heard from Sleeth. An exaggerated cough from Keith stopped Sleeth and distracted him as he was about to speak. Sleeth immediately lost interest in Jonathan, mumbled "Pass", to Tunk's great dismay, and moved on to the more attractive specimen at the end of the line.

Jonathan wanted to leap for joy, saved by Keith's intervention, but he wisely remained rigid.

Sleeth stood erect in front of Keith. Seconds passed before he looked straight into the boy's hazel eyes. Keith stared back unblinkingly. Sleeth flushed momentarily and moved on.

Tunk waved a hand to catch Sleeth's attention. "Is Cadet Rayner a Pass or a Fail, sir?"

"Can't you see?" Sleeth said matter-of-factly, "Cadet Rayner's turnout is exemplary. Pass!"

28

REVENGE

James Bhasin was conscious of increased hostility towards him in the House ever since he and Jonathan reported Tunk to the police. Tunk, without saying a word, expressed his fury in silent, diabolical ways. He'd shoot evil smirks at Jim, clench his fists, or slice his open palm across his throat when he caught Jim's eye.

Jim devised a strategy to get away from the House and avoid Tunk altogether. After lunch, Jim took a book with him and headed out on the south side of the House in the opposite direction from the old cemetery.

He stayed within Blackleigh grounds and took the same route each day following a narrow path through a sea of tall reeds. Some of the tall stems snapped when he trampled through them, and his running shoes squished on sodden ground. Ahead was a desolate swamp area with a clump of trees at the rear.

He walked around the water's edge and proceeded into a thicket.

Jim enjoyed the time alone, listening to the occasional birdsong and relaxing. He felt safe beyond Tunk's reach. He usually made his way to a wooden shack he'd discovered amongst the trees, the gardeners' tool shed. Inside were rakes, saws, spades, large bags of fertiliser and other gardening equipment; plus a folding chair and a small table where Jim could spend his afternoons reading without fear of intrusion.

Today there was a light drizzle. Bhasin took out his class book, *Middlemarch*, and began to read. After a few minutes, it became hard to focus; he had the strange sensation he wasn't alone. His body tensed; he looked out the window and was jolted by the flutter of ducks on the wing, rising upwards from the marsh. Something had disturbed them. He watched the flock soar into the clouded sky and disappear. Jim inhaled and exhaled deeply, wondering what he should do.

From behind a tree, Tunk watched the hut with ice-cold hatred. He could see Bhasin through the open window.

Jim decided to make a run for it. He bolted the shed, and turned onto the path back to Trafalgar. He'd gone about 20 metres when Tunk stepped onto the path, blocking his way.

"Wh-What are you doing here?" Jim stammered, sliding to a stop, an arm's length away.

"I'm going to settle things between us once and for all," Tunk said quietly, thoroughly savouring the look of panic on the junior's face. "That is if you can spare the time," he added with his usual sarcasm; then punched Jim in the stomach.

Jim clutched his gut, stumbling back a step. "What's your problem, Tunk?"

"No problem," Tunk said brassily, "but it would be a pleasure to hear you beg for mercy."

"That's not going to happen," Jim said firmly. Despite, or because of the threat, Jim gained absolute clarity. Jonathan was right. No matter the price, giving in to a bully was not an option. He'd take his beating if he had to.

The response took Tunk by surprise. "No little darky gets away with making me look a fool. Now, I repeat, I'd like to hear you beg for mercy."

Jim stared Tunk in the eye and said, "Save your breath."

Tunk hit Jim in the jaw, spinning him around. He grabbed Jim's arm from behind and twisted it up towards his shoulder blades and increased the pressure. "Beg, goddamit, beg!" Spittle formed at the corners of Tunk's mouth. "Beg for mercy, and I'll let you go," Tunk lied. He planned to humiliate Jim regardless. He'd make Bhasin strip off and hand over all his clothes, so he'd have to walk back to the House buck-naked.

Jim realised that if Tunk kept applying pressure, his arm would break or be dislocated. He was about to speak when Tunk inexplicably squealed like a girl then let go.

Jim turned around to see Dirk Williams, the owner of the booth at the fair. He was dragging Tunk backwards by the hair. Dirk kicked Tunk's legs out from under him, and he landed on the ground with a hard thud.

Tunk started to get up until Dirk pointed a finger at him like he was a dog, and commanded, "Stay!"

Dirk turned to Jim. "I'd hoped to thank you and Mr Simon for what you did for me and my brother. Now and then, I do a little poaching in these woods. And today I saw this ugly gent following you."

Dirk removed his jacket and rolled up his sleeves. "Now, young man," he said to Jim, "you best get yourself out of here. You don't wanna see what happens to a bully when he meets his match."

29

CELEBRATION

Flicker and Croat returned to their study, put their books away, and Flicker closed the door. Croat was anxious; Flicker had indicated they needed to discuss a serious matter.

"You went to see Tunk at the sanatorium, this morning," Croat said. "What's the latest?"

"It's a prefect's duty to follow up when a serious assault occurs," Flicker reminded him. "You know I'm no friend of Tunk."

"So, how's the ol' chap doing?" Croat said with indifference.

"Going home this afternoon with Mummy and Daddy. From what I could make out, Tunk, who knows how to spin a story, claims three huge thugs from Enderby attacked him in the woods." Flicker shook his head in amusement. "Tunk says he did his best to defend himself, but three brutes were too much, *even for him.*"

"If that is what really happened, it's outrageous," Croat declared. "Can he identify them?"

"Apparently not. He claims that…" Flicker made quote marks with his fingers. "'the cowards jumped me from behind and I never got a good look.' Lucky for Tunk, a gardener found him unconscious, laying in the grass near a toolshed. He was worked over badly, and his parents have decided to take him out of school. But he'll be back next term."

"I'm worried, James," Croat frowned. "Tunk knows about our drug operation."

"I've shut that down since becoming a prefect," Flicker reminded Croat, "there's no evidence. Besides, Tunk isn't a squealer. He was useful to us because he'd sometimes let slip what Sleeth was thinking. Tunk is loyal to himself only."

Flicker unlocked his bottom desk drawer and brought out a bottle of Moët champagne and two long-stem glasses. "I think his timely absence calls for a little celebration." Flicker found a corkscrew and popped the cork with a flourish, then poured the light golden liquid into Croat's glass and filled one for himself.

"Two toasts, William," Flicker said. "The first is good riddance to Tunk." They touched glasses and sipped the champagne. "Now, I've another more important toast."

Croat sat up in his chair and awaited Flicker's revelation.

"At the end of this term, Reece leaves Trafalgar. I plan to stay on for one more term *if* I'm appointed Head of House. At that time, there'll be an opening for my current prefect spot and I'll have influence in the choice. Let's drink to you, *the new prefect*, William Croat – your reward for loyalty to me."

Croat beamed and held up his glass. "I'll damn well drink to that. I'd do anything to be a prefect."

Flicker nodded. "You may have to. It's not a done deal."

They sat back in their armchairs, relishing the moment and the promise of the future.

Their celebration was interrupted by a rap at the door. Flicker quickly put away the bottle and the glasses. Croat went to open the door. He was taken aback to see Sleeth standing there.

"Greetings to two of my favourite people," Sleeth said in a hollow voice, brushing Croat aside as he walked into the study. His sleeves were rolled up revealing his massive arms. "Do I detect the smell of champagne? I'm not interrupting anything, am I?"

"What the hell do you want?" Flicker said irritably.

"Ah Flicker… I'd like a few moments of your time."

"Make it quick," Flicker snapped, not offering Sleeth a chair as Croat returned to his.

Sleeth ignored the rebuke and looked around the study at the changes in the décor. "Not my taste." He grabbed a chair over by the new meths stove and sat down.

"Get to the point," Flicker said.

"Reece just told me that he's going to recommend me as the next Head of House when he leaves. This doesn't affect you, Flicker, as rumour has it that you're leaving anyway, but it makes a real difference for Croat, here."

"How does this impact me?" Croat asked in surprise.

"The Head of House influences the choice of prefects. Sorry to disappoint you Croat, but there's no way I'd nominate you for anything, not even to clean my corps boots. Tunk will be back next term, and I'm looking forward to working with him. He and I will bring some much needed discipline."

Flicker let out a deep sigh of boredom as if he had no interest in anything Sleeth had to say.

"Furthermore, Croat," Sleeth said, "I know you *thought* you'd been promoted from corporal to sergeant along with Sergeant Tunk in the corps, but on second thought, I've decided to demote you back to corporal for the upcoming year."

Croat angrily slapped his armrests.

Flicker calmly asked, "What makes you so sure that I'm leaving at the end of this term?"

"It may not be your decision," Sleeth replied cryptically.

"I'm trying to think," Flicker mused out loud, "why Reece would support you for Head of House. I know of no area in which you excel, apart from how you bully juniors and cadets. Am I missing something?"

"I think so," Sleeth replied. "I also collect information about people. Tunk has been an invaluable aid to me in this regard."

Concern now appeared on Flicker's face. He looked at Sleeth as if he was seeing him for the first time. "Your point?"

"I've been asking questions…There are too many coincidences around here. Rodgers, Gracey and

Crown Junior all worked for you." Sleeth paused for dramatic effect. "Not to mention your *business* at the old church."

"What are you implying?" Flicker shifted in his chair.

"I thought I made that clear," Sleeth said, "*I* keep quiet about my suspicions, and in return, *you* leave Blackleigh for good at the end of this term."

"You forgot about the school code, you can't report me, it'll reflect worse on you," Flicker said.

"No I haven't," Sleeth grinned. "It'll be an *anonymous* tip."

Flicker sprang from his chair, gracefully moved to the wall and grabbed his foil, slashing it through the air, advancing on Sleeth. "Get out!"

Sleeth stood nonchalantly. "I'm done here anyway. I know when I'm not welcome." He exited at his own pace, leaving the door open behind him.

Croat waited while Flicker gained control of his temper.

"This time he's gone too far," Flicker said, seething with anger.

"Sleeth is dangerous *and* ambitious." Croat crossed over and closed the door. "What can we do?"

"I had an idea when we first discussed Sleeth's interest in Keith Rayner," Flicker replied. "But then the timing wasn't right."

"What are you thinking?"

"How to bring Sleeth down and finish him off. I've a plan, but I need your help to carry it out."

"Of course, I'll do whatever it takes." Croat reached out for a handshake.

Flicker squeezed Croat's hand tight enough to make him grimace. "You'll have to if you want to be a prefect."

30

OBSTACLE RACE

Officer Cadet Hugh Sleeth pulled on his shining corps boots and knotted the laces tightly. It was the annual obstacle race for first-year cadets from both Trafalgar and Plessey Houses, so he wore denims instead of his khaki uniform. He connected his glinting belt buckles and adjusted his beret to the correct angle over his reddish, acne-riddled face. But Sleeth had something much more diabolical on his mind than just supervision.

His tense expression reflected the hatred he felt inside. He was satisfied with the way he'd demoted Croat. Flicker was another matter. There was no way he could allow Flicker to stay on beyond the summer. Until now, Flicker held the cards, but things had changed. Perhaps for the first time in his life, Flicker was up against a stronger and more ruthless opponent. Sleeth would stop at nothing to bring a deserved disgrace upon his scar-faced enemy.

The attack on Tunk came at a bad time, but Sleeth never suspected it was anything other than a gang of Enderby hooligans, as Tunk had reported.

Simon irked Sleeth like no other junior ever had. So far, nothing he'd done had any effect on the rat. But this was about to change.

The hated junior was not the first person at Blackleigh he'd sought out for retribution. Sleeth recalled a string of arrogant weaklings who ended up with bloodied faces and smashed noses. In his mind, he saw them cowering before him in dark corners of the school. Despite their pleas, he'd never shown mercy. One of his most recent victims ended up in the school sanatorium, nursing a badly cracked rib. With his height, weight and muscular edge, Sleeth always prevailed. He thought about his hero, out of the pages of Shakespeare, whom he'd studied for his English "A" level exam. *Macbeth knew how to ruthlessly deal with his enemies.*

The coming obstacle race gave Sleeth the opportunity to settle his score with Simon. He'd find a way to catch the junior all alone somewhere along the course, then put his plan into effect. That would effectively end of the problem.

★★★

In the dining room, Jonathan fretted about the upcoming race, feeling too nervous to eat lunch. He was encouraged by Jim Bhasin's victory over Tunk,

230

but he knew there'd be many more battles in this war and they couldn't afford to lose even one. A feeling of nausea churned in his stomach. A week earlier he'd seen the dreaded announcement on the corps notice board: "Next week's obstacle race is compulsory for all first-year recruits in both Trafalgar and Plessey Houses."

Each recruit had to run separately, and the timed, arduous race averaged two hours, but would last longer for any recruit who encountered an impassable obstacle. Jonathan envisioned himself barely standing at the finish line, gasping for air. That was if he even made it to the end.

On his way back to Trafalgar, Jonathan ran into David Gold, who as usual looked pleased with himself. David was dressed in his impeccable school attire rather than corps denims.

"Hey David, what are you doing?" Jonathan said, looking him up and down. "The race starts in a few minutes. No one's excused. Not even you."

"I know… I was so looking forward to participate." David didn't miss a beat in his positive response. "Anthony Summers gave me tips on how to surmount many of the obstacles. He was training me for the race right up until I sprained my foot, yesterday."

"What? You're not taking part?" Jonathan shook his head in disbelief.

"Sadly, no. Despite my protests, the school doctor insisted on giving me a medical note to excuse me from corps activities for the next two weeks.

"How do you do it?" Jonathan exclaimed.

"What do you mean? I can't put any pressure on my left foot. How could I run?" David started to frown, but turned it into a wink. "You may be interested to know they've made me a civilian observer at one of the obstacles to ensure no one's cheating."

Jonathan cringed when David waved, and delivered his favourite quip, wriggling his fingers, "Don't do anything I wouldn't do."

At two o' clock Jonathan joined the other cadets moving in single file up to the starting line. He shuffled forward, feeling uneasy when his turn finally came.

The start was monitored by officers from each of the two Houses. Jonathan was unnerved to see Sleeth supervising and barking out instructions. Newly demoted, Corporal Croat, and a few sergeants stood around, acting busy. David Reece, the Head of House, also an officer in the corps, ticked off the names of all participants from the Trafalgar section.

Sergeant Rice, a timekeeper from Plessey, glanced at each cadet at the starting line, then looked at his stopwatch. When the second hand came around, he ordered, "Go!" and noted the exact time, minutes and seconds. Another timekeeper would record the finish time of all those who completed the zigzag course. The two times would be compared later, then posted on the school notice board the following day.

Keith Rayner was ahead of Jonathan. When Keith moved to the starting line, Sleeth came up and briefly took over from Sergeant Rice.

Sleeth leered at Rayner from top to toe before

commenting, "Good luck. I've no doubt that you'll have one of the best times. Okay, go!"

Keith sped off.

Jonathan advanced, toed the line, and waited for the start command.

"Cadet Simon," Sleeth snapped, "not so fast. Go to the end of the line. You're last."

"Why?" Jonathan asked curiously; not in protest.

"Unlike Rayner," Sleeth shot a thumb in Keith's direction, whose back was disappearing down the trail, "you'll hold the others up."

Jonathan was actually glad to be last, feeling that there'd be no pressure and he could set his own pace. Ten more boys set off, then Jonathan, bringing up the rear, was at the starting line again. Sleeth had taken off alongside the previous boy and was yelling encouragements – or more likely, insults – in his ear.

As he looked ahead, Jonathan and saw the race route was marked out in black signs with yellow arrows taped on them. His race began without incident. On the first obstacle, he had to crawl on his stomach under low-strung wires, then on all-fours through narrow concrete tunnels where he scraped his hands.

Clambering out of the tunnel, Jonathan knew that other obstacles included climbing over walls of various heights, leaping across water pits, swinging from one rope to another, Tarzan-style, without letting your feet touch the ground – otherwise, Sleeth or one of the civilian observers would make you start over.

Sleeth had steadily monitored Simon's progress all

afternoon, hoping for an opportunity to stage a severe accident. But there were always civilian observers too close to risk anything. He went on ahead to the last isolated obstacle.

The boathouse on Enderby Lake was a one-storey stone-faced building with a timber pitched roof. The front of the boathouse faced the open water of the lake with a horizontal beam fourteen feet long, eight inches wide, and ten feet high over water, supported on each end at the top of the structure walls.

For the race, two ladders had been placed against the outside walls so that cadets could climb up, reach the beam, and after passing, hand-over-hand along it, reach the ladder on the opposite side and climb down to the ground.

This obstacle proved to be the end of the race for the weaker recruits. Many fell into the watery sludge while trying to cross the high beam and ended up covered in green muck.

Sleeth, alone at the obstacle, was thrilled to discover that the civilian observer had apparently taken off. He figured that with sunset nearing, the boy must've gone home, not wanting to miss dinner. He took a handful of slimy algae, climbed up the far ladder and deposited it three feet from the end of the beam. He then hid in the nearby tall weeds and contemplated his next move.

A diabolical plan brewed in Sleeth's evil mind: When Simon fell from the beam into the water, he'd hurry out of the weeds and jump in as if to save the boy. Simon would be momentarily relieved – until Sleeth grabbed him by the neck and held Simon under, until he drowned.

Sleeth pictured himself coming out of this a hero: *I'll carry his limp body back in my arms and put on a command performance, with tears and the works. I'll say that I went to make sure the obstacle course was all clear, and found the poor boy floating face down in the lake. I tried to revive Simon with mouth-to-mouth, but it was too late.*

He was beside himself with anticipation. *This will make three: Gracey, Crown, and now Simon, all finally gone!*

31

THE BEAM

Jonathan clawed his way along the ground under a length of tight netting and came out in a clearing. It was turning dark, when he reached the last obstacle – the dreaded boathouse with the horizontal beam.

One thing Sleeth was right about, it'd taken Jonathan a long time to complete each obstacle and he'd have held others up, were they behind him. Just like the previous obstacle, there were no civilian observers to make sure he didn't cheat. Jonathan figured that due to the late hour they'd been sent home. It occurred to him that he could skip this obstacle – considered the hardest of them all – and no one would know. But his sense of honour got the better of him. He climbed to the top of the nearside ladder, leaned over to his left and grabbed hold of the beam.

Jonathan carefully inched along, swinging nervously in the air with his feet dangling down. He could hardly believe that he was completing the obstacle, and now wished he had a witness to congratulate him. Below, he saw a thick film of emerald green algae that held a strange fascination for him, almost as if inviting him to drop through the mottled surface and experience the cold, putrid depths. By now, Jonathan had managed to get over three-quarters of the way across.

Moving on slowly, he studied the grip of his hands. He firmed up his grasp and moved farther along. He was almost close enough to stretch and put his toe on the descending ladder when his left hand met the wet algae Sleeth had planted.

Jonathan's heart jumped, tension seized his body.

His left hand gradually slipped away until he was hanging by his right arm only. Jonathan tried to swing and reach the ladder with his foot. First try he missed; second try he got a toehold. But his body weight was too much for the one hand. He saw the tops of his fingers stretch and grow pale with strain. He knew he was going to fall even before it happened. His fingers vanished in front of his eyes; he was gone.

Jonathan crashed through the mucky green surface and was engulfed in darkness. Muddy water shot up his nose and blinded his vision. He found himself sitting on the slippery bottom, and began twisting and kicking to get his feet underneath him. He finally succeeded and rose up, breaking the surface and stood chest deep in the stagnant water.

Sleeth couldn't believe his luck. It had also occurred to him that Jonathan could have skipped this obstacle.

What an idiot! Sleeth thought. He stepped out of the tall weeds to head for Jonathan and hold him under – but not without gloating first. He had practised his speech: "Remember Simon! I warned you. You had the chance to get the hell out of Blackleigh. You should have listened. And now you'll pay… with your life!"

After three steps, Sleeth froze when he heard a loud noise issue from the rear of the boathouse. A moment later, the door opened. Sleeth retreated into the weeds to observe.

David Gold exited the boathouse, yawning and straightening his tie. He heard splashing in the water and saw Jonathan, his hair matted with algae, trying to grasp hold of reeds at the bank; but they kept snapping and he was unable to haul himself up.

David quipped, "Well, Jonathan, looks like you failed the last obstacle."

"Don't just stand there, help me out of here," Jonathan hollered.

David looked left and right. His eyes lit up when he found an oar. He went to the water's edge and extended it to Jonathan, being very careful not to get any slime on his clothes.

Sleeth shook his head in disappointment at the lost opportunity before him. *How I'd love to dispose of Gold as well! But two dead bodies will look way too suspicious.*

Once on dry land, Jonathan asked David, "What are you doing here?"

"I was assigned to this obstacle. But being an observer is so boring." David made a small frown. "Besides, standing on my sore ankle all afternoon was exacting a toll. Fortunately for me, there was a mattress in the boathouse, so I took a little nap."

Jonathan shook his head. "You're amazing David. Even standing around is too much for you."

David ignored the dig and said proudly, "Hey, if it wasn't for me, you'd still be in the water."

Jonathan laughed and nodded. He pointed homeward, "Yeah, you're right… C'mon David, let's get something to eat."

Sleeth would have to take an alternative route back to the House. He turned in the opposite direction, vowing, *It isn't over yet, Simon.*

32

SCHEME

May 1956

Warm weather came as uncertainty prevailed: Who would be the next Head of House? These were days when the promise of summer defiantly burst through May skies. The weeks seemed to briefly fly ahead to what felt like a hellish hot July before turning back in time to a tepid May once more.

On these unusually hot pre-summer days, a subtle difference settled in the air. White cricket attire appeared with batting pads, rock-leather covered maroon balls and wood grained bats, each stamped with the printed signature of a well-known cricketer. Some boys lay out in the grass, sunbathing in shorts, as if July had already arrived.

Keith Rayner, flat on his back, at the rear of the House, listened to the frequent clacks of bats hitting cricket balls. He looked up; a ball flew, streaking across the blue sky before it vanished into a pair of outstretched hands. Soon after, the same ball hurtled back overhead in the opposite direction.

He sweltered in the unusual heat. Beads of sweat glistened on his tanned torso. Like an Indian summer, poised between summer and autumn, Keith's physique was also on hold, lingering between youth and adulthood. He closed his eyes, felt the warmth of the sun caress his lids, and quietly cursed that he'd forgotten his sunglasses.

Keith became aware of a large figure hovering over him. He opened his eyes and sat up with a frown. Croat, in a shirt and tie, was flapping his right arm to catch Keith's attention. Sweat blotched Croat's shirt under his arms.

"Rayner… I need a word. Can you come to my study?" he requested.

Keith hesitated, though intrigued. "Sure, but I'll need to shower first. What's this about, then?"

"I'll explain inside. I can't talk here in this heat." Croat wiped his hand around the back of his neck. "I'll wait for you."

Keith watched Croat amble away. He knew that the senior was devious and always had an agenda. But he figured there was no harm in listening to what Croat had to say.

Rayner stood, towelled the sweat from his body and off the back of his legs, then rolled up the towel and wrapped it around his neck.

Keith showered, dressed casually in a T-shirt, shorts and running shoes, then went to Croat's study. He found the senior alone, sitting in an armchair, stuffing a jam doughnut in his mouth.

"Ah yes," Croat spluttered, wiping sugar from his lips, "take a chair."

Keith waited while Croat finished chewing and swallowing. Keith could almost hear Croat's brain turn and crank in the right configuration before he spoke.

"Thanks for coming, Rayner."

"What do you want, Croat?" Keith asked, precluding any small talk.

Croat slowly licked the last sugary icing and raspberry jam from his fingers. "I'll be frank," he said, opening his palms in a dramatic pose. "I need to discuss something with you… Can I call you Keith?"

"Tell me what you want, Croat?" Keith said, wary of Croat's motive for being on first name terms.

Croat chortled at the rebuke. "The subject is a delicate matter."

"Then why tell me? You're not a prefect. What are you angling for?" Keith snapped.

"Quite so," Croat mumbled uncomfortably. The interview was not going in the seamless way Croat had hoped. Flicker would be furious if he fucked up.

Croat lowered his voice as if others might overhear. "I can tell you that the prefects are always on the lookout for future leaders in the House. Between these four walls, they feel *you* have potential."

In the silence that followed, Croat studied Rayner.

The junior was more than good-looking. The mix of fair hair, hazel eyes, and golden physique was perfect. How the ancient Greeks would have worshipped a fine figure like this!

Croat coughed nervously. He had come to the pivotal moment in their meeting. "I'm telling you in confidence that a senior member of our House is acting with impunity. He may have serious mental problems, and is in need of professional help."

"Are you talking about *Flicker*?" Keith asked facetiously.

"Flicker! Of course not…" Croat snapped, missing Keith's stab at humour. "Flicker's our only hope. This has nothing to do with him."

"Then get to the point," Keith said in exasperation. "What the fuck has this to do with *me*?"

Croat shook his head. "I haven't made myself clear. I'm talking about Sleeth. Certainly, you know the brute is half-crazy."

Keith remained silent. Until now he had no intention of doing anything that'd benefit Croat or Flicker. But at the mention of Sleeth's hated name, the scourge of juniors, he became interested.

"I personally witnessed Sleeth take sadistic pleasure in humiliating Simon, Crown and Gracey at the rifle range," Croat disclosed.

While Jonathan hadn't gone into detail, Keith knew he'd been unspeakably brutalised. He swallowed his anger. "So, what's your idea?"

Croat sat back in his armchair pursing his fingers

together. "Whatever our differences, we need to be loyal to Trafalgar. I'm going to ask you to do something for the benefit of the House."

Keith eyed Croat warily.

"Here's the problem," Croat said, his beady eyes blazing. "Sleeth is a strong contender for Head of House when Reece departs, largely because of his lead position in the corps. Certain seniors think that as Head, he'd bring ruin to Trafalgar. The House would be run like a penal colony. We can't let that happen."

Keith's expression indicated that he agreed with Croat's assessment of Sleeth.

Croat felt emboldened and continued, "Every Friday, Sleeth spends his late afternoons up at the armoury doing paperwork for the corps. Let's say you were to pay him a visit. He'd welcome your company. Everyone knows that Sleeth has the hots for you. Play it cool, then get him to make a move on you."

Keith remained impassive, but he was thinking, *Croat's sicker than I thought but it's worth listening to see where he's going with this.*

"Bring someone with you to watch what happens through the north window," Croat went on. "Make sure Sleeth doesn't see him. Without a witness, it will be Sleeth's word against yours and he's a prefect. Then if Sleeth makes a rash move, which is highly likely, tell him 'no'. Knowing Sleeth, that won't stop him. Have your witness come into the armoury only when Sleeth has continued his advances. Then the two of you can get the hell out of there."

"Wait a minute. Not so fast, Croat. Remember the code?" Keith sneered, "I can't report him."

"Well, *I can*," Croat beamed. "The corps has a different set of rules regarding the conduct and integrity of its officers. I'll say you came back to the House visibly upset and that I demanded to know what happened. I'll report to Flicker. He will be obligated to confront Sleeth and demand he do the right thing… relinquish his campaign for Head of House next term."

Keith looked into Croat's eyes. This was a rare opportunity to get even with Sleeth on behalf of so many juniors. Maybe it was worth the risk? After a pause, he said, "I'll do what you ask, but I'm not doing it for you or Flicker."

The senior stood up, indicating that their meeting was over. To solemnise their agreement, he firmly grasped Keith's hand. There was no more to be said and Keith departed.

Croat sighed. Pessimist that he was, he began to envision all that could go wrong with his plan and sought comfort in the extra jam doughnut he'd put aside for himself.

33
ARMOURY

Keith's first action upon leaving the study was to wash his hands and rid himself of Croat's clammy touch. He then went into the Houseroom to find the one person he needed.

Jonathan was reading *The Enderby Times* at a table.

"I need to talk," Keith said ominously.

"Is it bad news?"

"Could be quite the opposite. Come with me up to the dorm."

Jonathan was intrigued and followed him upstairs. Keith sat on a bed, while Jonathan stood and listened.

"I know you've been looking for a way to get even with Sleeth," Keith proffered, "and so have I. There's something you and I can do together. Are you interested?"

Jonathan sat down next to Keith. "Why include me?"

"I just saw Croat. He detests Sleeth nearly as much as we do."

"And…" Jonathan prompted.

Keith relayed Croat's plan.

"Let me guess," Jonathan broke in, "you want me to be the witness."

"You're already ahead of me."

"But what if Sleeth doesn't take the bait?"

Keith smiled. "Don't worry. I've been at boarding schools since I was eight. Boys were always attracted to me. I had to learn fast. You're looking at an old pro at the seduction game."

Jonathan grabbed Keith's arm. "Maybe, but I still say it's dangerous. Sleeth is a loose cannon. No telling how…"

Keith cut him off, "We have a real opportunity to take this monster down. What do you say?"

"Our lives won't be worth living if we fail." Jonathan shuddered. "But I swore an Oath to Ian and Arthur that if I had the chance I'd get even with Sleeth. Count me in."

★★★

On Friday it was almost sundown when Jonathan and Keith left the House together. Keith had suggested they dress in running clothes. Beyond Blackleigh Hall they walked north on a path up Armoury Hill and reached the facility, located on a plateau at the hilltop. The building served as the school corps HQ for all cadets.

The armoury was isolated and looked like an ugly dark-red brick fortress, with barred windows on the north side, enveloped in a cluster of trees. Keith slipped through the undergrowth and cautiously approached the north window nearest the entrance. He stood alongside the outer wall and took a quick peek through the window. He could see the ground floor and a wide metal staircase leading to the level above. Sleeth was at his desk, where he and another senior were talking.

Jonathan waited for Keith in the bushes some twenty yards from the entry. He knew the interior of the building. The ground floor was kept in an immaculate state. The space was stocked with equipment and assorted corps clothes. In the centre of the room hung a single bulb over a wooden desk that Officer Cadet Sleeth used for office matters. A small room, at the rear, with a locked door, was used for storing ammunition. Only Sleeth and Chris Mercer, the Head of School had keys. The exception was a small ammo pouch containing six rounds that Sleeth wore on his belt whenever he was in uniform.

Sleeth couldn't tolerate disorder and arranged for a rotating group of cadets to come in over the weekend to dust, wash windows, and sweep the stone floor clean. On the upper floor, rows of metal racks were spaced out with passageways between them. In each rack, under a designated number, an old Enfield army rifle was allocated to each member of the corps, who was responsible for the cleaning and oiling.

Rumour had it that Blackleigh once considered the example of another prominent boys' school, where bayonets were also allocated to select cadets. One boy, taking this battlefield opportunity too seriously, proceeded to try and spear a few of the opposing forces in a corps exercise. Fortunately, the only injury was a lacerated thigh. Since then, Blackleigh, to the disappointment of Sleeth, abandoned the plan.

Keith returned to the cluster of shrubs where Jonathan waited. "There's someone with Sleeth. Looks like he's about to leave."

"Who?" Jonathan asked.

"I don't know. His back was to me."

The husky individual left the armoury, hesitated a moment, then took off walking down the hill. Jonathan immediately recognised Drub from the fair. His expression was fixed in a permanent scowl; the only emotion he showed on his box-like face was in the constant chewing movement of his mouth.

"I'm going in," Keith said. "When I yell 'Stop! Leave me alone!', come in right away."

He nodded and watched Keith head to the entrance and walk boldly inside. Jonathan could feel the hairs bristle on his arms. He hurried to position himself with his back up against the building, right next to the north window, hoping to hear what was being said and take an occasional quick glimpse inside.

He had to be patient, but the longer Jonathan waited, the more anxious he became. From brief glances through the window he saw Keith standing by the desk where Sleeth worked, but neither were talking.

He was afraid of being seen, and moved away, back against the wall and waited, uncertain what to do, when he heard muffled conversation. Jonathan half turned and began inching his way back towards the window. And that was when Drub's bulky arm wrapped around him from behind, squeezing Jonathan's small frame tightly as his left hand clamped over Jonathan's mouth.

Drub hissed. "I saw you and Rayner out of the corner of my eye, so I circled back. What do you two spastics think you're up to?"

At that moment, Keith screamed, "Stop! Leave me alone!"

Jonathan bit into the thick fingers over his mouth and Drub briefly released his hand. Simon struggled to break free. "Let me go."

Drub squeezed him tighter. "Only after I beat the shit out of you."

34

SEDUCTION

When Keith entered the armoury, Sleeth was writing an inventory list at his desk. Sleeth wore his corps uniform, shirt open at the collar, without a jacket or tie. The sleeves of his khaki shirt were rolled up in narrow folds, high enough to reveal his chiselled arms.

Sleeth looked up; his body jolted ever so slightly upon seeing Rayner. Though Sleeth was distracted and his body tense, he forced himself to focus on his paperwork.

Keith approached, uncertain whether to stand, or sit in the folding chair facing the desk until Sleeth acknowledged him. Rayner chose to remain standing to give himself more freedom of movement and silently waited.

Sleeth's mind was racing; he wondered why Rayner had come to the armoury alone. *Is it possible he wants the same thing I do?*

Tension seeped through Sleeth's body. Until now, Rayner had always steered clear of him in the House. Even so, Sleeth fantasised about the junior's body almost every night. The officer surreptitiously flopped a hand over his erect penis but resisted the urge to fondle himself.

Keith's reputation as a skilled fighter you didn't want to mess with had been concocted for self-preservation. Sure, he'd got into his share of scraps, largely out of jealousy over his good looks, but his win-loss record was about even. And if it had been true, Sleeth still outsized and outweighed him. Even in a fair fight, which he didn't believe Sleeth was capable of, Keith had no doubt he'd be overmatched.

The only constant noise in the room was the clank and ripple of a steel shutter, buffeted by the wind against an open window. The slamming noise was unsettling, and Rayner found himself distracted. Keith wondered whether he should speak up or wait. It was already a clear test of wills.

The silence was broken when, without looking up, Sleeth snapped, "What do you want, Rayner?"

Keith heard arrogance and a line of military forebears in Sleeth's gruff, commanding voice. He cleared his throat. "Is this a good time to talk?"

"That depends on why you're here," Sleeth replied. The officer twirled his gold-nib Schaeffer pen between his fingers.

"I was out for a run, near the armoury," Keith said, "and I decided to pop in."

"What's on your mind?" Sleeth now stared intently at Keith.

The junior waited for the rattling shutter to stop. For a moment, the room was silent. He had Sleeth's total attention. "Maybe you and I never got to know each other," Keith offered. "How can we make things right?"

"I don't understand." Sleeth could not believe his ears.

"Well, I'd like us to be friends," Keith said, eyes twinkling.

Sleeth's neck deepened in colour. Keith waited for his response. The damn shutter slapped again and jolted Keith's concentration. He wanted to rip it off the window frame and trample it under his feet.

After a pause, Sleeth replied in a firm voice, "That's a possibility… But my friendship has a condition."

"And what's that?" replied Keith, feigning innocence.

"That it's *my* definition of friends."

"What do you mean?" Keith said with faux naivety.

Sleeth understood the game. He dropped his pen and came around the desk. Sleeth casually touched Keith's arm, then moved his hands up over Keith's body to his face. "This is what I mean…" Sleeth leaned forward to kiss Keith.

Keith pulled away. "This isn't what I had in mind."

"Cut the crap," Sleeth chopped his hand through the air. "You want the same thing as I do, and you know it." *He's playing hard-to-get,* Sleeth surmised, *this is all part of the game.* He moved in again.

Keith realised that this was the pivotal moment. He

put his hands up, backed away and said, "You've got me all wrong."

Sleeth's expression twisted in anger. "You prick teaser. I know your kind… it's all about the chase… the thrill of getting them hard, then rejecting them. But not this time." In a lightning fast judo move, Sleeth grabbed Keith's arm, deftly twisted it behind his back and bent him over face down on the desk. While Sleeth applied painful pressure to keep Keith pinned, with his other hand he removed his own belt, then reached to unbuckle Keith's.

Keith never suspected that Sleeth could move so quickly. He cried out to alert Jonathan, "Stop! Leave me alone!" When there was no response, he shouted a second time. Keith then realised something had gone wrong; he was on his own.

He balled his free hand into a fist and swung it back into Sleeth's groin. Sleeth yelped and released his grip enough for Keith to free himself and start for the door. Though temporarily stunned, Sleeth moved to block the exit. He growled at Keith through gritted teeth, "You're not going anywhere till I get my due."

"Help!" Keith shouted at the top of his voice, then turned and fled up the metal staircase to the darkness of the floor above. Keith could barely see his way ahead. With his hands spread wide apart, he edged along a passage leading to the area where the rifles were stacked in rows.

Keith's hands knocked against an object and a rifle clattered heavily onto the floor. "Shit!" he muttered, having given away his location.

He made his way to the far wall, breathing heavily. *Where the hell is Jonathan?* Once more, Keith risked a shout, at the top of his voice, "Help… Help me!" His cries echoed off the walls. Then silence.

Keith wished he hadn't been looking up. In the next instant, he was practically blinded when the second floor became illuminated by three overhanging bulbs. One was directly over the alley from where he'd come. Keith grabbed the rifle and used the butt to smash it. He ran under the second bulb and knocked it out as well.

One bulb was left at the far end of another row of rifles. He hoped to get there, disable it, then outmanoeuvre Sleeth in the darkness.

Keith swivelled to the next corner and there stood Sleeth. Keith instinctively swung the rifle at him. In one motion, Sleeth blocked the stock, grabbed it, yanked it out of Keith's' hands and tossed it aside. Keith spun around and ran for his life as Sleeth hurtled after him.

Outside, Jonathan and Drub heard Keith's cries for help. Drub was still holding Jonathan, but his grip slackened.

"You hear that, Drub? It's Rayner," Jonathan spat. "If anything happens to him, I'll make sure you're also held responsible as an accomplice."

Drub gripped Jonathan tighter. "We've a code of silence at Blackleigh. It applies to fucks like you."

"To hell with the code," Jonathan yelled. "Let me go, or I swear I'll report you to the Headmaster. No matter what happens to me, you'll be finished here along with Sleeth."

Drub considered the seriousness of the situation. He dropped his hands, releasing his captive. He felt a kinship with Hugh Sleeth but not enough to go down with him.

When Jonathan ran towards the armoury door, Drub's first thought was to follow. Then he decided that the wisest course was to steer clear of trouble. Sleeth would have to handle whatever situation he'd caused by himself. Drub would mind his own business; he took off, double-time, for Plessey.

Jonathan raced into the armoury and came to a stop to assess the scene. A chair was turned over in front of the desk where Sleeth worked. Next to it lay Sleeth's belt. Sleeth and Rayner had to be on the floor above. He removed the ammo pouch and bolted up the stairs, two at a time, hearing a scuffling sound somewhere up ahead.

On the upper floor, Jonathan saw the solitary light at the rear. He grabbed the first rifle he saw, a single-shot bolt action, removed a cartridge from Sleeth's ammunition pouch, chambered it, then listened for any sound. To his right, he heard Keith, in a low voice, trying to talk sense into Sleeth. Jonathan hurried in that direction.

Rayner and Sleeth were at the end of an alley with rifles stacked on either side. With his back to Jonathan, Sleeth's muscular form was straddling his victim, face down on the floor. He had both of Keith's arms pinned behind his back; his shorts and underwear pulled down. With his free hand, Sleeth undid his zipper.

"You fucking tease… now you'll pay," Sleeth said devilishly.

Jonathan charged forward and pointed the rifle at the back of Sleeth's head. "Enough! Let him go! This gun is loaded."

Sleeth recognised the voice and slowly turned his head. "Well, well, if it isn't that pussy, Simon. You don't have the guts to shoot a man."

Sleeth turned, stood up and put his right foot on Keith's back to keep him immobilised. He grinned and said, "Give me that gun, you gutless wonder."

The officer was right. Shooting someone was not in Jonathan's blood – but self-defence was. Jonathan deftly spun the rifle, as Sleeth had taught him on the parade grounds, to grip the barrel end. He dropped to a crouch, swung hard with all his strength, aiming for Sleeth's left knee.

In his awkward stance, weight unbalanced, Sleeth was helpless to move and there was a sickening sound like a bone crunching.

Sleeth crumbled to his knees, yelling with pain. Jonathan jumped to the side and with a jabbing motion brought the butt crashing down on Sleeth's back, knocking the wind out of him.

Sleeth curled into a fetal position, gasping for breath, gripping his gashed and bleeding shin. Jonathan swung the rifle back over his shoulder, threatening to use it again like a club.

By this time, Keith had pulled up his shorts and got to his feet. He made a fist of his right hand, pulled it back in line with his shoulder, then smashed it into Sleeth's jaw. And it was lights out for the senior.

Jonathan was bursting with pride; he'd kept his Oath to Arthur and Ian.

"What took you so long?" Keith asked irritably.

"I was waylaid by Drub – tell you about it later. More important, are you all right?"

Keith nodded.

"What shall we do with him?" Jonathan indicated Sleeth.

Sleeth was coming back around. "I'll make sure both you fucks are expelled," he snarled groggily. "You attacked an officer with a loaded rifle."

Keith bent down and put his head alongside Sleeth's. He decided to take matters into his own hands and did a change-up on Croat's scheme. "Shut up and listen carefully: Within twenty-four hours, you'll see Flicker. Tell him that you've decided not to run for Head of House next term. I don't care what excuse you give. Simon and I will keep silent about what happened here. And if you don't, your attempted rape, and the fact that you're queer, will be all over the school. Do you understand?"

"What are you going to tell Croat?" Jonathan asked when he and Keith left the building.

"I'm not saying a word about what happened to Croat or anyone else. I'll just leave it that Flicker can expect to hear from Sleeth."

★★★

The next day, Flicker was reading in his study, when Sleeth knocked at the door. Sleeth walked in with a slight limp and a purple bruise on his jaw. They looked at each other warily, neither trying to conceal their enmity. Flicker waited for his rival to speak.

"There's something I want to discuss," Sleeth said grudgingly.

"What happened to you?" Flicker quipped, "Fell off your *high horse*?"

"Up yours," Sleeth shot back.

"To what do I owe this unexpected visit?" Flicker leaned back in his armchair, again without offering Sleeth a seat.

"There's a rumour going around that I'm running for Head of House."

Flicker played along. "I don't believe in *rumours*." He couldn't resist a stabbing smile.

"Neither do I." Sleeth's face grew red with anger as he struggled to quell the urge to slap the grin off Flicker's face. "I came to tell you that the rumour is false. I'm not running for anything."

"Why, Sleeth?" Flicker twisted the knife.

"Fuck you is why." And with that Sleeth left.

Flicker gloated, but only for a moment. The trap for Sleeth had worked, but he was not so naïve as to believe that everything would automatically be plain sailing from now on.

35

THE LETTER

In the senior changing room, Croat gazed at himself in the mirror. He hated the way he looked first thing in the morning. His eyeballs were bloodshot, tiny red wriggles crossed the white gelatinous matter; and puffy pouches of skin weighed below both eyes. He was dismayed to see that although he was younger than Flicker by three months, he looked a couple of years older, and strands of brown hair had already started to recede from his wrinkled forehead.

His task of clearing away the night's growth began. He applied a generous amount of foam to his face and neck. With his razor functioning like a lawnmower, he renewed swaths of clear sensitive skin, ready to face the day. He finished up, washed his face and put on his glasses. Croat made a mental note to avoid his tendency to open and close his mouth like a fish in water.

Croat felt uneasy. Rayner hadn't given him any

details about what occurred with Sleeth. But he knew Sleeth had gone to see Flicker yesterday. His unease was compounded by the haunting way Sleeth looked at him with undisguised hatred on the previous evening in the senior dorm. Croat wondered if Sleeth somehow knew he'd orchestrated the plot to take him out of the running for Head of House.

He joined the rest of the House in the dining room for breakfast and took his regular place at the head of the long table, facing Sleeth. Croat wished for the company of his study mate, but Flicker sat in another dining room supervising their breakfast.

A prefect stood at the high table and recited the usual short prayer. "Benedictus benedicat per Christum dominum nostrum."

Porridge was deposited at the heads of each table in heavy round metal containers. Croat would typically take turns with Sleeth to dollop out portions of the thick steamy sludge into bowls piled high in front of them. They'd then pass each helping down to the far ends of the table until all were served. Oversized white jugs of milk and bowls of sugar were already on the table, as were baskets of sliced bread.

Despite his bruises, Sleeth appeared to be in a buoyant mood. He turned to his left and right, sprinkling witticisms to his seated neighbours and frequently burst out in guffaws of raspy laughter. Even after his concession to Flicker, Sleeth seemed to have grown more dangerous, as if ambition still suffused him with power. Croat had known him for four years but had never seen him so energised. It was apparent that Sleeth made a point not to look in his direction. Croat sensed trouble brewing.

Croat handed Sleeth one of the two ladles. He took it without a word and winked at Steel, his study mate and smarmy smiling neighbour at the table, who had shiny greased black hair. "This porridge looks like last night's shag," Sleeth joked to Steel, and began serving. "I'll put an extra portion aside for Croat."

Steel responded with a chuckle.

Croat felt himself blush. He was never able to contest Sleeth's jocular mood so early in the morning. He worried that others at the table might soon notice and remark on the friction between them.

Croat served himself the last of the porridge. He looked for milk and sugar. A large foot-high jug was out of his reach to Sleeth's right.

"Sleeth, pass the milk," Croat said. But Sleeth was preoccupied, telling another crude joke. There was no reply from him or even a look of acknowledgement. "Sleeth, pass the milk." Croat repeated a little louder.

Sleeth continued talking as if Croat hadn't spoken.

Now others around the table noticed the impasse and became silent. Croat felt he had to act quickly to preserve his dignity. He leaned forward, touched Sleeth's arm and barked in exasperation, "Pass the fucking milk."

Sleeth's eyes flashed. A devilish expression spread over his face. He held the attention of his captive audience all the way down the length of the table. Jonathan, Jim Bhasin and Keith Rayner all looked up when Sleeth yelled, "Why didn't you say you wanted milk, Croat?"

With a swift movement, Sleeth stood, lifted the milk jug high in the air and poured the contents over Croat's head, saturating his hair and clothes. Sleeth placed the empty pitcher back on the table with a flourish. He clapped his hands with glee and announced, "Croat asked for milk… and he's fucking got it!"

Laughter erupted. Croat flung back his chair and hurried from the dining room along with his dashed reputation and standing in the House. He left behind a winding milky trail. Sleeth had provoked him and he'd fallen right into the trap. His hated adversary was out to destroy him and for once Croat, a master manipulator himself, didn't know what to do.

★★★

The post was delivered earlier than usual. Jonathan went into the Houseroom to see if there was anything addressed to him. He looked at the pile… Yes, an envelope. He recognised the bold rounded letters as Arthur's.

He went outside to be alone and opened it. The first page was a personal note to Jonathan explaining that Arthur had decided now was the time to reveal the truth. He gave Jonathan permission to show the second page to anyone he saw fit. It was a formal confession addressed to "Whomever it may concern".

Ten minutes later, Jonathan knocked on the door

to Flicker's study. He had the second page in his back pocket in case Flicker didn't believe what he had to tell him. He entered to find Croat alone, slumped in an armchair, looking demoralised.

Since breakfast, Croat had showered and changed his clothes; his crestfallen mood remained.

"What do you want?" Croat snapped.

"I came to see Flicker."

"He'll be back in a couple of minutes, but I don't want *you* waiting around here… Stay outside the door."

"What did I do to you?" Jonathan returned.

Croat took in a long gulp of air. "Did you go with Rayner to see Sleeth in the armoury last Friday?"

"Yes," Jonathan said, and delivered their agreed-upon story. "Rayner was hoping to try out another pair of boots, but the armoury was closed."

"Closed?" Croat repeated.

"Yes, closed. No one was there."

Croat sighed. He realised Simon wasn't going to reveal anything. "Look, just get out."

Jonathan complied and stood in the study corridor.

A minute later, Flicker strode towards him, glanced at Jonathan and opened the door of his study. When Flicker came in, Croat rose from his armchair. "James, you have company. Simon wants to see you. I'll leave you two alone. Later, I need to tell you what happened at breakfast with you-know-who."

Flicker nodded and Croat left the study.

The prefect had little patience for the junior who continuously made trouble in the House. Ever since

Simon reported Tunk to the police, and then forced his way through the Houseroom mob along with the Crown brothers, Bhasin, Rayner, and Wynn, resentment was on the rise against him.

"What you have to say better be important, Simon. Make it quick."

"I've come to see you because there's something you need to know. It's about that fire in your study. Everyone believes that Ian Gracey felt so guilty about starting the fire that he killed himself."

"That's ancient history," said Flicker, more abruptly than he intended.

"I just received a letter from Arthur Crown…"

"Get to the damn point."

Jonathan shifted uncomfortably from one foot to the other. "It wasn't Ian who caused the fire."

"What are you talking about?" Flicker said irritably.

"Arthur confessed to what really happened. He's kept it a secret until now."

Flicker felt his muscles tighten. *Could this be happening?* he asked himself silently. "But the police investigated," he protested weakly. "And Gracey wrote that note."

"But Arthur caused the fire," Jonathan insisted. "He was alone in your study messing with the meths stove. Ian happened along and helped him put out the fire. Arthur was so devastated that Ian decided to take the blame. Ian made Arthur swear not to…"

When Flicker reacted with profound shock, Jonathan asked, "What's wrong?"

Flicker made a superhuman effort to control himself. "I need to think this over. Do you have Crown's confession?"

"Yes, here it is." Jonathan took the folded envelope from his back pocket and gave it to Flicker.

"Thank you… Please leave."

"Are you going to be all right, Flicker?"

Jonathan considered telling Flicker about his own involvement that night but decided against it. He turned and left the study.

Moments later, the prefect was on his knees. Flicker's hands covered his face as he sobbed uncontrollably like a child. He was responsible for the death of another innocent boy.

36

TORMENT

Flicker slumped in his armchair. After staring woefully for a long time towards some distant horizon, he finally returned to reality.

He left his study and proceeded along the corridor like a sleepwalker, eyes half-closed, one foot dragging after the other. A senior attempted to engage him in conversation but he gazed straight ahead, ignoring those around him.

Flicker sought a place of refuge to be alone. He walked over to the chapel, opened a side door and entered the deserted sanctuary. All the interior lights were off. Flicker crossed over to his usual seat and dropped down.

James knew that he had to make the most important decision of his life. One choice was to turn himself in to the police for his role in Ian Gracey's death and Stephen Rodgers' suicide. Such action would result in his losing everything. He'd likely be looking at prison. His future would be bleak; the scandal would haunt him for the rest of his life, long after others had forgotten.

Another course was to try and live with the guilt. But Gracey's innocence was a new element that plagued his conscience. No one had tied him to either crime. Gracey's note of apology, referring to the fire, had been accepted by the authorities as a suicide note. Even Croat didn't suspect the truth.

Yet Flicker wondered if he could live with himself. He feared long nights of impossible sleep with images of Gracey, Stephens and even Nick tormenting his mind.

Flicker looked up at the vaulted ceiling of the chapel; he closed his eyes. He had the forlorn hope that when he opened them again, some heaven-sent sign might guide him to the right decision. He tried to pray, but his thoughts were jumbled.

Flicker opened his eyes to find nothing around him had changed. He was still sitting on his seat in the chapel unresolved about what to do. But he knew, whatever else, he'd have to try and make amends.

★★★

In the early afternoon, a notice in large, bold letters appeared on the House bulletin board, arousing great interest among members of the corps. Small groups hovered in the lobby to read the instructions.

"To first and second year members of the corps only – no seniors. Assemble outside at the rear of the House tonight, Saturday, Ten o'clock prompt. Corps dress: denims, boots, belts and berets. Briefing of this military exercise to be provided on a need-to-know basis. – Officer Cadet Hugh Sleeth"

Jonathan stopped Keith, about to leave on a run. "What's going on?"

Keith shook his head. "I don't know. Corps exercises are never planned for a Saturday night and on such short notice. Everyone else will be watching the movie… Shakespeare's *Richard the Third*. I don't like the sound of this. And I don't trust Sleeth."

37

NIGHT MANOEUVRES

At ten o' clock, Saturday evening, Jim Bhasin stood at the side door of the Houseroom watching members of the corps gather outside in the dark. The shadowy, denim-clad figures mingled and readied for the evening's exercise. Jim was relieved he hadn't been at the school long enough to be a member of the corps.

He looked up. The moon appeared from the cover of heavy cloud, casting a lazy glow over the young soldiers. The sound of boots on gravel fused with impatient voices.

The cadets, waiting for Sleeth, were annoyed to both miss the film and to be called for duty on a weekend evening. Sleeth alone had arranged for the unusual exercise. Reece, the departing Head of House, was in London; Alec Morton was attending a conference in York. Flicker had been absent all day. P. G. Ring, the ineffective acting Housemaster, was in charge.

Some cadets gathered in small groups; others flitted in the darkness from one group to another carrying their torches. One circled his torch around in a wheel and others followed. Fiery circle upon circle swung in the air. With concerted bursts of motion, the gathering moved their beams up and down. Some thrust them into nearby faces, pretending to gouge out the eyes of another as if with a red-hot poker. Jim could barely distinguish one boy from another in the passing flashes of light.

The cadets were nervous and wanted to know more about their night's mission. They talked in hushed tones. "What's Sleeth planning?" "What can be so important?"

Tempers frayed; hostility rose. Jim heard a cry of pain as a jabbing elbow found the ribs of another.

Jim noticed Jonathan and Keith standing apart from the others. He called out and caught Jonathan's attention, who left Rayner and came up the steps to the Houseroom door.

"What's going on?" Jim asked.

"I can't tell," Jonathan replied anxiously. "Most of them hardly talk to me anymore. It's as if I have leprosy."

"Can't you and Rayner get out of this exercise?"

"Not a chance."

"The mood of the corps is pretty grim," Jim said. "I saw Croat at the back. I don't think even he knows what's going on."

Sleeth arrived from the armoury with a small group of selected cadets. He swaggered ahead of them in full military dress, a rifle slung over his shoulder. Behind him, two cadets from Trafalgar, with Corporal Forrester in charge, pulled a flatbed wagon loaded with three knotted coils of climbing rope, a can of petrol, a large stack of firewood, and a large wooden steamer trunk. Sergeant Steel, the only senior from Trafalgar present, apart from Sleeth and Croat, brought up the rear, with a rifle over his shoulder.

"See that," Jonathan said to Jim, pointing, "the notice said nothing about bringing rifles but Sleeth and Steel are armed. Now I'm really worried. Wish me luck."

"Good luck, be brave," Jim called after him as Jonathan ran down the steps.

A minute later, Sleeth climbed the steps to the Houseroom door and at the lighted entry turned to face the cadets. He surveyed those present.

Jonathan was aware of Sleeth's eyes settling upon him. The officer's gaze moved away and found Keith Rayner, who stared back defiantly.

Sleeth surveyed the other dark figures assembled below. "Atten-SHUN!" he barked. Each of the thirty cadets present stomped their feet together and saluted. Then silence.

"Line up three abreast in columns," Sleeth ordered. "About-face from the House… Move it."

The cadets quickly formed columns while Steel read the roll. Each cadet snapped off a "Here!"

Sleeth flashed Sergeant Steel a sardonic smile, then gave his next order: "Squad… Quiiick march. Wheel to the right… left, left, left… right, left, right, left…"

The column marched forward; Sleeth in the lead, Steel and the wagon bringing up the rear. Jim saw them turn to the right and disappear in the darkness. The collective steps of the squad crunched on the gravel and became dull thuds upon reaching the grassy area. They marched on under the leaden sky away from the House and over the fields.

"I can guess where we're going," Jonathan whispered to Keith, marching beside him.

"Where?"

"To the cemetery grounds and then to the…"

"No talking, Cadet Simon!" Steel screamed from the rear.

Jonathan felt like he was being carried forward by a relentless tide with no will of his own to resist. He had no control over what might happen.

Is this a trap? Is Sleeth planning to exact a revenge on Keith and me for what happened at the armoury? Jonathan figured that Croat might also be due for extreme retaliation.

They'd marched three-quarters of a mile. All the way, Sleeth continued to bark out orders: "Increase the pace… left, right, left…"

Jonathan had guessed correctly. They were approaching the wire enclosure of the cemetery.

The derelict remains rose before them; the top of the bell tower appeared to reach upwards and almost disappear into the clouds.

"Squad halt." Steel ordered. "Stand at ease."

The cadets assumed relaxed postures as Sleeth removed a layout plan of the church grounds from his pocket and studied it with the aid of a torch. "Listen up," he commanded. "Proceed around the fenced area until you reach the cemetery on the far side. There's a wire gate in the fence. Remain outside until I give further orders."

The cadets, using their torches, hurried along the outside of the enclosure. Upon reaching their destination, one after another, they dropped down and sat cross-legged, waiting. The door in the fence was broken off its hinges and lay on the ground.

With the arrival of Sleeth, Steel, and the cart, the seated cadets shone their torches up at the two standing figures.

Sleeth raised his arms high and wide to command attention. "I'm sending three of you ahead along with Sergeant Steel and Corporal Forrester. They are designated as Squad A. The rest of you, Squad B, will join them soon. Squad A will secure a climbing rope from the top of the tower down to the ground. When Squad B arrives, our drill begins. Any questions?"

"What's the purpose of this drill?" a cadet called out.

"You'll be informed in due time. Sergeant Steel is in charge, and Corporal Forrester will supervise his orders. Corporal Croat, Cadet Rayner and Cadet Simon, you're Squad A. Fall in."

Jonathan and Keith came forward, followed reluctantly by Croat. Jonathan was confused by the fast-moving events. He and Rayner went through the opening in the fence, pulling the wagon behind them into the cemetery. Croat followed. Steel barked out orders: "Cadets Simon, Rayner, and Croat, head in the direction of the tower."

★★★

James Flicker returned to the House around nine. His day was spent in the chapel, and later he contemplated his terrible dilemma while walking the outer grounds of the school. Only a few juniors were sitting at Houseroom tables. James went to his study to talk to Croat about the corps notice he'd just seen on the bulletin board. He was dismayed to discover that Croat wasn't there.

Flicker changed into warm clothes and went to check out the dormitories. It wasn't quite time for lights-out and he wondered if he'd find anyone there.

The first dorm was in darkness. He turned on the lights. Only one person lay in his bed.

Flicker bent over Jim Bhasin, who was sound asleep, and gazed down at the Indian boy with his mop of black, shiny hair. He recalled the angelic face of Ian Gracey on his bed that fateful night after the study fire.

Jim felt someone shaking him and opened his eyes to see a menacing face with a savage scar across the cheek. He sat up with alarm.

Flicker said calmly, "I need to talk to you. Don't worry, you haven't done anything wrong. Where the hell's everyone?"

"Th-They've gone," Jim stammered.

"I saw the message on the notice board. Do you know where they went?"

"Sleeth and Steel scheduled a night corps exercise. I saw the cadets head in the direction of the cemetery."

"Was Croat with them?"

"Yes," Jim said, "but if you ask me he wasn't too happy about it."

"When did they leave?"

"I don't know, an hour ago, maybe less?" Bhasin tried to read his alarm clock, but to no avail in the dark. "I'll say this though, Jonathan Simon looked plenty worried."

"Get dressed and bring a torch." He easily pulled Jim up to a standing position. "You're coming with me. I have a use for you."

★★★

Sleeth stood to address the remaining cadets. Five minutes had passed since he'd sent Squad A ahead with Steel and Forrester. "I speak to you as loyal cadets. Tonight's exercise is no drill. It's for real, an army manoeuvre. There's a crisis in the House with our honoured traditions under attack." Sleeth weighed the reaction of his listeners. He had to connect fast… make them understand. "You in the corps are the first line of defence in times of trouble. This means it's up to us to take action against anyone attempting to undermine our school."

The cadets murmured their approval. Sleeth sensed heightened interest. "It's our duty to identify our enemies and make them pay."

The response to this call to action began as a slow

handclap and evolved into raucous chanting in unison, "Make them pay! Make them pay!"

Sleeth raised his hands to command silence. "Yes, they'll pay. I've already sent the three traitors ahead. The first is William Croat, who schemed to bring down a future Head of House. Next is Keith Rayner, a co-conspirator. And worst of all, Jonathan Simon, who broke our code of silence. These three are a disgrace to everything that the school and the corps stand for."

Amid the shouting, Harry Crown hopped to his feet to make himself heard. Whatever Sleeth might do to him in retaliation was worth the risk to stand up for his friends. "Look, I don't know if Simon going to the police was right or wrong. But we all know that what he said about Tunk cheating at the fair was true."

Sleeth was momentarily at a loss for words but soon gathered himself together and pointed his torch at Harry. "Look what we have here… another traitor trying to spread lies!"

A cadet poked Harry in the back with a torch while others booed.

"Cadets Davies and Hawk, restrain Crown," Sleeth commanded. "Tie his hands behind him with his own belt and escort him back to the armoury. Hold him there until you're given further orders."

The boys rushed to comply. Harry tried to resist but was soon overpowered by the bigger cadets. Sleeth raised his hand for silence. "Is there anyone else who isn't with us?" He looked right and left. "If so, step forward."

Everyone remained still.

"You make me proud." Sleeth snapped off a salute. "Let's crush those who dishonour Blackleigh. Squad B… assemble on the other side of the fence until we hear from Sergeant Steel that the rope is secured… Move." he shouted, pumping his rifle up and down.

38

BELL TOWER

Croat trailed after Jonathan and Keith as they pulled the T-shaped handle of the flatbed wagon along the decrepit church wall and on to the bell tower. Sergeant Steel and Corporal Forrester brought up the rear. Jonathan looked up at the opening atop the tower and tried to imagine how Ian felt before he fell to his death. He pressed his hand against the base of the edifice to test whether he was awake or having a nightmare. What he touched was real; cold stone covered with lichens.

Steel directed them to park the wagon twenty yards in front of the tower. Jonathan shone his torch into the small entry and recalled how the steps zig-zagged up into darkness.

Croat and Rayner, loathe to be in each other's company, avoided eye contact. Croat was angry at Keith for not revealing to him what happened at the armoury.

And Keith was pissed that he'd almost got raped carrying out Croat's absurd scheme.

"Corporal Forrester," Sergeant Steel called out, "select one of the cadets to go with you and haul a rope up the steps to the top. Then make sure the rope is well secured to the bell's crossbeam. Toss the rest of the rope from the opening down to the ground."

Croat complained to Forrester, "I'm too heavy to climb those rickety stairs, let alone carry rope."

Keith shot Jonathan a look as if to say, *That's about what I'd expect from him.*

Sergeant Steel realised that Keith was the most athletic of the three and that the rope needed to be secured fast. "Cadet Rayner," he ordered, "you take the rope and follow Corporal Forrester to the top."

Keith grabbed one of the ropes off the wagon, slung it over his shoulder, then and he and Forester started their climb.

After climbing what seemed like endless steps, he and Forrester reached the platform.

On the ground, Croat wrung his hands together. He knew that Sleeth had singled him out for a specific purpose, and deliberately put Steel in charge. But now he realised that Sleeth suspected he was behind the plan to entrap him using Rayner.

Keith dropped the rope on the floor. Just below the roof was a high crossbeam, that at one time supported a bell. The bell itself was stolen years ago, probably as a prank or on a dare. Together, they secured the rope, tossed the loose end out of the opening of the tower and watched it dangle in the air below until it stopped short about a foot from the ground.

Forrester put his weight on the rope and was confident it would hold. "We're done. Let's go."

Four minutes later, Keith and Forrester came out at the base of the tower and saluted Sergeant Steel.

"Right," Steel said, returning the salutes, "Forrester, you stay here and keep an eye on these three. I'll report to Officer Sleeth that his orders have been carried out." Sergeant Steel promptly left.

Jonathan took Keith aside. "Now what?"

Forrester was taking a pee, several feet away, with his back to them, as Jonathan and Keith huddled together.

"It's no coincidence that Sleeth selected us for Squad A. But why?" Keith pondered aloud.

"I'll bet the answer is in that trunk," Jonathan said, pointing.

The two of them snuck over to the wagon. The single hasp on the trunk was tied shut with heavy gauge bailing string. Rather take the time to undo the knot, Jonathan removed his constant companion, the Swiss Army knife, sawed through and opened the lid. The trunk was filled to the brim with rotten vegetables: heads of brown, slimy lettuce and cauliflower, rotten tomatoes, mouldy potatoes and several cartons of eggs, all castoffs from the school kitchen. The stench made them want to puke. A gallon-sized petrol can with a screw-top lid was in plain sight next to the firewood.

"What do you think Sleeth intends?" Jonathan asked, closing the lid fast.

"I don't know, but whatever it is, I don't want to find out," Keith replied.

"Look," Jonathan said, quickly devising a plan, "there's only one gate in and out of here. We can't escape without running into the other cadets. I know of a sarcophagus where Ian, Arthur and I sat when we came here. How about we hide behind it? If we can remain undiscovered until sunup Sunday morning, since everyone is supposed to attend chapel, the cadets will have to give up and go home."

"Hiding doesn't make sense," Croat said, joining them.

Jonathan gestured to the trunk's contents. "Well, it beats the alternative. At least it gives us a chance."

"I agree," Keith nodded. "Jonathan and I are going. You can stay here if you want, Croat."

"But what about our guard?" Croat bobbed his head in Forrester's direction.

"I'll take care of him," Keith said and approached the corporal, who was zipping up his pants.

When Forrester turned back around, before him stood Keith in a boxer's stance with his fists cocked. Forrester, like the other boys, still held the belief in Keith's reputation as a fierce fighter.

"Get the hell out of here, Forrester, or I'll mess you up." Keith snapped off a left jab and a right uppercut, each stopping an inch short of Forrester's face.

Without a second thought, Forrester took off running.

The three hurried over rock-strewn ground. Waist high weeds swayed around them in the wind.

Croat stopped, leaned against a tree trunk and tried to catch his breath. "I'm not cut out for this," he moaned.

"Move it! We've lost time on your account," Keith snapped. "The corps are probably on our tails."

Croat lurched forward and tried to keep up.

Jonathan continued to lead, stopping only briefly to listen for sounds. Even with his torch, he could barely make out the location of his companions, who'd fallen behind.

"Keith, over here," Jonathan called softly, shining the beam of his torch on his lower body. Keith hurried to his side.

"Where's Croat?" Jonathan asked, peering into the dark.

"Dragging his fat arse. He keeps stopping." Keith shook his head in frustration.

"Keith, I know where we are!" Jonathan said. "I remember now. For a while, I was going in the wrong direction. But I recognise this chestnut tree. It's near the sarcophagus. We're almost there."

"We'd move twice as fast without Croat," Keith suggested.

Jonathan briefly considered this. "No. Even though he deserves it, we can't leave him behind. The sarcophagus is right up ahead."

"C'mon, Croat," Keith called, "we've made it."

Croat came up wheezing and joined Keith and Jonathan already squatting behind the sarcophagus.

The moon disappeared behind churning black

clouds. They could hear the cadets noisily fanning out through the cemetery. Jonathan saw beams from torches approaching and warned the other two to remain quiet and stay still. Minutes later a cadet stood within inches of where they hid – but Sleeth yelled an order and the cadet turned to go.

The wind kicked up and Croat, who had hay fever, got a whiff of mugwort pollen and sneezed.

The cadet yelled, "They're over here!"

Seconds later the three of them were blinded by ten or more torch beams shining in their faces. Sleeth promptly appeared accompanied by Sergeant Steel.

"Look here… We have fucking deserters on top of everything else," Sleeth scowled. He reached down, grabbed Jonathan by his shirt collar and yanked him to his feet. "Your orders were to stay at the tower."

"Guess we got lost," Jonathan said sarcastically.

Sleeth slapped Jonathan's face.

His cheek hurt and his eyes watered, but Jonathan just stared back, undaunted, at Sleeth.

Croat stepped up to Sleeth and pleaded in a high-pitched whine, "Officer Sleeth, you've gone too far this time. Let's call off this exercise and…"

Croat yelped as he received a stinging backhand slap across his face.

"I say when this exercise is over," Sleeth sneered, "you fat lump of shit. All right, you three… March!"

They tramped back to the tower in silence, bordered on all sides by fellow cadets so they couldn't make a break for it.

Sergeant Steel joined Sleeth at the rear. "What's your plan, sir?"

"First, we build a bonfire near the tower for light," Sleeth replied with relish. "We'll send Simon up the tower first and as he climbs down the rope, ten cadets will pelt him with the rotten vegetables and eggs. Rayner will go next and get the same treatment."

"What about Croat?"

"He's too fucking fat for the rope. We'll pelt him on the ground. Then to destroy the evidence, we'll make the three of them strip naked and toss their clothes into the fire.

"Too bad Tunk couldn't be here," Sleeth added, "he has such fondness for making boys strip naked. Get this: When I spoke to him on the phone and told him my plan, he had another idea... We march the naked traitors back to the House chain-gang style. But instead of tying string to their ankles – it'll be penis to penis." Sleeth grinned maniacally. "What a mind Tunk has! Whenever any one of them falls out of step, they'll all get a painful jerk to their dicks!"

Steel laughed uproariously. "When it comes to torture and humiliation, Tunk is an unappreciated genius."

They reached the bell tower and Squad B formed a semi-circle in front. Sleeth ordered four cadets to pile up the wood. Meanwhile, he and Steel unslung their cumbersome rifles and handed them off to a cadet for safekeeping.

Steel grabbed the can of petrol, poured it on the wood and set it ablaze with the flick of a match. The cadets cheered with excitement.

"Corporal Croat, Cadet Simon and Cadet Rayner… You three are a disgrace to Blackleigh," Sleeth declared pacing back and forth in front of them. "Only you will participate in this corps exercise. One at a time, you'll ascend the steps of the tower to the top. You'll then climb down the rope to the ground on the outside of the tower. On your way down, the corps will throw kitchen refuse at you to remind you exactly what you are… filthy rotten garbage." Sleeth pointed to the trunk and the cadets cheered once again.

"Simon, you first. Rayner will be next."

Before Jonathan could take a step, Sleeth held up a hand to stop him, then rotated it and made a *gimme* gesture. "Cadet Simon, I'll take that Swiss knife I know you're carrying." He made a head gesture towards the cut string on the hasp. "Don't want you to get any bright ideas."

Jonathan had no choice but to hand it over. Sleeth's eyes rested on Croat. "I haven't forgotten you… you conniving, spineless shit."

"Why me?" Croat whined.

"I know it was you who set me up at the armoury," Sleeth said, sotto voce. "You'll get yours right here."

Now Croat knew for sure. This night's exercise was all about revenge. His stomach began to cramp with pangs of fear.

Jonathan dreaded having to be the first but saw no way out.

The voices of Squad B swelled as they repeated Sleeth's exhortation: "Make them pay!"

Jonathan entered the church and shone his torch over the dirty interior walls. A wave of fear swept over him. He closed his eyes and prayed under his breath, "Ian... help me... guide me." He looked up grimly at the first few ragged flights of stairs and started his ascent.

His mind flashed with memories. He recalled how his mother, illuminated by a shaft of light, waved goodbye to him at Paddington station. He saw himself, a fretting schoolboy, cowering in the train compartment on his first journey to Blackleigh.

He climbed higher and the faces of new friends came to mind: Ian, Jim Bhasin, Peter Wynn and David Gold. He imagined Arthur with his hangdog expression, flashing a smile and exclaiming, "What a fucking school!"

He thought of those he hated: Sleeth, Tunk, Drub, and the enigma that was Flicker. Both good and evil were with him as if he'd known them forever. He'd wanted to belong to Blackleigh and the House, but his sense of justice conflicted with the traditions of the school.

Still climbing, Jonathan last reflected on the Oath that changed his life. Since then, he'd found the strength to face even this trial. When he reached the platform at the top, he resolved to look down defiantly at Sleeth, Steel and the cadets. He'd make no plea for mercy.

Jonathan mounted ever higher until he reached the last step and the base of the platform. He shone his torch and was about to step onto the floor when he stumbled, shocked by what he saw.

39

INFERNO

Jim Bhasin sat cross-legged on the floor of the platform.

"You took your time getting here," Jim said casually.

The shock of seeing Jim had caused Jonathan to misstep; he reached out and sprained his wrist in breaking his fall.

Jonathan looked up in pain from where he lay. He knew he wasn't dreaming when Jim rushed forward and helped him to his feet. They hugged as though they'd never expected to see each other again.

"It's a miracle… How did you get here?" Jonathan wiped away tears of joy.

"While no one was around, I just climbed the steps."

"But I left you back at the House?" Jonathan said, still finding it hard to believe he was talking to Jim. "How come you're even here?"

"You're not going to believe this," Jim said, clutching Jonathan's arm. "I was asleep in the dorm when Flicker woke me, told me to dress and to come here with him. When we reached the cemetery, the cadets were fanning out in a search party. It was easy to get past them without being seen. We saw a single rope dangling from the top of the tower. Flicker opened the trunk, figured out what Sleeth had in mind and came up with a plan. He grabbed another rope off the wagon and we climbed together and reached the platform, just before the corps returned along with you three prisoners.

"Flicker tied one end of his rope to the beam and tossed it through the rear opening and down to the ground."

"Where's Flicker now?" Jonathan looked back down the stairs, thinking he might be somewhere in the church.

"On the back rope… said he wanted to do a practice run. He's an experienced rope climber, did you know?"

"Why did he bring you here?"

"Because he didn't think you'd trust him unless I came too."

"I still don't," Jonathan said, dead serious.

"We haven't much choice," Jim said. "But when two outsiders like you and I join up, that changes the odds." They hugged again.

Two hands appeared on the climbing rope of the rear aperture. In a blink, Flicker swung onto the platform and nodded at Jonathan.

"If you two can tear yourselves away from each other," he quipped, "the corps are gathered below. We have to go."

"How?" Jim asked, looking hopefully at the stairs.

"What's your plan?" Jonathan asked tentatively.

"I'm not exactly sure," Flicker replied. "I'm making it up as I go. But first things first: I need to get *you* out of harm's way. That's my ace in the hole. Then I'll deal with Sleeth." Flicker observed Jonathan holding his sore wrist and turned to Bhasin. "You first. Ready?"

Flicker climbed down the rope, reached the ground and stood at the bottom as a spotter for Jim. Flicker called up softly, "Don't worry, I'll break your fall if you slip."

"I should have gone to Calcutta." Jim's dusky face took on a pale hue. He grabbed the rope with both hands and scissored his legs around the nearest knot.

"Hold on tight, Bhasin," Flicker said, "let yourself down one knot at a time. And don't look down."

Jim carefully began to descend hand under hand, his feet stepping against the outside stones of the tower.

Jonathan found it difficult to look over the edge, but he was encouraged to see Jim making steady progress. When Flicker could reach up to him, he said, "Let go." And he lowered Jim the rest of the way to the ground.

Jonathan was relieved to see Jim look up and wave with both feet on terra firma.

Flicker immediately grabbed hold of the rope, deftly climbed right back up, and stood facing Jonathan on the windswept platform.

Jonathan could hear the cadets below shouting for him. "What now?"

Flicker spoke in a calm voice. "We need to create a diversion. Turn on your torch. Shine it on your face and carefully step forward just long enough for them to see you."

Jonathan cautiously moved to the edge of the front opening. He felt faint seeing the blazing fire buffeted by the wind far below. A chorus of hissing greeted his appearance.

Despite Jim's assurance, Jonathan didn't trust the prefect. He considered that one small nudge from Flicker would send him tumbling over the edge. And at that moment, just as had happened to Ian, a sudden gust of wind hit Jonathan from behind. He lost his balance and pitched forward.

In a fraction of a second, Flicker's hand snapped out, grabbed hold of Jonathan's cross-belt from behind and pulled him back to safety. How Flicker wished he could have done the same for Ian. Jonathan turned to Flicker with a look of surprise. The prefect's quick reflexes had saved his life.

"I don't see you, Simon!" Sleeth shouted. "Come forward! Move to the edge and get on the rope. That's an order!"

Jonathan turned to Flicker for guidance.

"Tell Sleeth that if he wants you, he'll have to come and get you."

"But I don't want that wacko anywhere near me," Jonathan protested.

"Don't worry about Sleeth. You'll be long gone before he can get up here."

Sleeth's harsh voice rang out from below, "Cadet Simon, start climbing down the rope... Now!"

Reassured by Flicker, Jonathan yelled back, as loud as he could, "Officer Sleeth, can you hear me?"

"I hear you, now get your arse on the rope!"

"Sleeth… You're out of your fucking mind. If you want me, come and get me." As he spoke, Jonathan wished that Ian and Arthur could've heard him.

"How dare you defy me!" Sleeth roared back.

That insolent son of a bitch! Steel seethed. He'd finally lost patience with Jonathan's stalling. While everyone else was looking up, waiting, he grabbed the petrol can. *I'll smoke Simon out.*

He ran to the tower entry, unscrewed the lid and splashed the rest of the petrol over the first flight of steps and onto the floor. After backing away, he flicked a lighted match into the entry. Steel watched in fascination as a whirling sheet of flame shot across the floor and engulfed the stairs.

Jonathan and Flicker saw smoke rising from below and realised the stairs were on fire. Flicker turned to Jonathan. "Time to go. Are you ready Simon – I mean, Jonathan?"

Flicker called me by my first name! Jonathan held up his now swollen wrist for Flicker to see. "I fell… can't grip the rope."

"I know," Flicker said, "that's why I had Bhasin go first. I'll carry you down in a fireman's lift."

Again, Jonathan hesitated. Flicker sensed and understood, "C'mon trust me… there's no other safe way out of here."

He's calling this 'safe'? Jonathan shrugged his shoulders

and allowed Flicker to lift him onto his back. Jonathan knew they were near the rear edge as Flicker turned. Flicker grasped the rope and slowly, hand under hand, one knot at a time, they descended.

As Flicker climbed down with Jonathan holding onto him, he saw himself, years earlier. He'd been subsumed with guilt over Nick's death. Now Flicker realised that if anyone was to blame, it was his father, the adult, who bore responsibility. His father, not him, was the one who had delayed by not opening the connecting door to their rooms, and had also left him standing in the corridor doorway, at first refusing to believe him, rather than acting immediately. Then his father had held back from going into Nick's burning room. Flicker would never allow his father to use guilt over Nick's death as a weapon against him again.

Jonathan felt his feet touch the ground. His legs buckled; he fell over, then quickly got to his feet. Jim rushed to his side and said, "You're a typical Englishman… You want to be carried around first class."

Jonathan laughed more in relief than at Jim's humour.

Flicker patted Jonathan on the back, "Well done. You two best get back to the House. Don't let the others see you go."

"What about you?" asked Jonathan.

"It's time to deal with Sleeth."

"You saved us both… I'll never forget that." Jonathan gave Flicker a grateful smile.

"Go, now," Flicker said and left them.

Jim dug into his pocket and pulled out a Swiss Army knife. "I found it up there while I was waiting for you. It was in a crack in the floor."

"My God, I recognise this," Jonathan gasped. "It's Ian's! He was watching over us." Jonathan hesitated, then said, "I want you to keep it. I've got one of my own. Hopefully, somehow, I'll be able to get it back from Sleeth. C'mon let's get the hell out of here."

★★★

Flicker stole around the tower and was immediately confronted by two cadets, blocking his path.

"What are you doing here? You're not a member of the corps," one said tentatively.

"This is a private, corps-only exercise," said the other.

Flicker looked at them wickedly. "You better get out of my way, or I just might lose my temper. You don't want that to happen."

They stepped aside fast and let Flicker pass. He came around to the front of the tower and saw Bill Croat standing with Rayner. His study mate wore a look of despair. A short distance away, Sleeth and Steel were looking up at the aperture for any sign of Simon. The ground entrance of the tower was illuminated by flames. Black smoke and sparks belched from the opening at the top.

Flicker tapped Croat on the back. Croat turned and gasped at the sight of his friend. "James… it's a miracle… you're here. They sent Simon to the top of the tower."

Flicker held a finger to his mouth and turned to Rayner. "Jonathan's fine," he whispered, "don't say a word."

Flicker approached Steel from behind and heard him say to Sleeth, "The stairs are gone but the walls are holding… Simon has only one way down."

Flicker grabbed Steel's shoulder and spun him around. His fist smashed into Steel's face. The sergeant fell back and lay flat on the ground, out cold.

Sleeth turned to Flicker in surprise. "I didn't expect you," he said quietly, "but I've been waiting for this moment a long time." He assumed a judo stance.

The cadets, already cheering and shouting, formed a ragged circle around Flicker and Sleeth. One yelled, "Get him, Officer Sleeth!" and a couple of others echoed it. But with Flicker's regal presence and the possibility of a showdown between him and Sleeth, the calls quickly petered out and the cadets looked on in a fusion of excitement and uncertainty.

Sleeth tried to throw a punch, but Flicker's fencing reflexes allowed him to dodge the blow. Sleeth then attempted a roundhouse kick; but again Flicker deftly evaded it. Sleeth went back to trying to land jabs and punches.

Flicker remained on the defensive. Twice he had the opportunity to punch Sleeth in the face but didn't.

After several misses, Sleeth, in frustration, leapt at Flicker to tackle him. Flicker easily dodged him leaving Sleeth sprawling on the ground. A couple of cadets laughed. Jonathan's knife had fallen fell out of Sleeth's pocket. He grabbed it, opened the large blade, sprang to his feet and advanced on Flicker. To his surprise, Flicker put up no defence but stood rigid, staring Sleeth square in the eyes. Sleeth perceived this as resignation and put his knife up against Flicker's right cheek.

"How'd you like a matching scar?"

Flicker, in a low voice that only Sleeth could hear, replied, "Go ahead. But consider the consequences of using a deadly weapon on a fellow prefect. With what you've done here, you've already dug yourself a hole so deep you could never get out of it. But I'll give you a way out – and allow you to save face at the same time."

Flicker dropped to one knee and bowed his head, giving the appearance of a surrender pose.

Sleeth, shocked by Flicker's response, quickly recovered. He turned to the cadets and said, "This exercise is over."

Sleeth was again taken aback when Flicker, in a conciliatory gesture of respect, stood, clicked his heels and saluted him.

"Awaiting further orders, sir," Flicker said solemnly.

"Atten-SHUN!" Sleeth barked to his troops. "Stand at ease… Squad Dismissed."

En masse the cadets obeyed his command. Sleeth turned to Flicker, still standing at attention, flashed a grin and said, "Let's get the hell out of here." He was as much relieved as Flicker.

This was the first and only time Flicker had ever seen Sleeth smile at him.

The cadets headed back to Trafalgar, some at leisurely pace, others at a sprint. Sleeth detained two cadets, Bell and France, and ordered them to take the trunk off the cart and heave it with the contents on top of the bonfire.

Sleeth helped Steel to his feet. Steel, still foggy, asked, "What's going on?"

"We're done here," Sleeth replied and they left together.

Croat turned to Keith, "Let's go you arsehole."

"It takes one to know one," Keith shot back. They put their arms around each other's shoulders and walked away.

Flicker remained standing where he was, as if mesmerised by all that happened and amazed that his on-the-fly plan had worked. Bell and France had finished with the disposal and were pulling the empty wagon back to the armoury when Flicker put up a hand to stop them. "Bell, France, listen up. The cadets were going to punish Simon, but he's the bravest among you. He knows right from wrong and acts upon what he believes. That deserves respect not hatred. Spread the word."

They nodded their agreement and trudged on.

Flicker went to the tower entry and stamped out a few smouldering embers from the staircase, fallen from above. The stone edifice remained intact, as it had through the ages.

He looked up at the tower. When the flames had reached the top, the ropes burnt lose. He watched the front rope cascade through the air and land in a heap directly in front of him. The sight gave him a start; he had an eerie flashback of Ian falling through space.

A snowy owl circled overhead, then swooped down to land on top of the tower. Was he imagining this, or did Ian speak to him in his head? Flicker thought he heard Ian's voice say, *We all do things we regret… But you've made up for it.* Flicker's eyes welled up with tears of great relief.

As the dark clouds overhead scudded away, Flicker turned and walked home in the moonlight, but not before reaching down to pick something up off the ground.

40

EPILOGUE

1 July 1956

A week later, at midday, bright sunlight streamed through the high windows emblazoning the Assembly Hall. The massed students occupied a respectful distance around the Headmaster and the faculty, who stood in the centre circle.

In Blackleigh tradition, at this last assembly of the school year, the Headmaster revealed the names of any new Heads of House and those elevated to be prefects. He'd already thanked the leaving head of school, Chris Mercer, for his service.

The school listened anxiously. Infrequent bursts of applause followed the appointment of a popular new prefect, but most announcements were met with silent disapproval.

The large faculty was grouped separately in black

gowns over their daily attire. Each of them wore distinctive fur-lined or silk collars that marked their various achievements in academia. Among them were Alec Morton and P. G. Ring, his Assistant Housemaster, who silently contemplated the Headmaster's words.

While Stewart spoke of the school's accomplishments, Morton inwardly reflected how the school year began when he saw three new boys in his study, Arthur Crown, Keith Rayner and Jonathan Simon, along with Ian Gracey.

Since the year had passed, he wasn't surprised that Crown Junior had washed out. The boy had "failure" written all over him... poor study habits, bottom of his class, and his participation in team sports was nonexistent.

Keith Rayner was a worthy addition to the House. The young man's confidence had grown. With his speed, Rayner might have a future in the first fifteen rugby team; and with his maturity, as a future prefect.

Jonathan Simon had surprised him. The self-conscious and nervous boy started out making enemies of all but a few of his peers. However, of late, Morton noticed that this had changed, and the boy appeared to have somehow gained their respect. This was evident when boys passed Jonathan in the hallways and greeted him by his first name. Some even smiled at him. Jonathan had developed an independent streak and possessed a clear sense of right and wrong.

Alec Morton recalled Ian Gracey with affection. He'd recently learnt that Ian's tragic death was connected to his covering up for Arthur Crown. Alec Morton doubted that Ian had a mean bone in his body. The boy was taken from them before he got to experience all that life had to offer. Morton would not forget Ian, his smiling, eager face, suspended in time… forever young. Morton was glad that Flicker had proposed a memorial plaque be made for Ian and placed on the trophy shelf in the Houseroom.

Jonathan, standing in the Trafalgar section, looked across at David Gold, immaculately dressed as usual. David made eye contact, pointed a finger at Jonathan and mouthed, "Are *you* the next Head of House?"

Jonathan smiled, shook his head and mouthed back, "No, but I bet *you* are!"

William Croat straightened his tie. He was determined to look his best when the Head called his name as a new prefect; he'd walk to the front showing a modest demeanour.

Thank you, sir, he silently practised, *I'm grateful for your trust.* Then he'd stand with dignity and pride among the other prefects.

Croat didn't expect to receive much applause. But he'd look around and make a mental note of anyone who booed him from Trafalgar. They'd be on his shit list – no favours allotted.

Jonathan turned to Jim. "Who's it going to be?"

"Have hope, I still believe in justice," Jim said with conviction.

Stewart continued to read from his handwritten notes. "In Trafalgar, we're departing from our practice of keeping the number of House prefects at five… and one Head of House.”

“What’s the old man jawing about?” Croat mumbled, feeling outrage. *I’ll shit in my pants if they make Tunk a prefect when he returns in the autumn.* Croat edged forward to be nearer the podium.

Stewart looked up. “After consultation with the Trafalgar Housemaster, Alec Morton and P. G. Ring…”

The Assistant Housemaster opened his eyes and wondered who’d called his name. He distinctly heard the Head say, “We will not be appointing *any* new prefects in Trafalgar next term.”

A murmur of surprise arose. Croat almost keeled over; his look of confidence vanished. He could imagine Tunk, if here, would delight in giving him a gap-toothed grin.

Stewart continued, “We wish David Reece, who leaves for Oxford, every success. Our search for a new Head of House at Trafalgar came down to a couple of outstanding young men.”

Stewart went on, “Ours was a hard choice for the new Trafalgar Head but we finally decided on… James Martin Flicker.”

The assembly burst into applause and waited for Flicker to appear.

Sleeth clapped along with the rest, but he was musing: *Flicker thinks I’m an ally now. How perfect! When I retaliate, he won’t see it coming.*

When Flicker heard his name called, he was thinking of Croat and how Alec Morton had overruled him when he put forward Bill's name as a prefect. But he'd find a way to pacify his roly-poly friend.

The midday sunlight flooded the space where Flicker stood. He closed his eyes to ward off the bright light.

Winning, Flicker discovered, wasn't all it was made out to be. The greatest satisfaction came in helping others. On the night of Sleeth's corps exercise, he'd managed to save Simon and aid both Rayner and Croat. He liked young Jim Bhasin. If other foreign kids were anything like Bhasin, with his strong sense of justice and right and wrong, they could be a credit to the school.

Weighed down by emotion, Flicker felt himself pushed forward. Others made way for him. He heard voices laud him from all sides, but they seemed far away. He strode on with assurance and pride, gradually increasing his pace.

Flicker shook hands with the Headmaster.

"We were waiting. We thought we'd lost you, James," Stewart said.

"I thought so too, sir… But I found myself in time," he quipped.

Flicker caught the eye of Chris Mercer, Head of School, who nodded in his direction… Flicker smiled back. Life was giving him a second chance.

A. S. Stewart cleared his throat. "My last announcement is of a personal nature. I am retiring at the end of this school year. It's been a privilege to serve as your Headmaster and I will look back on my days at Blackleigh with pride and gratitude. I wish you all every success in your endeavours.

"My replacement, Dr Macleod, is currently Headmaster of a prominent boys' school in Scotland, known for its demanding curriculum and strict disciplinary standards. I know you all will make him feel welcome."

The assembly over, students ambled into their dining rooms for lunch. With a new and unpredictable Headmaster, they had much to discuss.

Jonathan stayed behind, thinking of Ian and Arthur and how he missed them. He left the building and stood outside, at the top of the steps, admiring the panoramic view. *How great*, he thought, *to have survived Blackleigh and to have formed such genuine friendships*. He'd see Arthur, Jim and David over the holidays. Keith lived too far away.

He looked out towards the horizon, heard steps behind him, and turned to see Flicker. Jonathan was uncertain how to acknowledge the new Head of House. "I'm glad the Sleeth situation turned out well," he finally said, "thank you for all you did."

"And I thank *you* for your courage," Flicker replied. "There'll be changes in the House next year. I intend to lead out of respect, not fear. I want juniors to feel comfortable coming to me with their problems. As the new head of Trafalgar, one of the benefits is that I get a study all to myself. I'm going to put an extra armchair in there, where you and others can sit and feel safe and open to talk. Your being there occasionally will break the ice.

"Also, I'm interested in your perspective on how things can be made different around here. I want Trafalgar to be the House all other Houses envy." Flicker hesitated, then said, "There's something I'd like to say."

"Yes?"

"You handled the Arthur Crown problem as best you could, given that Gracey made you swear to keep Crown's secret… " Flicker prompted.

"Thank you," Jonathan replied, feeling relaxed enough to confess his part in the fire. He told Flicker the whole story. That Arthur concocted the idea on his own to repay Ian and himself for helping with his homework. They were Arthur's guests that night. Ian Gracey and he arrived *after* the fire started and saved the study from being further damaged.

Flicker listened as Jonathan spoke, then broke into a smile. "There's a way to make up for your part in this… Agree to take charge of the two juniors scheduled to be cleaning my study next term. How about it? I trust you to do a good job."

"Why not?" Jonathan laughed, "I owe you anyway."

"One more thing, Jonathan. I seriously doubt you'll ever need this from now on. But here…" Flicker retrieved Jonathan's Swiss Army knife from his pocket and handed it to him.

"Where did you get this?" Jonathan gasped.

"Sleeth dropped it on the ground at the tower," Flicker replied.

"How'd you know it was mine?"

"I have my sources," Flicker said with a sly grin. "The wealth of what I know about this place would astound you."

"Thanks so much!" Jonathan shook his head in astonishment. "This means so much to me."

The Head of House and the junior shook hands. When Flicker pulled him close for a brief hug, Jonathan felt like time stood still. He'd long remember this special moment.

"Have a good holiday, Jonathan." Flicker turned and entered the main building.

Simon looked out over the green fields. He felt his heart soaring. Blackleigh and its buildings stood on his left; Enderby on lower ground. A new housing estate was under construction near the school boundary wall. Nothing at Blackleigh, with a new, iron-fisted Headmaster coming, remained constant. Everything was in flux.

Jonathan planned to spend some of the afternoon packing and saying goodbye to several of his new friends. He'd soon be in London for the summer holiday and then return to Blackleigh.

Yes, he thought, *I finally belong.*

ACKNOWLEDGEMENT

My thanks to my editor, Cliff Carle, for his guidance and unfailing confidence in this first book in a three part series. Cliff gave me insightful input and suggestions page by page. I so appreciate his precision and our resolving of loose ends.

Any errors left over are mine.

ABOUT THE AUTHOR

Michael Leon Lewis was born in London, England, and educated at the Hall School in London, then at Stowe School, where he won the annual school poetry prize.

In 1968, he immigrated to Los Angeles and graduated from UCLA, Phi Beta Kappa, with a BA in English and subsequently from Loyola Law School, passing the California State Bar.

In 1979, he founded a real estate investment company with his brother and won numerous beautification awards for projects undertaken on the Los Angeles Westside.

Michael served as vice-president on the board of trustees at UCLA Royce 270 for the Performing Arts, and as president for two years on the board of trustees for the Los Angeles High School for the Arts.

Michael Leon Lewis is devoted full-time to writing, is a long-time member of a literary group, and plays the classical guitar.